THE QUARRY

SKULLDIGGERY
BOOK 2

DM GRITZMACHER

PIQUED PUBLISHING

PRAISE FOR DM GRITZMACHER
THE QUARRY

"If you want blood, you've got it! More savage gore! Curvier twists! More menacing villain!"
caffeinatedbabbles.com Book Blog

"I love a book that can bring me into their world where I feel like I am right there as part of the story and that is how this book made me feel."
Deanna

"This series has me hooked! From the fantastic imagery to the way the author makes me care about the characters, to the surprises, I could not put it down. The waiting is the hardest part, I cannot wait for the next book!"
Angie-Goodreads

"Whoa, this book grabbed my attention and wouldn't let go, no matter how much I begged and pleaded!"
Erik

"DM Gritzmacher delivers again. The Quarry is every bit as terrifying as the first installment in the series."
Brian-Bookbub

PRAISE FOR DM GRITZMACHER
THE RELICT

"…powerful occult thriller… a gripping blend of horror, thriller, and investigative mystery…"
D. Donovan, Senior Reviewer, Midwest Book Review

"Captivating Beyond Anything I've Read Before!"
Shelley

"…vivid descriptions, that are grotesque and frightening…"
The Customer

"Part horror story, part supernatural thriller, all excellent!"
Eloise

"…a great debut novel for all fans of horror fiction!"
Iowa Girl

"I LOVED it! Be prepared to hunker down, close the curtains, cuddle up and enjoy…"
Rebecca

CONTENT WARNING

The Quarry contains graphic depictions of violence, sexual assault, and gore that may not be suitable for some readers.

QUARRY

Quarry-1: a place, typically a large, deep pit, from which stone or other materials are or have been extracted. 2: the person or an animal pursued by a hunter, hound, predatory mammal, or bird of prey. 3: a square or diamond-shaped piece of glass, tile, etc...

PROLOGUE

FRANCE–14TH CENTURY

A DISPIRITING FOG began to roll in, and a wet mist blanketed the gathered men in its damp embrace. On only the third military campaign of his life and his first accompanying the King and the Prince, a pale young man wiped his dripping nose with a soggy sleeve. He watched along with the others from near the top of the knoll, anxious to move on from this place of misery. While the archer waited with his wood longbow strapped across his back, sopping weeds heavy with dew swished lazily around him in the cool morning breeze. Darkening his worn leather boots and keeping him chilled and uncomfortable. Grey clouds covered the sky and filtered what meager sunlight dared to brighten the day. Rain, thought the fledgling longbowman, seemed likely once King Edward's army finally did resume its march across France. He sighed and shifted uncomfortably on his feet. His fitful sleep of the night before left him still weary.

Though miles away, the archer caught the faint scent of the sea and its salt in the air as he stood. He turned slightly and faced the wall of shadowed forest at his back, raising his nose and inhaling deeply, trying to fill himself with something natural and unsoiled. It seemed as if all he had seen, heard, and tasted for more days than he dared remember had now left him tainted somehow. With eyes closed, he conjured up an image of the pure green sea, and in his heart, he wished they were turning back to those cleansing waters now. But he knew the invasion on these shores was only just beginning. He thought of his family across the sea and longed to return to them. Already ashamed of his actions and what he'd taken part in.

Wondering if he could ever look either of his sisters in the eye again…

———

The indentured foot soldier moved away from the dark opening. The little hair remaining on his head blew listlessly about him as he walked. In one hand, he held the worn leather reins of the towering black horse he'd led back and forth over this same trail the last several days. The simple wood wagon, now empty and with one cracked wheel, thumped noisily behind them both. The foot soldier spoke soothingly and in low tones to the heavily muscled beast at his side. The man felt bad for the burdened animal. The horrid sights, sounds, and smells they'd witnessed together had forged a strong bond between them. Both were equally restless and ready to leave this place now that they'd finally emptied the last of the ghastly cargo they had been hauling.

The pace of the horse's clomping hooves picked up once they left the black of the cavern. As had been their habit, they both walked faster away from that dank and stony place than when they had approached it. Although now back outside once again, the soldier never felt genuinely comfortable until they were completely past the white Roman ruins and toppled granite pillars near the top of the hill. When they finally crested that earthen rise, leaving the yawning mouth of the ancient quarry behind for the last time, a sluggish rain began to come down. The man turned his grimy face from the drops that fell around them. Eyes lowered to the dirt path.

The drops, he felt, were God spitting down on him in disgust…

———

The white-bearded knight was one of the last still left deep inside the long abandoned quarry. When they had all descended together, he'd marveled at what the Romans had achieved centuries before. The endless channels and passageways, the depth at which the ground was plundered, and the detail -though disturbing and blasphemous- of the statues and art that had remained untouched for so long. But his opinion changed as days passed and the orders received were followed. His marvel turning to unease.

The knight could not say if the disquiet he felt was from the fevered frenzy he'd taken part in days before or the disturbing task only just finished. But now, nearly alone and far below ground, the blackness around him seemed to have a life of its own. The emptiness was heavy and thick with a quality of motion that seemed to stalk him. Eyes wide, he pirouetted once before backing against the twisted, wolf-like statue that dominated the hollow cavern where he stood. Despite the profane image chiseled into the large stone, he felt better with his back against the twisted effigy.

Less exposed.

The grizzled and battle-tested knight steeled himself as if in combat again, tense and feeling watched. His heralded history of unquestioned bravery and pride refused to allow him to call out for the help his rising fear clamored for. Certain something circled about him in the quivering shadows, he swiftly withdrew his weapon and strained his eyes in the flickering, weak candlelight. Whatever it was seemed to abruptly close on him, and he spun his weapon. But the upswing of the blade sliced nothing but air.

The veteran warrior held his breath. Stationary for long moments, his every sense heightened. Exhaling only when he heard several of his fellow knights' voices growing louder and echoing down the long tunnels. He relaxed, lowering his arm and sword, forcing himself to laugh, which somehow felt necessary. The approaching armored soldiers never saw the brave knight again nor heard his laughter.

The only sound was the clatter of his weapon as it hit the stone floor of the quarry…

CHAPTER
ONE

VIEUX, FRANCE 1944

WHEN THE GROUND SHOOK, Jeanne was sure she would fall again. The upheaval under her small feet felt like the whole earth was conspiring to knock her over as she ran. A thunderous blast erupted nearby, knocking her mother off her feet. The mother and daughter were holding hands tightly as they ran, and four-year-old Jeanne tumbled down on top of her mother when she lost her balance. As Jeanne tried to scramble back to her feet, another explosion rocked the ground and sent her tiny body sprawling backward, heels-over-head. The barrage of sounds that had pummeled and hurt Jeanne's ears for the last several hours was gone.

As Jeanne tried to right herself, she did so both dizzy and deaf. The previous flood of booming detonations, crashes, and collapsing buildings was replaced by a steady hum. An unrelenting buzzing in her ears filled her head and seemed to shut everything else out. The little girl shook her head back and forth while poking at her ears with tiny fingers, trying to loosen the angry hive of bees that had somehow nestled inside each of them. When Jeanne withdrew a finger from her left ear, there was a smudge of wet blood on the end of it. Seeing it squeezed more tears out of her eyes, even though she felt no pain.

Kneeling down, Jeanne's father suddenly appeared in front of her. His mouth moved, but she couldn't hear what he was saying. Jeanne shook her head once more as her father rapidly swept her up in his arms. The little girl's head bobbed violently against his shoulder as her dad began to run again, now with her in his arms. Jeanne looked up and saw her mother had regained her feet and was following close behind them. Blood ran down one of her arms, and, like Jeanne, she was crying as well.

Behind her mother were other faces Jeanne recognized from Vieux, the small French village they all called home. Each face, usually kind, untroubled, and warm, was now pinched and grimaced. Mouths open and gasping, legs pumping up and down, everyone running together in the same direction like a panicked herd of animals. Jeanne could see jagged, red gashes on some of her neighbors' arms and legs, and many were crying. Even at four years old, Jeanne could recognize the alarm and desperation etched across the mass of villagers as they ran in the fading light of dusk. Their visible fear scared Jeanne, and she buried her head in her father's sweaty neck. Desperately wishing things to return as they were just days before.

With her eyes closed, Jeanne clung tightly to her father as she was jostled from side to side. He periodically swung her from hip to hip while darting between buildings and hurtling over various obstacles in their path. The rough ride and his labored breathing were only felt by the blessedly unhearing tiny girl and, with her face buried, unseeing the chaos falling around them. Jeanne was crying and didn't really understand what was happening or why, but she could feel the collective panic and anxiety all around her.

Jeanne had been told earlier they were all heading someplace safe. Despite the deluge of firepower raining down around them, the remaining villagers agreed to wait until the sun began to set before moving. Betting the dying daylight would help provide cover and not draw the attention of any German soldiers still left in the area. Soldiers they'd lived side by side with for as long as Jeanne could remember. She understood her father blamed these same uniformed men for this confused violence. The loud noises, the fires, and the buildings and homes being destroyed one after another all day long. The unseen airplanes far above their village, he said, were trying to drive the funny-talking men away from their homeland. Her papa told her the men in the planes were helping them, but none of that made sense to the terrified little girl.

Jeanne raised her head timidly and quickly peeked out. The acrid burning smells of the battle slowly fading away. In a glance, through the hazy, smoke-filled lingering daylight, the young girl saw they had made their way outside of their little town. In the distance, back where the panicked journey began, she could see their village's burning homes and demolished buildings as her father continued to lead her and her mother farther away from the destruction. The wreckage of what had been home was barely recognizable to her now. As she looked back, Jeanne watched helplessly as a lone donkey tethered to a standing post bucked desperately to escape as flames encircled the doomed creature. The fire engulfed the entire area in seconds.

The unfortunate farm animal consumed by the blaze.

Jeanne tore her eyes from the fiery scene and tried to focus on the people who ran beside her mother and father. She could tell many of the villagers running with them from the beginning of the aerial assault were still following closely, but a few were now missing. Either falling behind or not making it past the barrage falling indiscriminately from above. The remaining men, women, and children were all moving quickly across a small barley field that had barely begun to sprout from the earth. All of them raced toward the dense forest just beyond the farmland.

Jeanne's mother limped dramatically but was still keeping pace. Scrambling desperately across the field in her torn clothing. The dirty green dress she wore was now stained with black soot. As the group crashed into the cover of the wooded area, Jeanne gave her a little scared wave, and her mother returned a weary, fleeting smile.

Abruptly, barely into the timber on the outskirts of their village, Jeanne's father stopped running. For the first time since being picked up by him, Jeanne began to recognize sounds once again. The speech was muffled, but her father's rich and deep voice was unmistakable as he spoke to those crowded in and around him in the woods. Jeanne still could not clearly make out all the words, but it was evident the men in the group were searching for something nearby in the encroaching darkness.

Michel, the kindly town baker who often shared samples of his sweet treats with Jeanne and her friends, stepped forward. The huddled and gasping group split down the middle for him, and Michel strode purposefully forward as Jeanne looked on. A few yards away from the assembled villagers, he dropped to his knees and thrust his hands into a pile of long skinny tree branches and leaves lying on the ground in a heap. Sweeping the camouflage aside, revealing a jagged and rocky hole hidden beneath the pile. From this dark crack, a thick rope snaked along the forest floor, the opposite end tied to a sturdy tree nearby.

Grabbing the rough, textured cord, Michel moved directly over the wide crevice, straddling the gap and holding himself aloft by the rope held in each fist. With a practiced hand, he slowly lowered himself into the ground. His legs, plump waist, and chest were gradually lost from view. When Jeanne could no longer see his head, another villager grabbed the long cord where it rose from the dark hole and began their descent. One by one, the group who ran together from the destruction plummeting from the sky dropped themselves down into the opening. As tremors continued to shake the land, Jeanne watched as entire families were swallowed up. The relief of the adults as they reached the rope balanced out the terror of the smallest children. A few of Jeanne's little friends had to be dragged down the black entrance by their parents and siblings. Terrified by the dark and the unknown, kicking and screaming as they went.

As Jeanne and her mother and father's turn drew near, her papa once again knelt in front of her. He gave her a tired smile, licked his finger, and used it to wipe some soot off her cheek. When he spoke, Jeanne could hear him clearly again, the buzzing in her head replaced by a dull ache. "Now be brave, my little flower. It is not safe for us up here right now with all the bombings. We need to get someplace deep and hidden where the explosions and soldiers can't reach us." Jeanne's father pointed to the black hole, still devouring their friends and neighbors one by one. "We will all be safe and together down there. I will help you, but you must be strong for me, little flower. It will be dark at first when we start down, but already Michel is lighting the way for us below."

In the distance, a series of blasts rocked the forest's ground, and the towering trees above them swayed ever so slightly. A cascade of green leaves floated unhurriedly down all around them. Her father looked skyward briefly as the roar of an unseen airplane somewhere overhead passed close by. Jeanne's bottom lip quivered, and it took everything she had to keep from bursting out in tears. She was determined to be brave and make her father proud. "But… But what is down there?" Tears welled up in her eyes. Courageously she held them there.

"Ah, my little flower, that is the best hiding place ever!" Her father lifted her chin and smiled reassuringly at her. "This is the grandest cave you have ever seen, Jeanne. It is an old stone quarry only a few of us knew was here. But once, a long, long time ago, many men worked there. They dug under where we are standing now and carved out gigantic rocks other men used to build magnificent palaces and even some of God's churches." Jeanne's father turned and motioned for Jeanne's mother to start down the rope. He rose and picked his only child up into his arms once more. He kissed her on the cheek, and as he walked towards the crack, he said, "Now hold tightly to me, and we will be down there and safe again in no time."

Jeanne trembled and clutched tightly to her father as she was told, digging her heels into his back. Her teeth chattered, and fresh tears streamed down her face, but she hid them in her father's soft shirt. Pressing her tiny face against his chest and breathing in her dad's comforting and familiar smell. She could feel the two of them moving as one, her back briefly scratched by the jagged edges along the crevice wall as they dropped lower and lower. A brisk breeze floated up below them, and the temperature grew cooler and cooler the lower they went.

Halfway down, Jeanne got brave again and pulled her face away from her father's chest. She looked up at where they had come from and watched the last of the smoky and fading sunlight streaming down the shaft's opening gradually disappear. She sobbed when the form of the next villager coming down the hole above her blotted out the dim daylight from overhead. She tried to look down and see where they were headed, but her father's body blocked her sight from their destination below. Jeanne could not see anything in the pitch-black passageway now.

Another explosion from the outside world above sent dust and small rocks clattering down the sides of the tunnel as they continued their descent. Her father grunted as a torrent of small stones and dirt filled the enclosed space from the force of the detonation. He stopped momentarily until the shaking passed before beginning to lower them both once more. Jeanne reburied her head in his chest and held on without looking out again until they reached the bottom of the deep hole.

As father and daughter landed together, the long climb from above complete, Jeanne slid gently down from her father's protective grasp. Her small buckled shoes shuffled in the dirt as they both promptly backed away from the rope to allow the remaining villagers, still descending, to enter the cavern. Jeanne's mother bent down and hugged her tightly, relieved at her safe passage from above. Simone planted kisses across her daughter's dirty face before briefly hugging Marcel as well.

Jeanne stood beside her parents and looked in wonder at the sanctuary they had been so desperate to arrive at. It didn't feel safe to Jeanne at all. But instead, a scary, foreboding, and foreign place. It was very dark and cool and smelled funny and damp; the earth she stood on an uneven dirt and rock floor. Sharp stones of all sizes protruded out from the ground. A gigantic set of squared-off boulders in the far corner lay cracked and broken.

Several small wax candles had been lit and were held aloft by Michel and a few other men in the group. The flickering flames provided a dim, wavering light and exposed the walls, roof, and floor where the villagers huddled. The cramped space was starkly bare, and the new arrivals crowded together in an almost colorless and dull grey cavity. The cave ceiling had been evened out cleanly sometime in the distant past. Dimples on the surface gave it a textured look and feel, and in places, water dripped from natural sources flowing somewhere above. Dust floated in the air, angry at being disturbed by the intruding, exhausted villagers. A single wide tunnel beckoned out of the darkness behind the new arrivals, the only path leading away from the hanging rope and entrance.

From out of this black channel, several small, dim lights appeared, floating in the air like fireflies and gradually growing larger and larger. Soon grim but familiar faces of men, young and old, appeared behind each of the dull yellow lanterns they held aloft. These men were all fellow neighbors and townsfolk from communities and rural areas near their home and the village of Vieux. Many of the men emerging out of the darkness beyond the entrance were elated to see the newest arrivals. Happy and relieved faces appeared, soon followed by rounds of hugs and kisses sprinkled in amongst hearty greetings as the two groups came together. Scattered among the joyous reunions were also several disappointed expressions from those still missing and waiting on their loved ones to arrive. Dwindling hope scarring their eyes.

Once the last of the latest newcomers landed and the rope remained slack, everyone made their way together back down the long, black tunnel. Jeanne walked between her two parents holding the hand of each, anxious to see what lay ahead.

THE SMALL VILLAGE of Vieux France borders the twisting Orne River and sits near the ancient forest of Grimbosq. The largest city of any real size or population close to Vieux is Caen which sits a few miles north, closer to the English Channel. Both the village of Vieux and the city of Caen are roughly 150 miles east of Paris in the French countryside.

The Butte family were farmers that, for generations, lived off the land near the edge of the small French village of Vieux. The rural area and small community of neighbors had been an idyllic setting in which to grow up in. Four-year-old Jeanne Butte was an only child and lived with her mother and father in a small and modest home. Jeanne was raised in the same home her father, Marcel Butte, had been. A simple family farm in the north of France passed down to him when Jeanne's grandfather died shortly after she'd been born.

Marcel worked almost every day from dawn to sundown to provide for his small family of three. Jeanne's mother, Simone, had been married to Marcel for just over ten years. The couple had almost given up ever being blessed with children when Jeanne was finally born. The daughter closely resembled her mother except for her blue eyes and much lighter hair color. It was almost blonde in the sunlight, and the contrast to both of her parents' black hair color had sparked her father's nickname for her. Jeanne was his "Little Flower," named after the yellow gentian flowers that grew wild in clusters all around the pastures and fields surrounding the small French village they called home. Though Jeanne looked much like her mother, it was her father's fondness, attention, and approval she sought the most. The father and daughter were almost inseparable when Marcel wasn't working and farming in the fields.

As the Second World War ravaged the European continent and Hitler's German army conquered and occupied France, the village of Vieux was left relatively unscathed. However, German soldiers, officers, and their Nazi counterparts commonly traveled along the small lanes connecting the rural village to the whole of France. The simple men of the village resented the presence of the Germans, who they considered arrogant and unruly, and at times this caused disturbances. But for the most part, the conquering soldiers kept to themselves, and the village existed much as it had before the foreign invasion.

For Jeanne, these uniformed men had been a part of her entire life. She was born less than a year after their arrival and never knew a time before their presence and nomadic movements. As Jeanne grew, she became aware of the tense relationship between most of her neighbors and these men who spoke in a language she did not understand. While the friction was palpable, even to one at such a young age, this army of foreign men traveling back and forth from the village never presented a danger or threat to her. Most smiled and waved if they passed near her, sometimes even sharing a bit of chocolate if she was with her mother, Simone. Her mom explained to Jeanne that many soldiers were simply lonely and missed their own families who lived very far away. Seeing the children of Vieux helped the soldiers remember what waited for them when they were finally able to return home.

With these words in mind, Jeanne struggled to understand why her papa treated the soldiers' presence so differently than her mother. Marcel, her father, frowned and often pulled Jeanne away from any cluster of soldiers if he was nearby or if he felt his daughter was too close to them. Despite the mixed messages from her parents, Jeanne did not question or fear the uniformed men. So far in her short life, the only time she ever felt fear was when her parents started to argue if the soldiers lingered within the village for a very long. In those moments, her dad would often become uncharacteristically loud, red-faced, and harshly slam doors in the house. Her mother was often sad and left crying after these outbursts. The loud bickering between the two left Jeanne feeling she was somehow to blame. Often intuitively, before a bitter word was uttered, the little girl would find an excuse to leave the house and play outside alone. Or visit the farm animals in their barn, avoiding the joyless conflict that often played out between her parents.

There were no soldiers Jeanne could see anywhere in the cavern now as the group moved forward and deeper into the big, dark tunnel. The cluster of newcomers passed several tunnels of various-sized openings on either side as they made their way. None of them were lit; some seemed to have collapsed entirely, while others yawned widely as if inviting deeper inspection. Walking between her mother and father, Jeanne tightly squeezed both of her parents' hands as the three of them moved past these and farther down the long underground shaft.

In the far distance above, explosions could still be heard, but Jeanne no longer felt the ground shake under her. However, with each step, despite escaping the bombs and fires above, Jeanne did not feel more comfortable as her father had promised. Instead, she shivered in the cold, underground air, and each time Jeanne breathed, the air smelled funny. Grown men, women, and other children from their village walked in front and behind her, making it impossible for Jeanne to see where they were headed. The dust kicked up by all the marching feet tickled her nose as they trudged in silence among the dim, flickering light of the lanterns. She turned her face and rubbed her nose along the cloth of her shoulder to keep from sneezing.

As she did this, Jeanne froze when a single, mournful cry echoed and bounced among the walls of the cavern around her. The apparent pain and anguish in the sound sent chills bubbling across Jeanne's arms. In unison, the motley group of villagers and rural farmers stopped in their tracks within the tunnel at this sudden and unex-pected outburst. After a moment of silence, when no one in the group seemed to breathe, a second wail erupted somewhere off in the distance. It was a shriek unlike any sound Jeanne had ever heard before. Pulling her hand from her mother's, she turned with outstretched arms up to her father. Eyes wide in the darkness and panicked, she reached up desperately for him, terrified and wanting to be held. Certain whatever made that awful sound would soon be upon them.

In the shadows thrown by the yellow light of the nearby lanterns, Jeanne could see that the unexpected sound had also scared her papa. The look on his face pushed aside the bravery the four-year-old had barely clung to since first descending inside the underground shelter. Raw fear leaped up and out of the small girl, and Jeanne began to cry loudly. Soon, a chorus of terrified crying rose from the other children in the group. The crescendo built as each voice added to the cacophony of sound dominating and reverberating inside the tiny enclosed space. Jeanne sobbed loudly and jumped up into her startled father, who clutched at her. Nearly dropping Jeanne before getting a firm grip under each of her arms and hoisting her up and into his chest. Somewhere at the front of the group, a man's voice shouted loudly and confidently, cutting across the cries of frightened children.

"Please calm yourselves," the man's voice said in French. "We are very close now, and many are already wounded here. The cries you hear are those who have been injured by the bombing. The sound echoes strangely inside these rock walls, but I assure you there is nothing to fear down here. Please," the man continued, "we are almost there, and you can see for yourselves. Do not be afraid, my friends…"

Jeanne's father hugged her tightly and bent his face to her ear even as she continued to cry. "Hush, hush, little flower. See? It is only someone else scared, just like you, making that sound. I think they are hurt too. Maybe we can help them?" Jeanne's papa moved his hand to her cheek and wiped the tears before tilting her face up to his. "Now, now… You mustn't be afraid. Down here, we are all safe. I promise." Jeanne looked into her father's face and saw his fear was truly gone again. Slowly her terror began to melt away as well.

"But what of the Beast? The fiend that makes this dark place its home?" The question had originated somewhere behind where Jeanne and her mother and father stood among the group. Jeanne could not see who was talking, but the voice was coarse and dry like crumbling leaves in the fall. It uttered questions, but the words were accusatory. "Why do you think you belong down here…?" The small group turned one by one and saw it was Laurent who had spoken up.

The woman seemed impossibly old and tiny in stature, hunched over and frail looking but with fierce eyes that burned lively. A shapeless, colorless, and unflattering dress hung limply from her rounded shoulders. Jeanne was sure Laurent had not been included in the group that entered the cave system with her family. Yet she was bringing up the back as if she had always been part of the assembled refugees.

"The demon that dwells within this maze will end you all. Just ask all those around us now. This is the doorway to hell." Her hair was white, long, and stringy under a dirty knit cap. Laurent's face was lined deeply with pox and crevices, marking both her hard life and the long years it had taken to live it. The few teeth left in her head were dirty, cragged, and jutted out at odd angles from tight lips bleached of color.

Hers was an odd but familiar face within the village of Vieux but one shunned by those who lived there. Jeanne had only seen the ancient woman herself a handful of times during her entire life and had always been afraid of the strange lady. Older kids had once told Jeanne that Laurent was a witch living in a shack somewhere within the thick woods bordering the village. Seeing and hearing her now in this scary place only confirmed their whispered fears and suspicions. "It knows. It knows our sins and will come for you. You will see." She barked a cackle that ended in a throaty and dry coughing fit. "A sin collector this one is, a devourer of lost souls…"

With all eyes turned towards her, Laurent suddenly grew silent once more. She looked down at the cavern floor as if ashamed of what she had reported. Abruptly she turned and shuffled awkwardly back down the dark-lined rock walls in the direction they had just come from. Mumbling to herself as she often did when she wandered the village streets, one arm spasmed and twitched against her side as she made her way from the assembled group. She was quickly out of sight in the soft light of the few oil lanterns.

Michel, the usually friendly baker, called after her. "Nonsense, you crazy old bat! Always babbling about dark creatures roaming underground or the Beast of Gévaudan… Nothing but old wives tales." He then raised his voice, shouting in the tight quarters of the dark tunnel. "The monsters aren't down here! They are all up there!" Gesturing above his head where they had all escaped minutes earlier. "Those Nazi bastards are getting their collective sins rammed down their own throats now. Not us!" Michel's voice lowered once more, and turning back, he muttered, "You old witch…" Anything else was cut off once more by the return of the ethereal wail that first stopped the group's progress. Nervous glances were exchanged among the adults before the shuffling march resumed.

Still carried by her father, Jeanne looked hopefully over at her mother, longing to see more assurance that where they were headed was indeed a sanctuary and not damnation. But instead, her mother stood rigid even as others pressed against her to move forward. Jeanne's mama pulled at her long black hair and looked down the tunnel where Laurent had melted into the darkness. Jeanne saw other villagers brush past her mother without looking directly at her. When her mother finally faced forward once more, the look in her eyes was not one of assurance. But of blank desperation even a child understood. Jeanne buried her face once more against her father as another anguished scream rebounded around the group.

Together they all headed toward the sound of madness.

CHAPTER
THREE

JEANNE DID NOT OPEN her eyes again until she heard a few of
the older children from the ragtag group of refugees begin talking.
Finally daring to peek out from her father's chest, she was surprised to
see they had entered a grand, oval-shaped chamber. Multiple fires
were lit along the ground of the immense underground room, and
groups of adults and children sat huddled around each of them. Above
one of the larger fires, a single black kettle sat engulfed among dancing
orange flames. More lanterns lined the walls of the stone cavern, some
hanging from steel spikes pounded into the rock walls and others
resting on the tops of large boulders scattered along the ground of the
carved-out cavity.

Dirty faces peered up at the group of newcomers as they walked
past the survivors who had made their way below the surface before
them. Although cries and screams of pain and anguish were still audible, the sounds were muted among the groups of families now
greeting the newest arrivals. Jeanne immediately felt safer among the
larger number of people, many of whom she recognized from her
village above. Compared to the black, hauntingly twisted tunnels the
group had just exited, the additional lighting eased the very active and
wild running of the four-year-old's imagination.

Jeanne's father, still carrying his daughter, strode beside Michel.

Michel spoke to the entire group as they walked, assuring them they would all be safe together. He explained fresh air, even though they were far underground, still flowed in and out of various vents sprinkled among the maze of tunnels. The small hidden openings at the surface were dug out by the original men who had labored to extract the stone and carve out the quarry. Proper air circulation was crucial when working or staying below ground for any length of time.

Michel then spoke directly to Jeanne's papa, showing him where his family would temporarily be making their home. He led the three Buttes to a place near the back of the gigantic cavity where several large stones made a natural boundary. Within that space were two dented and rusted oil lanterns and several ragged blankets lying on the ground next to a pile of straw. The baker pointed in various directions around the cavern, speaking briefly with Jeanne's papa before moving forward with the rest of the group. Michel led the remaining newcomers towards similar, empty spaces within the old underground stone quarry. At each stop, other families peeled off the larger group one by one, filling in their designated spots until everyone was finally situated.

Jeanne sat on one of the large rocks in their area while her father and mother stepped a few feet away and began whispering amongst themselves. Still in shock from the sudden and unexpected changes over the last several hours, Jeanne looked at neighboring spaces while her parents talked. Stealing glances and discreetly peering over to where other families nearby had carved out their place before the Butte family arrived.

Those families each took over sections of the quarry that were, just like the one Jeanne was now sitting in, a few square yards wide and across. Some had made clearer boundaries along the ground of their area by using loose stones to create tiny borders only a few inches high. Others, using brown cord and pieces of rope, hung up aprons and blankets between large boulders as a flimsy wall that provided some privacy. The fraying twine tucked inside cracks along the walls to hold up the cloth barriers. As Jeanne slowly looked back and forth, taking in her new surroundings, she was disappointed to see that the closest families did not include young children like herself. It seemed to Jeanne that all her village friends were at the opposite end of the giant cavern. She waved to several of them from where she sat, but they did not see her or wave back in all the commotion of the newcomers settling and the gloom of the shadowy cave.

With her parents and the groups of families closest to the Buttes focused on conversation and other things, Jeanne began to notice the items some of these families brought with them. At her age only inquisitive, not yet old enough to question how these families knew what to bring. Or how they managed to get their belongings down into the cavern. Instead, naturally curious and looking for clues as to how these neighboring families were going about living down in the cavern.

Jeanne's eyes swept across many different sections and the various assorted possessions that folks brought with them. One family had a full set of plates, cups, and even forks, spoons, and knives for eating. Another brought bedding, including pillows and quilts of many colors. There were suitcases and old wooden chests with heavy lids closed to prying eyes. Many families had one or two pots and pans in their area, most dented and already blackened by fire. Jeanne saw leaning against a far stone wall a single bicycle sitting next to a broken wood wheelbarrow. Three spaces away, Jeanne was tickled to spy a wind-up gramophone like the one in her house. The thought of music being played here, and maybe even dancing with her father again, made Jeanne smile despite the conditions and uncertainty surrounding her. She looked over at her parents and saw they were now done talking and, like her, looking at all the people that made up this new underground community. Jeanne walked over to them, tugging her mother's dress.

"I have to pee, Mama..." Jeanne whispered faintly. "Where can I go?"

"I am not sure, sweetie," her mother admitted. Then looking at Marcel, she asked, "Should we go see where everything is? Maybe we all should use the bathroom before we turn in tonight. I know it is not that late yet, but I'm exhausted." Jeanne's father seemed distracted but nodded his head in agreement.

"Michel said there is a collapsed tunnel back this way," he gestured deeper into the cavern and away from where they entered. "He said across from that is one of the tunnels to…uh… do that. Let's go see what we can find." Circling around the cave wall, the three of them picked their way carefully across the cavern's rocky floor. They stopped briefly to talk with other villagers they knew and shared what they each had seen or heard so far. Accepting offers of help from some and extending the same to others. Although anxious to relieve herself, Jeanne began to feel better with each familiar face they encountered. However, that blossoming comfort soon disappeared when they stepped into the entrance of the near-black tunnel.

"Do we… Why do we have to go down here, Papa? I don't want to." Jeanne could see a few yellow lights ahead of them in the darkness. But she also could hear movement somewhere down the winding passageway and could not tell what it was. A hacking cough echoed around them, and groaning seemed to come from the rock walls themselves. Jeanne stopped walking and pulled her hand out of her mother's. It was only half a lie when she started to say, "I don't have to go anymore…" Marcel and Simone both turned back and looked down at their daughter. Parental concern on the mother's face and a bemused half-smile on the father's. Both were blissfully unaware of the gnarled hand that had begun to reach out of the black tunnel behind them.

The disembodied, spectral hand slowly moved toward all three of them.

Jeanne's eyes grew wide, looking past her parents, unable to breathe as the shriveled pale fingers crept closer to them. The shadows in the passageway ahead hid what (if anything, thought Jeanne!) the hand was attached to. The dim lights from the larger cavern behind Jeanne only illuminated the lone, still-reaching appendage. The knotted fist contorted, and two fingers extended out, each with long, dirty yellow fingernails. As the fingers pointed, a bony wrist slowly became visible, and the floating hand turned to reach for Jeanne's father, surely to snatch him and drag him back into the black tunnel, never to be seen again. Jeanne screeched in fear, soiling and soaking her panties as her full bladder involuntarily emptied itself. Her sudden exclamation startled her parents, who quickly stepped to their young daughter and kneeled down. Crying and blubbering, Jeanne pointed at the hand behind her mom and dad as it inched forward out of the darkness.

Jeanne's father turned and stood once more. Seeing the hand emerging out of the darkness, he extended his own, grabbing the skeletal hand and eliciting another piercing scream from his four-year-old daughter. Undeterred, Marcel pulled gently, and soon the crippled form of an elderly man hunched over at his waist became visible in the meager light. Behind him, the village doctor patiently walked out of the shadows with the absurdly thin figure, half holding him upright as the old man struggled with each step. Drool dripped from the side of the wrinkled mouth, and his emaciated chest heaved once before a hollow cough cut off Jeanne's screams.

Despite his relatively young age, Dr. Criqui, well-known and liked in the village of Vieux and the surrounding areas, began apologizing. "I am so sorry we frightened you, my dear," he started. "Jacque needed to relieve himself, so I was helping him find the closest place." Seeing the young child's fear and understanding the stressful circumstance they all were in, he quickly added, "This place seems scary, I know. But, Jeanne, everyone being here together is our protection. And I am so happy to see you and your family have made it down here safely. Think of this old quarry just like you do a closet at home. Dark, maybe smelly and seldom opened, but useful and always surrounded by a loving family." The doctor winked and smiled at Jeanne as he continued behind the slow, hobbling old man. Both men gradually moved past the Butte family. "If you are looking for a toilet, keep going down this tunnel and look for the three clustered lanterns on the right," Dr. Criqui added over his shoulder.

After Jeanne composed herself, the Butte family descended the long tunnel. As promised, one of the spots used as a community bathroom in the quarry was soon located. Her mother peeled off Jeanne's dripping panties, helping the little girl clean and dry herself. "You'll have to go without these until we can clean them later," she said with a reassuring nod and smile. Simone rung the cloth dry as best she could before tucking the damp underwear away in the pocket of her own dress. Then briefly squatted above the make-shift latrine.

While Jeanne and her mother waited for Marcel to finish his turn, they walked deeper into the earthen tunnel together. Her mother showed no fear as she held her daughter's hand, saying she just wanted to see what else was back that way. After a few more steps, they came to a fork in the tunnel, and her mother stopped, seemingly satisfied with what she saw, much to Jeanne's relief. Then turning quickly, they both began to make their way back towards the toilet and where they'd left Jeanne's father. Her mother took long strides, making it hard for Jeanne to keep up.

"What were you doing down there?" Jeanne's father was already waiting, and Jeanne ran to him in the flickering shadows. She was beginning to feel a little better now that she'd seen a few familiar faces on their walk to the bathroom and explored a bit more of the cavern. Her spirit of adventure slowly overtook her earlier fears. But when her father continued talking to her mother, it was in a tone Jeanne instantly recognized. Slightly higher and louder than her father's usual deep voice and more demanding. The one that often preceded her parents' arguments and fights. "Is someone down there? Who were you talking with?" Jeanne's brief respite from her fears evaporated. "What were you looking for?"

"Nothing, no one was down there. I was just… just seeing where it went. That's all." Jeanne recognized the defensive tone of her mother as well. But unlike at home, Jeanne could not run outside or away. She cringed and felt trapped between the two, now more afraid than ever.

"Jeanne!" Her father's face was suddenly thrust into her own, and she flinched as he bent over her. Jeanne desperately wanted to be anywhere but where she was at that moment. Her father peppered her with questions. "What did you see down there, huh? Who did mama talk with? Did you see anybody?" Jeanne shook her head no. "What does that mean, sweetie? Didn't you recognize the man?"

"God, Marcel, leave her alone. Can't you see she is scared?"

"Don't make me into the bad guy here!" Jeanne's father's voice was thunderous as he talked directly into Jeanne's face.

"Nnn…No one, Papa… There was no one. Just… just two more tunnels. It was real dark…" Jeanne tried to think how she could make it better. Sure, again, she was really the problem. Now regretting and feeling guilty for having wet herself. "I was scared. Can we go back now? I don't want the beast demon swallower thing to hear us. Maybe… maybe it lives down one of those tunnels." Burning tears were streaming down her face once again. She looked up at her father pleadingly. Willing the one she loved more than anything in the world to return. Not the father that yelled at her mother. She didn't like him as much…

"Demon swallower, what are you… Oh god, Laurent. Do you mean what Laurent was babbling on about when we first came in? The Beast of Gévaudan and all that nonsense, ha! That old…" Jeanne's father looked over at her mother, shaking his head. His face broke, and once again, the father Jeanne loved returned, and his eyes grew soft once more. He bent down and picked Jeanne up again. Over her shoulder, he said, "I'm sorry, Simone. It's just this bombing and running. I was so scared we wouldn't even get here. It is just making me crazy, that's all. It's the Germans, all the damn Germans. And I'm just exhausted."

Jeanne's mother moved over to them but risked saying nothing to her husband. Instead, laying a hand on the top of Jeanne's head, shushing her gently. "Hush now, baby girl. There is no beast or demon down here. Mama is not scared, is she? We even walked down farther together, didn't we?" Pointedly she added, more for Marcel's benefit than her daughter's, "And we didn't see anything down there, did we?" Jeanne shook her head once more, her chin rubbing against her father's shoulder.

Together, the three headed back to their new place deep inside the once long-forgotten old stone quarry. Still being carried by her father, Jeanne looked back at her mother over his shoulder. "Believe me, Jeanne, I would know if there was a demon down here. I would fight and beat him back to hell before letting him get you."

CHAPTER
FOUR

AFTER A SHARED meal among their fellow refugees of lukewarm onion soup and stale bread, the Butte family settled in for the night. Dividing up the ratty blankets and making the most of the meager straw afforded them, Simone lay with her daughter and tried to help soothe the day's tumultuous events. Reciting some simple stories to her and humming into the four-year-old's ear. Hoping to calm Jeanne's mind and restore some semblance of normalcy despite the almost unimaginable chaos of the day.

As mother and daughter lay together, renewed but mercifully muted sounds came again from above their heads. Twice in the glimmering lantern light, cave dust cascades down from the ceiling, swirling around them like dandelion seeds in the summer breeze. Soon, however, the sounds become familiar enough, even in the dim light, much like faraway thunder in a storm that slowly passes. The uniqueness lost and consequence unseen, Jeanne could eventually feel herself drifting off. Only the occasional outburst or moan from the wounded kept the peace from settling completely among the ancient stone quarry's new inhabitants.

Jeanne closed her eyes tightly and chased after the serenity of sleep until she finally caught it. She dreamed of the farm animals back home she had always considered her pets, especially the frequent visiting cats she loved most. Chasing and rolling with them in the tall grass of the fields, searching out their hiding places under porches and among the hay strewn about their barn. At times, sneaking her favorite ones scraps of food when her parents weren't looking, and, in this dream, being able to talk with each of them. Soon the group of cats grew large. Newcomers of all sizes and colors sprung from cracks in the ground. So many at once that Jeanne stands and begins to nervously back away. As she looks on, a gigantic dog with radiant yellow eyes emerges from the throngs and moves deftly among them. Padding forward and herding the furry mob towards Jeanne as the felines' yowls crescendo. The cat's chatter becomes so loud and endless that Jeanne finds she can no longer sleep.

She wakes alone and confused. The straw all around her merging the dream of barnyard cats with the reality of where she is. Turning over, Jeanne sees that her mother had moved just a few feet away from her while sleeping. The outline of her body was buried and unmoving under the worn and thin blue blanket. Jeanne has no idea whether it is morning or night in the manmade cavern. Even the pace of time seems bewildering to the four-year-old. With no clues from the outside world and puzzled why she has woken, Jeanne props her elbows under herself and looks around the cavern. All is quiet; in the distance, she can see only a few small fires still lit, most barely embers glowing orange among grey and blackened ash. Neighboring families are sleeping together, and although impossible to tell the hour in the deep, dark cavern, Jeanne feels it must still be nighttime. She rolls over and closes her eyes once again when movement catches her attention.

It is her father. He has risen, and at his side, he holds one of their dimly lit lanterns in hand. It gives off only a meager circle of light, a yellow halo that barely reaches the ground in front of his steps. He has begun to carefully make his way along the outer rock wall of the cave next to their space. Jeanne sits up and calls out to him. "Papa," she whispers loudly, "where are you going?" Startled at his daughter's voice, Marcel stops, turns around, and silently shuffles back to where Jeanne is. Dropping down on his hands and knees in front of her, he whispers in the silence of the cave.

"Go back to sleep, Jeanne. I am just going to… uh…" He pauses and looks away momentarily before finishing. "I am just going to use the bathroom, and then I'll be right back." He gently nudges his daughter and helps her lie back down again. "Now close your eyes and go back to sleep. It is not time to get up yet. So you must stay here, understand?" Pulling her thin blanket up, he kisses her and rises, making his way again along the cave's wall toward the black tunnels.

After a few moments, Jeanne flips over and wiggles closer to the form of her sleeping mother. Intent on cuddling up against her in the cool of the underground cavern. The movement, however, disturbs her mother's blanket, and it falls away. Underneath the old blanket, Jeanne sees only straw clumped tightly together. Confused, Jeanne tugs at the blue blanket some more before realizing her mother is not anywhere underneath. Sitting up again and quickly looking around her, Jeanne couldn't find her mother anywhere.

Alarmed, she tries to call after her father. But as Jeanne does so, he rounds the cave wall and disappears down the tunnel leading to the toilet they'd used earlier. Afraid she'll get in trouble if she wakes the others, Jeanne quickly buckles her dusty leather shoes and rises to follow after her papa. Feeling she must urgently alert him that mother is missing. Jeanne fears the sin-swallowing demon beast has somehow whisked her away while they slept. Her concern for her mama outweighs her fears of the cavern as she rapidly trails after her father.

As Jeanne makes her way into the tunnel her father had entered, the waving black shadows that dominate the walls and the echoing sounds of the cavern crowd in on her. She begins to doubt herself and calls out for her papa to wait for her. But at that moment, yet another low wail reverberates off the walls and drowns her tiny plea.

Courage deserts her.

Jeanne becomes terrified that if she calls out again, the beasts or demons living down here will realize she is alone and find her. She stands paralyzed and mute, eyes wide and filling with tears.

Watching the light of the lantern her father carries moving farther away, Jeanne makes a desperate decision. Throwing her weight forward silently and swiftly, she rushes after her papa, eyes trained on the ever-growing smaller, bobbing, yellow light. Desperation and fear drive her, unwittingly, deeper down into the earth. Jeanne is so focused on not losing sight of her papa's dim lantern that she is unaware of how far she travels down the cavern's underground tunnel. Or that she has long passed the three lanterns illuminating the toilet.

Jeanne follows the small, swaying light, stumbling in the dark of the tunnel and brushing against its rigid, roughly hewn walls. Several times tripping over rocks that litter the floor of the ancient rock channel. Crying silently as the light begins to grow smaller and smaller with each step she takes. When it briefly disappears, she loses her breath, and her little heart, though pounding wildly, nearly stops. She sobs and runs until it miraculously appears again, then grows larger as she approaches. Relief floods over her, and she is about to call out for her papa to tell him the news about her mother when she hears faint voices.

As she approaches, Jeanne sees a second light visible in the black of the underground tunnel. Confused by the sight of a new light, her steps become tentative, and Jeanne slows to a halt as she hears two distinctly different voices. The rushed cadence of the ongoing conversation echoes within the chamber, making the words blend together and hard for her to understand. Just beyond the reach of the twin dim lantern lights, Jeanne can see two adults speaking loudly and talking over each other. Their raised voices and sharp words make her wince. Unsure yet who they are, she inches forward as quietly as possible. Terrified at being alone in the dark, strange tunnel. Yet intimidated at the thought of interrupting adults talking. She creeps ahead, eyes wide, looking for any clue or hint of the familiar form or clothes of her father. The murky shadows of both adults dance on the stony tunnel walls, shapelessly intertwining like smoke in the poor illumination of the lanterns.

Jeanne begins to make out the angry words she hears. Words she doesn't really understand. The harsh exchange scorches her young ears, and as Jeanne timidly treads forward, the discussion only gets louder and more heated. An unwelcome recognition dawns on Jeanne moments later: her father and mother are arguing loudly.

"You fucking whore! You told him about this, didn't you? The one place of safety the village had. Now you have endangered everyone hiding down here, so you can spread your legs for him again. Even now, with the entire world coming down all around us, you can only think of is yourself! Stupid pig! You are nothing but a filthy slut, Simone!"

"What do you know of it, Marcel, huh? What do you know about what I want or what I do? All you think about is your stupid fields and dumb friends in Vieux. All of you are so angry at the Germans! But not one of you with the courage to do anything about it. Never even picking a side, so weak and spineless. I don't know what is more worthless. That broken-down old farm or the worthless piece of meat between your legs."

At this insult, Marcel advanced on his wife, grabbing her by the throat and causing her to stumble backward. Marcel moved three steps forward and pushed his wife ahead of him and out of what little light the two lanterns on the ground gave.

Ignoring any light he still felt in his life, deeper into the darkness they both went.

"Don't you talk to me that way! You are supposed to be my wife!" Simone clawed with her hands at her husband's single hand, a calloused grip strengthened by years of toiling among the French fields. The hand remained wrapped around her throat and forced her back. She finally gained space between her neck and his fingers but only croaked out more taunts.

"That's right, Marcel." Simone was gasping but still defiant. Her grimace had become a sneer. "I am a whore, his whore, not yours. You know what I like best, Marcel? Huh? He doesn't fuck me like just a man. Oh no... Not that you could ever even do that. No, he is an animal, a beast even. And when he is done with me, I walk slowly back home to our tiny little house. The whole time I walk, I can feel what we did running slowly down my thighs, making me smile. Then you know what I do, Marcel? Huh? Since I know you won't touch me, I touch myself right in our bed. I lay back and play with what I still have of his, what he emptied inside me. I think about him..."

Simone gulps more air into her lungs, gagging but still talking. "Right after, I can still smell him on me and feel where he touched me. Where he was. But that only makes me long even more for the next time I can see him again." Simone relished her confession; seeing her husband's shock and the hurt etched across his features gave her a sense of power. Simone long thought this war would end the world, or at least the world she felt trapped in. She was done feeling impotent. "See you… you can't even get it up, much less make me cum. But him? All I have to do is think about him, and from miles away, he can make…"

"Shut up, god damn you!! You, you shut up right now!!" Marcel pushes violently backward again, and Simone stumbles on the loose rock scattered on the cavern floor. She desperately pulls and clutches at her husband's hands, coughing while slowly sagging to her knees. "Shut up! Shut your whore mouth!" Marcel adds his other hand to her throat. Squeezing in a fury, letting years of pent-up frustration flow out of him in a flurry of blind rage. "Don't you talk… Stop saying that! You shut your mouth!" Simone falls silent as the life is choked out of her. Marcel's greasy, jet-black hair falls across his face as he looks down at his wife of ten years.

Obscuring his vision of the murder he commits.

Even as Simone's hands fall lifeless at her sides, he continues muttering and gripping tightly at the pale white throat that spewed the insults.

At last, as if yanked out of his hands, his wife and Jeanne's mother limply collapsed to the floor of the stone quarry. Frozen, Marcel stands like a statue with his arms still outstretched in front of him. He looks dumbly at the empty hands used to throttle his wife, then down at the empty, crumpled shell of who he once loved. His legs were shaking, yet rooted, like two saplings caught in a terrible storm.

Marcel takes one shuddering breath. The last one he ever will.

Out of the darkness, to his right, a runaway train of rage tears into him. Uttering a bestial grunt as it descends, covered in black, the attack as savage as it was definitive. One limb after another fell upon the murderous husband with a swift and frightening power. A skilled blitz as brutal as it was short. In less than a minute, the victim and the whirlwind of destruction that hit him were gone. All that was left in the flickering light of the two lanterns where Marcel Butte stood just moments earlier was a red pool of murky liquid scattered with a few hard bits.

Jeanne watched all this unfold mutely, still just outside the reach of the twin lantern's fading illumination. Uncomprehending and unmoving beside the slowly dying lantern flame. Surrounded by utter darkness, the final echoes of her papa's violent end were the last sounds that reached her ears. The four-year-old girl, her father's "little flower," was far beyond gone. Blank eyes stared unseeing, breath barely taken, lips trembling, and eyes watering. Expressionless, eyes so wide the eyelashes were no longer visible, limbs stiff... Her body slowly shutting down and sagging.

Swooping down, all in black, what took Marcel into the next world now came for Jeanne. It swept her away without a sound...

CHAPTER
FIVE

KANKAKEE, ILLINOIS 1979

WHITE PAPER FELL from the sky around her like snow. Giant, oversized flakes all of a single shape, size, and design. As if Mother Nature had grown tired of churning out the endless miracles individual snowflakes required of her each and every winter. Hazy, grey smoke circulated and blotted out the sun above the paper-filled air fluttering around Jeanne. Fires licked at the dropping sheets from smoldering, caved-in buildings on either side of her, touching them and blazing in the air as they burst into flames. The bright, paper-fueled fires briefly hurt Jeanne's blue eyes as she wandered across the deserted roads of her abandoned village.

Jeanne marched steadily forward, looking desperately for her father and mother. Fearful for them and unsettled by the empty homes and buildings surrounding her. Black, gaping doorways and empty, blown-out windows stared at her as she passed each structure. Jeanne understood something terrible was happening and was powerless to stop it. A low rumble echoed off the abandoned storefronts and alleyways she passed. The sound grew in intensity, and Jeanne began to walk faster. Afraid to stay where she was, yet fearful of running blindly in the dense smoke obscuring her vision beyond just a few short yards. She tried calling out for her parents, but her voice was swallowed whole by the encroaching roar above her. Jeanne could not hear her own voice at all. Her chest thundered, and she felt the sound as much as she heard it.

Gracefully, a single sheet of white paper floated directly before her. Swaying back and forth in the windless day, slowly dropping lower and lower. Jeanne reached up and snatched it out of the air. Rescuing the drifting text and quickly examining the words in black printed across the white paper. She struggled to understand the foreign language until she realized the strange characters were English, and she could read it. Relieved, she scanned the page, knowing each piece of paper falling had the same thing written. Even as she read the words, Jeanne understood she already knew what the plummeting leaflets would say.

It read, "The vital objective near which you find yourself will be continuously attacked. Leave now! You don't have a minute to lose." The earth under her began to shake violently. As Jeanne released the leaflet and let it spiral to the ground, the intensity of the falling papers from the sky above increased. Tumbling so thickly she could barely see each step she took.

Jeanne began to run in a panic.

Heedless of the direction of her path or her blindness among the flurry of papers threatening to bury her. She ran as hard and as fast as her legs would carry her. Her feet slipped on the bed of papers on the ground; it was like running on top of wet leaves dropped by early autumn trees in a dense and dewy forest. The road she traversed under her trembled, and the non-stop shaking blurred her vision as she sprinted across it. She ran headlong into a sea of smoke and frantically swiped at the floating papers that dogged her path. Buildings crashed down around her violently as bomb after bomb exploded across the French countryside.

Jeanne briefly catches sight of her mother in the distance among the cascade of dropping papers. She was also running in the same direction as Jeanne, away from the explosions and falling rubble. Jeanne calls out for her mother, asking where her father is, but her mother never hears or turns around. Instead, she disappears down a rock-lined pit in the ground, recklessly diving headfirst so that Jeanne can see only the bottoms of her bare feet vanishing into the blackness.

Sure her mother has led her to safety, Jeanne launched herself after her. Scrambling over the small ledge on her hands and knees, pitching face first over the side after her. At the last moment, too late to stop her forward momentum, Jeanne notes that the jagged rocks lining the hole's opening resemble very sharp teeth. She is swallowed up and tumbles downward into empty space. Her arms pinwheel wildly at her sides, reaching for anything to break her fall but finding nothing. Jeanne falls and falls endlessly.

Her hollow screams echoing...

———

Jeanne wakes from the weightless fall, startling herself from the dream with an arm outstretched on either side of her empty bed. She sits up quickly, emerging from the all too familiar vision, and swings both legs over the side of her mattress, instantly comforted by the cool, hard-wood floor and the return of gravity. Jeanne groggily opens her eyes wider, trying to shake the disorientation of the disturbing nightmare. Her blonde hair is damp with sweat, and her light cotton nightgown sticks to her back. Her heart still pounding in her chest, Jeanne reaches shakily for the glass of water at her bedside nightstand. The additional touch with reality helps her clear the stark images from her restless sleep.

Pushing herself off the bed, she glances at the small, red numbers of her digital alarm clock that read 6:28 AM. Although earlier than she usually rises, Jeanne decides she would rather face the upcoming day than more dreams. She pulls the fuzzy, blue bathrobe off the back of the single chair in her bedroom, dipping her bare shoulders and arms into each of its sleeves and pulling the robe's belt tightly around her. Jeanne opens her bedroom door and is instantly besieged by a yowling, overweight black cat with light green eyes. Springing to its feet, the obese feline's accusatory complaints are loud and persistent. Ensuring Jeanne is well aware that an empty food bowl needs to be addressed in the kitchen.

Jeanne makes her way downstairs as the fat cat pads softly behind her on the carpeted steps. Undoubtedly hoping to herd its owner directly to the kitchen and the barren dish. Arriving, Jeanne first fills and turns her Mr. Coffee coffeemaker on, anxious for a dose of caffeine to help get her day moving. While she waits for the brewer to warm up, she takes a small cup of Good Mews cat food out of the pantry and pours it into a plastic bowl on her kitchen counter. Lowering it to the floor, the cat at her feet purrs loudly and nudges Jeanne's hand with his head, clearly pleased to get attention and an early jump on breakfast. With the obligatory feeding and first petting of the housecat complete, Jeanne turns back to the kitchen counter. She watches the stream of black java pour into the glass carafe. Soon she has a warm cup of coffee in her hand and sips at it gingerly, replaying in her mind the scenes from her dream before they dissipate entirely.

The dream itself was not new but rather a frequent flyer from somewhere in her subconscious mind as of late. Its origins were of no mystery either, just an echo from an early childhood spent in war-torn France that still reverberated inside her head. As a child, Jeanne had many sleepless nights haunted by dark and terrible images. As she got older, Jeanne finally began to control her emotions, and the dreams faded for the most part. But now, a divorcee and a mother of one at almost 40 years of age, they had begun to surge again.

Jeanne knew the anticipation and anxiety surrounding the upcoming trip back to the country of her birth was the main reason for these reoccurring dreams. She supposed planning for this trip, all the while knowing she would be leaving behind Russell, her only child, may also be triggering her. Jeanne was, in a way, abandoned as a child and left without a mother or father at a very young age. Now she was, though only temporarily, doing the same thing to her own child. Jeanne had been trying really hard to connect with Russell as a mother was supposed to.

Yet here she was, deserting him.

Everyone from family members, friends, and school staff understood Russell was a very sensitive boy. The angst during the earlier divorce from his father, Tim, often easily read upon his young face. Despite this, for Jeanne, being motherly or trying to comfort her son always felt forced and unnatural to her. Jeanne was only four when she lost both parents in the war. Little Russell was already ten but in many ways less mature than she had been at that same age. Of course, Jeanne had seen and experienced more by ten years of age than most kids or even adults would their entire lives.

Jeanne drank her coffee while Samson, the big black cat named by Russell three years ago when he'd shown up on her porch, sprang into her lap. He circled the top of her thighs several times and pushed his head into her empty hand. Demanding additional attention and purring loudly to either tempt or guilt her into complying with his desire. Jeanne obliged with several strokes under his chin as the cat raised his face and closed his eyes contently while she drank her coffee. Against her will, Jeanne's mind wandered back to the old stone quarry where her entire childhood village hid during the Allied invasion and liberation of France. A place she had somehow never really been able to leave. The manmade cavern, a tomb that she was only now beginning to understand, trapped her life deep underground before she ever had a chance to live it.

Sighing deeply, Jeanne finished the last of her coffee before rising and switching on a small transistor radio beside a tall glass vase of yellow flowers on her kitchen counter. Jeanne glanced up at the hands of the clock on the wall above the sink. It was almost 7:00, so she turned the AM radio dial up a little louder so she wouldn't miss the local on-the-hour weather report out of Chicago for today. The DJ reported nothing new from what Jeanne heard last night on the 10:00 news. The forecast continued calling for clear skies with no storms imminent or coming out of the Great Lakes region. With such a big day of travel ahead, she was relieved.

She soon flipped off the radio and, humming softly, made her way upstairs to finish the packing she'd started earlier in the week. Her flight to France was that afternoon. She soon found herself double and triple checking her suitcases, hoping she remembered everything she needed for her first trip back to France since leaving the country at almost five years of age. When she closed and locked her bags for the final time, it did not occur to her that she had not packed a single picture of her son, Russell Stander.

CHAPTER
SIX

WITH THE DAY TO embark finally here, Jeanne became increasingly anxious. After getting the obligatory hugs, kisses, and promises that Russell would take care of Samson, Jeanne was driven to O'Hare International Airport to catch the overseas Air France flight by her ex-husband. She promised Tim she would call his house once she reached her hotel and drop a few postcards in the mail for Russell if she could. Tim stayed with her until she checked her bags and had her boarding pass in hand. When he turned to walk away, Jeanne felt a flood of emotions that were hard for her to hold back. Her eyes unexpectedly welled with tears, and embarrassed, she looked for something to distract herself from blubbering and ruining her eye makeup.

Spying a small newsstand nearby, Jeanne darted in and scoured a paperback rack near the entrance. The red and white sign on top of the spinning wire rack declared the books were all new releases, but many of the metal pockets were empty. Looking at the picked-over titles, she was drawn to a relatively new author she'd read before named Stephen King. His latest novel, "The Dead Zone," had just been released in paperback form. Despite its morbid title, she impulsively grabbed a copy. She paid the ogling, Coke bottle glasses-wearing cashier before heading to her gate. She skimmed over the book while she sat on the hard and uncomfortable, though brightly colored, plastic chairs in the crowded seating area. Straining to hear the garbled gate announcements on the PA over the screeching baby two seats away from her.

Upon closer inspection of the book's content, Jeanne began having second thoughts about reading something so intense right before returning to her own "dead zone." But she spies early on in the book that one of the central characters, like Jeanne, lost his parents during the Second World War. That was intriguing to her, and knowing how much she identified with the ostracized main character in one of the author's earlier books, "Carrie," she decided to give the novel a chance. Jeanne begins reading it in earnest once she hears her Air France flight will be delayed by 20 minutes. Hoping to appear absorbed in the paperback, she flips the pages without looking up to avoid being sucked into the banality of the conversation of her fellow air travelers seated near her.

When her flight finally does begin boarding, Jeanne continues this well-practiced ploy. Artfully avoiding speaking or making eye contact with those alongside her as the passengers trudged slowly into and down the main corridors of the gate and gigantic intercontinental plane. The jumbo jet had four rows of aisles across, and Jeanne's window seat was halfway down the aircraft's belly. Finally seated, she notes her view of the huge movie screen in the middle of her section would be compromised during the nine-hour transatlantic flight to Paris. However, she is relieved to find the seat next to her unoccupied. As a bonus, the wailing baby from the gate is many rows ahead of her and hopefully out of earshot.

Although usually both an avid and fast reader, Jeanne finds it hard to concentrate on the story once the flight gets underway. Her mind wanders, and after the early meal is served and cleared, she is disappointed with the inflight movie. John Travolta and Olivia Newton-John danced across the blurry screen in "Grease," but she'd seen the picture when it first came out last year. Restless and a little bored, Jeanne replays the events leading up to her journey back to the country of her birth. A trip both Tim and her current therapist actually encouraged her to take. Both agreed it would be a positive step forward in her life.

Jeanne initially started seeing a psychologist years ago while still married. At Tim's urging, they started marriage counseling in hopes of saving what turned out to be a doomed union. But from the beginning, deep down, Jeanne hadn't really shared the same hopes with her husband. Even so, in the early seventies, any divorce had a stigma attached to it. In the Midwest - a hop, skip, and jump from the Bible Belt – it was not that common either. So Jeanne hadn't opposed Tim's appeal to work together and make an effort any more than she had resisted his initial marriage proposal. She hadn't loved Tim then, nor did she hate him once the counseling, and even the inevitable divorce, started. She felt, as with all relationships in her life, nothing. Part of her was amazed that it took the man so long to figure that out about her.

Tim was Dr. Stander: a widowed family practitioner ten years her senior that, when she'd first met him, had an eight-year-old daughter named Sherry from his previous marriage and an office in Kankakee, Illinois. Kankakee was a hardworking, primarily blue-collar factory town back then, just an hour south of bustling Chicago. Bordering the neighboring state of Indiana, and surrounded by flat and unremarkable farmland and fields to its south. The city itself sprang up initially along the banks of the meandering river the town was named after. Kankakee was where Jeanne immigrated after the war in 1945 at five years of age to live with her mom's sister, the childless Aunt, and Uncle Finney.

Jeanne had never left.

After graduating high school, Jeanne worked in the typing pool for the local General Mills plant before taking other secretarial jobs in and around Kankakee. She did this not out of a desire to be a career secretary but because she knew it was expected of her. She had felt an obligation to contribute income to the home of the aunt and uncle who had adopted her at such a young age. They were both older, kind, and giving, so the thought of taking advantage of them never entered Jeanne's mind. A good portion of the money she earned over the years went to them in the form of rent, her share of utilities, and the groceries she often purchased for all of them.

Jeanne's only splurges, outside the car her uncle helped her pick out, were on books and going out to the movies. She found both of these mediums endlessly fascinating. Spending time studying the written word and the actresses on the silver screen for clues on how to behave properly and act in social situations. For this reason, she always preferred to attend the daytime matinees on the weekends when the theatre was rarely full. Usually going by herself if she could get away with it, buttery popcorn in her lap and a soda in the cup holder. Of course, to keep up proper appearances, she also went to the movies on dates with random male suitors who sometimes asked her out. Always with a ready excuse to end any budding relationship after three or four dates at most.

Jeanne had answered a "Help Wanted" ad in the local newspaper and had started working for Dr. Stander in 1968 as a twenty-eight-year-old receptionist. By the end of her first interview with the older doctor, she knew he'd been smitten with her. While that may have seemed like an almost scandalous revelation to an outsider, theirs was hardly a romantic, passionate courtship nor a torrid office affair.

Instead, for her, at least, it was simply convenient. The path of least resistance towards what Jeanne understood she should desire and strive for in America. Growing up, she was taught to dream of horses, Elvis, and making the cheerleading squad at school. But, after escaping the suffocating hierarchy and cliques of high school and as an adult woman teetering toward "spinsterdom," Jeanne realized she needed to relearn what her dreams should be made of. At least if she wanted to continue to fit in and not raise eyebrows.

So she educated herself.

As an adult woman, her aspirations, Jeanne learned, should be the proverbial white picket fence: marriage, ideally with a successful lawyer or doctor, and, of course, a family of her own. Jeanne knew that if guilt had been an emotion she could feel, she should feel guilty for not thwarting Dr. Stander's fumbling advances right out of the gate. But the widowed doctor was nice enough, fairly easily manipulated, came with Sherry, an adorable daughter, and owned a thriving medical practice. Jeanne understood she could easily step into this ready-made family and thought, as a much younger, attractive blue-eyed, blonde woman, it seemed like a fair trade to her. Tim had been almost 40 at the time, balding, and with a slight paunch around the middle. His chances were most likely running out by then, anyway.

Dr. Tim Stander owned a number of properties, businesses, and several houses in the local area. In addition, he had built a picturesque summer place right on Lake Superior in northern Michigan. But the lovely house he currently called home, right along the Kankakee River on the city's outskirts, was idyllic. The epitome of the American dream home without being overly flashy or drawing unwanted attention. A brown and white A-frame house with four bedrooms and three bathrooms set off from any major roads and sitting on five acres of land. So Jeanne married Dr. Stander in 1969, becoming a mom to Sherry the same day, and continued cultivating a life mirroring what she saw around her.

Jeanne had spent her entire life knowing she was different. Disconnected and never trusting those around her, unfeeling, cold, and aloof. It was not how she wanted to be but simply how she was. Early on, she had recognized in grade school that she was different from others. Part of that was being an immigrant and struggling to switch from French to English as her primary language. But still, even at that young age, she intuitively recognized a need to mimic others to fill in the gaps and holes in herself she feared otherwise might become evident to classmates. Jeanne always made sure she had popular and successful friends to help pattern herself after in each phase of her life. None of them would have considered her a close friend from school or later from her work. It was of no consequence; only a few had ever tried to keep in touch with her.

Likewise, though she tried, she never understood the boys in school or, later, the men around town. Often leering and pestering her date after date for more than she was willing or even capable of giving. So it should have been no surprise to her that marriage and the wifely duties expected of her were uncomfortable at best. It wasn't the sex which she found mercifully short and perhaps equally embarrassing for Tim. Instead, it was the constant attention her husband, in-laws, neighbors, and seemingly everyone who knew the popular Dr. Stander expected of her. Jeanne found it exhausting having to pretend daily and, once away from her aunt and uncle's house, even in her own home. When she became pregnant a few short months into her marriage, it only worsened matters. She found herself counting down the days to the expected delivery date, not in joyful anticipation but rather to finally be done with the chore. Her boobs had ached, her back perpetually hurt, her legs swelled, and the lack of bladder control had been infuriating.

When Russell was finally born - in her mind, finally out of her - the increased attention she hoped would end instead actually grew. Soon becoming nearly unbearable. She avoided breastfeeding, much to her husband's chagrin, claiming over-sensitivity. For proof, she had discreetly cut her nipples in the shower with one of the slim, silver blades of her pink, Bic razor. The ensuing arguments over the value of breastfeeding a newborn ended when she casually left her new, white nursing bras with pink-tinged inner cups out in plain sight for her husband. Tim, then concerned, asked forgiveness for doubting her claims of discomfort.

That had been that...

Likewise, the temporary nanny, employed initially for only the first few weeks after the birth to help Jeanne recover, was soon hired full-time. Helping take care of eight-year-old Sherry as well as the new baby boy. The extended service clinched after Jeanne claimed a few dizzy spells and hints of perpetual exhaustion and the baby blues. The icing on the cake being the well-timed faint in front of Dr. Stander's much older sister Madeleine during one of her constant intrusions into Jeanne's home. As anticipated, she soon expressed to Tim her concern for Jeanne. Imploring him to reconsider the initial terms of the nanny's employment and extend her agreement. Insisting on Jeanne's behalf, he did not really understand the stress new motherhood brings.

Within six months of new baby Russell's birth, Jeanne finally began to feel like herself again. Now for merely a few hours each evening and on the weekends, Jeanne had to produce her live-action, one-woman, theatre-quality production of a content Midwest housewife and mother of two. With satisfaction, she mentally scratched off her to-do list the construed dreams of the masses. She was proud of her struc-tured outward appearance and, admitted inwardly only, full of pride for a job well done at pulling it all off. Even the few friends she kept tethered to her life over the years as ornaments seemed envious.

Perhaps even a little surprised at the successful metamorphosis undergone by their loner friend.

With each precious piece of this form-fitted, well-tailored life seemingly in place, Jeanne was then caught utterly by surprise when Tim asserted six years into their marriage that all was not as it appeared for him. That she had indeed missed something after all. Over the next two years, in marriage counseling and at home, Jeanne engaged in a cat-and-mouse game with not just one but two worthy adversaries. Matching wits weekly with her doctor/husband and the psychologist they saw together and, sometimes, individually. During these sessions, Jeanne came to the slow realization that her orchestrations of those around her only extended a game she could never truly win. And as it turned out, she didn't even understand the rules.

Toying with human emotions she couldn't even feel herself always seemed like playing chess, but now the game pieces felt like they were made of smoke. When both doctors finally whittled away all her strategically placed chessmen, they forced her into a checkmate. Then they upended the empty, hollow game board where Jeanne thought she was master. Pointing the emptiness out to her. Forcing her to face her true self for the first time and the shallow void where she should be the most human.

At this, Jeanne had fled.

CHAPTER
SEVEN

LIKE MOST THINGS throughout Jeanne's life, the split itself had been perfunctory. It was kept as quiet as possible to protect both Tim's practice and reputation. He also then, in turn, had done all the heavy lifting, and the divorce itself was quickly drawn up and uncontested by them both. Tim, as it turned out, was generous to a fault. Paying Jeanne a monthly alimony that more than met her needs and allowing her to move into one of the old houses in Kankakee his family had owned for years. They both agreed Russell would stay with his father and his half-sister Sherry who adored him and raised in the home he was born in. Jeanne would still see him, of course, coming to the house for visits occasionally. The entire divorce and her move had been awkward and confusing for the then eight year-old-boy. But in the end, it was clearly better for all involved, little Russell included.

After what was ultimately revealed during the marriage counseling sessions, the one caveat or demand Tim had - to which Jeanne readily agreed - was that she must now focus on herself. He even helped, along with a recommendation from their marriage counselor, to arrange weekly sessions with a well-renowned, forward-thinking therapist in the neighboring town of Bourbonnais. The overall grace with which her ex-husband handled everything moved Jeanne in a way she last felt as a small child when she was taken in sight unseen, unable to speak English, and from a foreign country by her own aunt and uncle years before. Ironically, she began to feel for the first time what may have bordered on love for the man she had just divorced. When her stepdaughter Sherry, by then a rambunctious teenager, either ran off or just plain disappeared in 1977, Jeanne had even briefly moved back and stayed with Tim to help out. The more she explored the entire relationship and marriage, the more she later appreciated what a sweet soul Tim truly was.

Jeanne had now been seeing her own therapist for several years. Jeanne was very comfortable with her, and the sessions helped clarify some of what had begun to come out during the earlier marriage counseling. For the first time, Jeanne started to understand how twisted her approach to life had been. But, crucially, she began to see a path out of the carefully contrived life she'd built. Her therapist gave Jeanne hope for real change and the strength to lift the weight of what often felt like impossible days. Detailing how much richer life could be if Jeanne allowed herself to feel and not force or control every aspect of it.

For most of the last year, working together, they started narrowly focusing and reexamining some of Jeanne's earliest memories. Pulling these suppressed, hidden, and near-dead things out of a woman nearing forty was hard work. A woman who spent a lifetime avoiding, burying, and minimizing any feelings, much less the uncomfortable ones. Jeanne understood that this "ability to compartmentalize," as her therapist liked to call it, caused her feelings of isolation and fed her lack of empathy. Only now was she slowly piecing together how the trauma of being raised in France during the Second World War impacted and shaped her entire perception of life. How it molded and shaped both the little girl's upbringing here in the US and the woman she eventually became. The ultimate goal, which Jeanne longed for, was to learn how to live as a mentally healthy adult, despite witnessing firsthand the horrific nature of man's darkest side as a child of war.

For the first time, navigating the confluence of the past and present.

For all her life, Jeanne only knew her parents were killed during the bombing in the allied invasion of France on D-day. That in itself, an orphaned refugee of war, was the story she understood, embraced, and told. The one she always believed in and thought served both herself and those she shared it with well. But, with the therapist's help, Jeanne understood she often used that as a blunt tool in the past when it would benefit her. Either to explain away any odd behavior by her or to solicit a particular response from another. A well-rehearsed instrument she played unabashedly and without shame. Only after years of intense therapy had she come to grips with what actually happened. She had watched her own father kill her mother right in front of her eyes.

That impact on a four-year-old, Jeanne realized, was frightening to even imagine. It was no wonder everything after that was blank. Her remaining time in France after the murder had been and stayed, at best, a blur.

She also really only knew, secondhand from her aunt, the story of her own arrival on America's shores. After her parents' death, Dr. Criqui, the local village's doctor, finally tracked down and contacted her only remaining relative: her mother's older sister. Aunt Finney had met and married an American sailor who was part of the US fleet bringing supplies to France well before the German invasion. She had moved to the US with her new husband years before Jeanne was born. That same local doctor, Jeanne now believed, was perhaps unaware or carefully omitted the circumstances regarding her mother's death. Instead perpetuated a lie Jeanne grabbed and lived with the rest of her life: that Jeanne's parents, like so many others from the small villages and surrounding communities of northern France, were killed in the Allied force's bombings.

But now, in the trusted, relaxed, familiar, and comfortable sessions, more memories of that time had emerged. Jeanne recalled the ancient stone quarry where they hid during the air raids. The cold, the funny smells, the sense of dread among the group deep underground. Most monstrous of all, she witnessed her father strangle her mother in a fit of rage somewhere down in the twisting labyrinth of the cavern.

Once that revelation came to the surface, and the initial shock subsided, Jeanne found herself hungry to learn more. A fire began to burn deep within Jeanne for more answers and perhaps even justice for her mother. Did anyone besides herself know what happened so deep underground? Was her mother's body ever recovered? If so, where was her mother buried? What happened to her father? Had he truly been killed in the war? Or was that yet another lie? Had he ever faced judgment for his terrible deed? Jeanne had so many unanswered questions… But, perhaps most troubling of all, had he somehow gotten away with it and spent the last 30-odd years living somewhere in peace? Maybe even remarrying and starting a new family? Could Jeanne even have a half-brother or sister somewhere in France? This new family blissfully unaware of what Marcel Butte had done to his first wife and, by extension, his daughter.

He had, in essence, snuffed out Jeanne's life that day as well.

As time went on, now living with these new memories for the last three years, Jeanne found it harder and harder to let go of what had happened to her mother. As a shell-shocked four-year-old, she wasn't given any time to deal with the loss of both parents before being shipped off to America. She certainly didn't have the maturity or a close and trusted friend or family member to confide in or share her feelings. The idea of counseling services in the face of trauma was still rare now in the 70's and was almost entirely unheard of back in 1945.

Jeanne understood her way of coping with the loss and accompanying emotions was to keep everyone at arm's length. Never allowing anyone to get close to her. Or, ironically, considering the underground cavern where it all happened, to bury her feelings at a depth she thought would never be excavated. But now, with all this finally unearthed, Jeanne found herself grasping for her true feelings. At times she even sobbed over the twin losses. The tragedy of her mother's brutal ending and the loss of some of her most cherished memories: the images of a loving papa that she'd clung to all these years. Somehow she still loved him…

Often raging at the duality of his ghost.

Ultimately Jeanne decided she must finally find out what happened, understand the entire story, and hopefully gain the proverbial closure needed to move on. It felt like the only way to have peace between her old self and her new, emotionally born-again self. To somehow bind the scared little four-year-old girl who, in many ways, was still lost in that quarry in France with this new, whole woman of forty and mother struggling to emerge. To no longer live as a haunted shell of a person merely pretending and acting as a real human being because of something that happened to her 35 years ago.

With her therapist's help, Jeanne now recognized what she'd been exposed to was not her fault, nor had she caused it. Yet she had carried and bared the raw wounds from it her entire life, never acknowledging them or tending them and never healing. They couldn't even be called scars. It seemed to Jeanne that the only way she would ever truly reconcile everything was for her to return to France. Discover and face the place where it all happened. Perhaps even find and confront her own father. Or, at the very least, those still alive who twisted her family's story to find out why they concealed the truth.

So, with her therapist's and her ex-husband's blessing, Jeanne purchased a single, one-way ticket to Paris. She had not booked a return flight, unsure if she would only need to stay mere days or weeks to find the answers she needed. Jeanne also reserved a room at an Inn in the nearby town of Caen, about eight miles from the village of Vieux, where she was born. Then secured a rental car from Hertz International ahead of time instead of waiting to arrive and taking a chance on the local rental car companies. After exchanging cash for several traveler's checks and some smaller denomination Francs, she felt ready for her big trip.

Though her Aunt Finney had not been back to her home country for over 40 years, Jeanne found her aunt was a wonderful resource for learning both typical French customs and re-learning some of the most common French phrases and words. While never having traveled alone much, Jeanne found herself excited at the prospects of such an adventure. She honestly looked at this trip as her rebirth in many ways. The palpable anxiety and excitement were still both new enough emotions for her that she had trouble sleeping at night. Her counselor agreed this combination was the likely reason for her recurring dreams and nightmares of late.

———

As the long flight continues and the jet engines drone on and on, Jeanne shakes out of her reverie. She looked around the plane and, absurdly, she knew, pulled out her boarding pass to confirm she was really making this trip. The thought of it was unimaginable just a few short years before.

Still unable to sleep, Jeanne continued to read her new book off and on during the remainder of the long flight. Stopping only to rest her eyes and sip at her water periodically. The book, mostly about a man miraculously escaping his fate but out of place in the world, struck a chord with Jeanne.

Near the end of the tiresome but uneventful flight, composed of three trips to the claustrophobic bathroom and two surprisingly good meals, Jeanne finally gets her first glimpse of her home country out the tiny window of the plane. The seemingly endless ocean she traversed over most of the flight turned into a lush bed of green below her, and soon the seat buckle light was lit.

Jeanne began her descent.

CHAPTER
EIGHT

WHEN JEANNE finally cleared customs and navigated the modern Charles de Gaulle Paris Airport, she felt exhausted. Knowing she still had a long drive ahead of her, Jeanne rested briefly at a small and hectic airport café where she could grab some coffee and another small bite to eat.

Collecting her wits about her, Jeanne made her way to the row of rental car counters at the airport by following the international pictograms and, blessedly, the English language signs she found accompanying the ones in French. Luckily, the Hertz rental car desk employee was kind enough to both speak and supply a map in English on which he outlined the best route to Caen. Jeanne was relieved that she didn't need to navigate or fight through the frantic Paris traffic. Both the five-year-old airport and her destination were located north of Paris. That kept her out of the notoriously log-jammed city byways. Jeanne was anxious to visit the fabled "City of Lights" and see the Eifel Tower, Notre Dame, museums, etc... Just not on her first day in the country. After such a long day and hours of driving still ahead of her, she longed only for a hot bath and a soft bed.

Traffic was mercifully light once she exited the immediate airport area, and the roads she traveled were well-maintained and easy to follow. Jeanne booked her stay at the hotel Domaine de la Tour Emeraude because it was located between the Caen city center and the village of Vieux, where she expected to start her search for answers. After a nearly three-hour drive, she finally pulled into the hotel's parking lot and killed the car's engine at a spot near the front entrance of the hotel.

She checked in at the front desk and found her clean and cozy room. The single bed was smaller than expected, and Jeanne was confused by the facilities in her tightly quartered bathroom. The porcelain toilet bowl was without a seat and, oddly to her, square-shaped. Directly beside the toilet was what looked like a men's urinal, but upon closer inspection, Jeanne realized it was a bidet. She unpacked and, as promised, made a quick phone call home to let Tim know she'd arrived safely. After a steamy bath, the rest of the evening was spent reading, relaxing, and trying her best to acclimate to the dramatic time change. Eventually, exhaustion won out, and Jeanne slept dream free.

After a light breakfast the following day, Jeanne made the short eight-mile drive south into the small village of Vieux, where she was born. The day was sunny and bright, and the French landscape was breathtakingly beautiful and lush compared to her mostly featureless home state of Illinois.

Arriving at the village, Jeanne drove around the small community to get her bearings. Whether it was the destruction during the allied air raids, the ensuing 30-plus years of progress, or the fact she was barely five years old when she'd last set foot here, Jeanne struggled to recognize much of anything. Where she thought her family's house and farm should be was only an open field. The small schoolhouse she remembered being impatient to attend with the "big kids" had also disappeared. The lone exception was the primarily flat, squared, and jumbled white granite Roman-era ruins at the outskirts of the village. They seemed to have miraculously escaped the worst of the D-Day bombing during the summer of 1944 and were much as Jeanne recalled. Fleeting images of a family picnic and her father holding her hand while she walked along the tops of the ancient carved stones came quickly to mind. As did running around the broken pillars that, though small, seemed so enormous to her as a child playing and darting in and out among them.

Bittersweet memories considering the purpose of her return.

Jeanne learned before leaving for France that the village's entire population was barely 500. She could drive through the whole town in just a few minutes. She stopped and parked on the brick-paved street outside a huge church near the town center. The house of God seemed familiar to Jeanne, but she could not place its location from when she was a child. The name on the sign in front of the old cathedral read "L'église Saint-Laurent."

Exiting the car, Jeanne found herself intimidated at the prospect of boldly charging into the sanctuary, unsure of local protocol and wanting to avoid making a bad first impression in town. So instead, she decided to watch the church incognito and see if it was indeed open to the public and if anyone seemed to be around that might be able to help her.

To pass the time, she casually made her way up a series of small crumbling concrete steps, grasping the wobbly rusted metal handrail that led her to a cemetery bordering the large church. Cresting the top stair, Jeanne was surprised by a large number of mausoleums and aboveground graves made out of marble and stone that greeted her. Some were ornate and of an impressive size, while many others were more modest in appearance. Jeanne knew aboveground burials and plots were a common practice in Paris. Still, she was unaware the custom was also prevalent in the rural French countryside. Statues dotted the graveyard and were plentiful in the small plot dedicated to the local dead of Vieux. At each turn, though, Jeanne felt like the impassive, unblinking stone faces were watching her. Judging her as perhaps an outsider who didn't belong or, more morbidly, as if Jeanne were somehow guilty of escaping their clutches.

Keeping one eye on the church, Jeanne passed each marker and read the names, surreally looking for her own: Butte. The headstones were a mixture of newer and older markers, and, at first, she focused only on the less weathered ones. Skimming over ones dating from the 19th century or appearing more than 100 years old if unable to be read. She soon realized, however, that the quality of the stone used for each marker badly altered the individual gravestone's aging process. Some of the headstones that looked new were very old, and some of the most weathered and mossy-covered were only a few decades old.

The deeper she ventured into the cemetery, the more prevalent the scars of war became. It was clear many markers were either missing or partially destroyed. After 30 minutes of wandering alone in the stone garden with nary a Butte to be seen, Jeanne became discouraged. She finally made her way back down to the street, trying to decide if she should venture into the church or not. Standing alone, she noticed a few locals discreetly peering at her as they passed by. Embarrassed at the attention she was garnering, Jeanne finally conquered her fears of being rebuffed at the local house of worship. Or at the outside possibility of interrupting a service of some sort inside the church on a weekday morning.

Jeanne climbed the steps to the front entrance of the church and entered. The heavy wood door shut tightly behind her, and its closing echoed off the vaulted ceilings. Gigantic, stained glass windows contained images of saints and angels peering upwards with predictably serene faces. Rich, dark wood pews lined the slightly sloping floor, and a thick crimson carpet ran down the middle of the church, splitting the two rows of seating and stretching to the altar like a river of blood. Near the front, a single-robed clergy with what appeared to be a stack of old hymnals was busy placing the blue-covered books in each row of seats.

The sanctuary was otherwise deserted.

Spying Jeanne, the man of God, stopped his task and walked up the central aisle to greet her. Jeanne judged him to be much younger than herself, perhaps still not even out of his twenties. The young man approached, smiling pleasantly under his jet-black hair with both hands clasped before him. In greeting he said, "Bonjour, Madame."

"Bonjour. English?" Jeanne asked hopefully.

"Yes, if you prefer, and be patient with me." The clergyman answered modestly and smiled with a nod while gesturing at the wood pew next to him. "Would you please like to sit?"

"Oh, wonderful! Thank you so much." Jeanne extended her hand. As they shook, she introduced herself before sitting, "My name is Jeanne Butte, and I was hoping maybe you could help me."

"So nice to meet you, Jeanne. I am Father Leo. I will do my best to help you." The friendly priest smiled openly, then added, "You are American, yes?" Jeanne nodded but then wavered slightly, unsure how to start the conversation now that she was finally here. In a comforting tone, Father Leo intuitively helped nudge her along. "Ah… Yet Butte is a most French name, yes? Perhaps you seek someone here with that name?"

Jeanne was instantly relieved and laughed nervously. "Oh, Father, you must be clairvoyant!"

"Ah… well no, not clairvoyant. But an American visiting this small place as a tourist? With the last name Butte?" Shrugging his shoulders, he added, "Maybe more deduction like American TV detective Columbo. Instead of our own fumbling, bumbling Inspector Clouseau…" Jeanne found herself immediately drawn to the man's slight French enunciations in his English. His calm demeanor put her at ease, and Jeanne instantly felt relaxed in his company.

She leaned forward excitedly. "Do you, Father? Do you know the Butte family…? My family, that lived here before the war?"

"Alas, Butte is a very common French name, Madame. I know a few, but," adding quickly as he watched Jeanne's face brighten in anticipation, "none that live here or near Vieux." Jeanne's smile faltered, a bit crestfallen, but then again, had she really expected it to be that easy? Seeing her disappointment, the cleric added, "But I have only come to now be here recently. You say the war? You mean the Second World War, yes?"

Jeanne nodded, "I was actually born here in Vieux but moved to the states to live with my aunt when I was very young. I was, well, I was hoping to find out about my time and family here." Blushing slightly, she added, "I know that sounds silly, but…"

"Not at all, Madame! To make such a trip is full of honor, not grandiose. But you know no one? Is that why you stopped here at the church?"

"Yes, and I saw the cemetery. I know… I know my mother died during the war, and I thought seeing her grave would, well, resolve some things for me." Feeling flustered again, Jeanne struggled to explain herself. "I was looking next door before I came in, but the headstones and markers were hard to read. There are so many of them, and I didn't want to be disrespectful..." Again the young priest seemed to understand.

"That was a very good idea you had. But yes, many markers have been lost over the years, and many more are nearly impossible to read now. But I would be happy to see what I can find in the church's records. That may take some time, and I have an appointment soon coming here."

"Of course, I am so sorry to keep you, Father." Jeanne began to rise, worried she had kept him from his duties.

"Not at all, no, no need to apologize. Hopefully, on such a beautiful day as this, you can wait a bit more before feeling you must wander the graveyard looking at old headstones." The clergy smiled and stood as they shook hands goodbye. "Can you come back again in a day or two?" Jeanne agreed eagerly and thanked him again for his efforts.

Turning to leave, Jeanne stopped, having nearly forgotten to ask about the doctor who had contacted her aunt all those years before. His name was the only solid lead she really had. She was both desperate to ask about him but also anxiety-ridden. What if the doctor was unknown or already dead? She was grateful for the church's offer of help. But at best, it would only lead to a dead end consisting of a gravesite or two. It discouraged Jeanne to realize her options for getting the resolution she craved was so precarious. But again, she thought to herself, had she really thought it would be easy to reclaim her ancestry? Fearful at the answer, she asked the kindly man of God before leaving.

"Do you happen to have heard of the doctor that once served this community? I am told his name was Criqui. Dr. Criqui. I may be pronouncing that wrong, and I don't have any idea how it would be spelled. But my family in America said he was the one that helped find me a new home in the states by tracking down my aunt who had married and moved over there at a young age."

Under a beam of sunlight streaming down from the colorfully stained windows, the Father's face lit up equally as brightly. "Ah, Mademoiselle. Why did you not ask right off? Dr. Criqui's office is just down the street, and I happen to know he is in today. The good doctor has indeed been here for a very, very long time. And you are right. He was here before and after the war. Perhaps he knows more of what became of your family. Here, let me point you to his office."

Holding open the church's front door for Jeanne as she exited, the priest pointed at a modest white building across the street at a bend in the brick-paved road. Jeanne thanked the clergyman and promised to return in a few days to see what the old church records knew of the Butte family. Walking purposefully, Jeanne strode across and down the street. Hesitating only briefly at the office door to read the small sign that said simply, "Eugene Criqui, MD." She opened the door to the tinkling of a small brass bell that hung across the top of the doorway and stepped inside.

CHAPTER
NINE

"JUSTE UN MOMENT," came a raspy voice from somewhere out of sight behind a half-opened door near the back of the small waiting room.

"OK!" Jeanne replied cheerily in English first before reminding herself of where she was and adding, "C'est Bon," the French equivalent, a little less confidently.

As she stood waiting, Jeanne looked across at the three cushioned brown metal chairs sitting unoccupied in a row along the far wall. They did not look particularly comfortable, and Jeanne felt too nervous to sit. In the corner, where she stood now, was a free-standing wood coat rack that held only a single black umbrella. In the room's opposite corner stood a wooden desk adorned with a small pot of colorful flowers, a beige-colored rotary phone, and a black electric typewriter. Both the desk and the much more comfortable-looking office-style chair - like the three other chairs in the room - were unoccupied. White ceiling tiles helped make the room brighter under the flickering fluorescent bulbs in the overhead lights. The entire office was simple, clean, and neat. Much smaller and less modern looking than the doctor's office where Tim, her ex-husband, currently practiced medicine.

"Bonjour. Comment puis-je vous aider?" Looking up, Jeanne did not immediately recognize the man in the white coat who entered the room. He was gaunt, hunched with age, and with only a thin line of white hair crowning the edge of his otherwise bald head. He smiled expectantly at Jeanne and held both hands behind his back. She started the conversation as she did with the priest, who directed her to the office of the elderly village physician.

"Bonjour. English?" Jeanne gave him her brightest smile, trying to hide the racing of her heart as she stood face to face with the man she had hoped so much from. This very moment was one she'd played out in her mind many different times and ways once her trip overseas was finalized. Now that it was here, at last, she felt vaguely lightheaded. Robotically, she extended her hand in greeting.

"No, I am French," he said as they shook. It was not the reply Jeanne expected, and her startled confusion clearly delighted the old doctor. He laughed heartily while apologizing. "Sorry, just an old joke that, like me, should probably be retired. I do speak English, so please go ahead. How can I help you, my dear?" Slowly Jeanne caught onto the joke and smiled along with the welcoming physician.

"Well, in fairness, I'm not English either, and although I live there now, I am also not actually American. I was born here in France." Jeanne paused, feeling her anticipation building and, at least inside, struggling to get her well-practiced speech out now that the time had finally come. She breathed in and out deeply to calm herself before continuing. "In fact, I was born here in Vieux, and I am pretty sure you attended my birth and delivered me."

The doctor cocked his head quizzically before again quick-wittedly countering with, "And you have now discovered a problem with the procedure? Perhaps dissatisfied and flew back here before I retired for good, heh? Well, well, my dear..." He "tsked-tsked" dramatically with one finger raised, "There are no refunds, and I only guide you at the onset. Anything after that, outside of this village anyway, and you are on your own." At this, Dr. Criqui laughed gregariously again. Clearly, he was a man enjoying his place in life and comfortable that he had lived it well. Jeanne could not help but be taken in by the old physician's gentlemanly mannerisms and obvious amusement. Her vague recollections of the friendly doctor from her childhood instantly solidified for Jeanne. She now questioned how the man in front of her squared with her recent musings of a nefarious villain who somehow sold her aunt a lie about Jeanne and the tragic end of the Butte family.

"I am not looking for a refund or to lodge any complaints, Dr. Criqui. But I have come a long way, hoping to talk with you." She paused. "My name is Jeanne Butte, and I wonder if you could answer some questions for me?" Unmistakably, recognition came across the face of the village doctor at the mention of Jeanne's last name. A fleeting shadow draped across his face and tugged briefly at the corners of his mouth. The smile ran away from his face, and Jeanne could feel his eyes focus more intently on her. He exhaled loudly, and for a moment, both the sound and his body resembled a deflating balloon. However, he quickly regained his composure. In another moment, his demeanor reverted to how it had been just moments before.

Dr. Criqui opened his hands and arms invitingly, and his infectious smile returned. "Oh, my dear! How wonderful! I have so often wondered after you. My, what a beautiful woman you have turned into. Why… Why the last time I saw you, you were just so high." The old doctor bent slightly at the waist, briefly holding one hand down near his belt before straightening once again. "So you have come to see your hometown, heh? Oh, such a trip! You must have been very successful in America to travel so freely." The gracious physician turned slightly, gesturing with one hand towards the door he'd just walked through. "Would you like to come to sit in my office with me, my dear? We could talk in there. I have some coffee we can share…"

"Um… yes, thank you, Dr. Criqui. That would be wonderful. But I don't want to intrude or anything. I could also come back another time if you are busy?"

"Bah… It is no problem at all!" He shook his head dismissively at the thought. "I was just reviewing some billing paperwork that was probably better left for my secretary anyway." Jeanne followed behind the doctor as he returned to his office.

Like the waiting room, the doctor's private office was small and old-fashioned but tastefully decorated. Beautiful, original oil-based landscape paintings hung on two walls, and behind his large mahogany desk, several certificates were framed and hung prominently. Three metal filing cabinets crowded together and filled the wall next to the door they entered. The bottom drawer of one hung open slightly, and the doctor casually kicked it shut as he walked past, winking at Jeanne as he did so. As Dr. Criqui sat behind his desk on a creaking, high-backed leather chair, he closed two manila file folders that held the paperwork he'd obviously been working on. Then, spinning around in his chair, the old physician grabbed an insulated, white coffee carafe off the credenza behind his desk and pulled a very small ceramic cup out of a drawer beneath it. Still seated, he turned around to face Jeanne and, without asking, poured her a cup out of the carafe before doing the same into the matching coffee cup already on his desk.

Pushing the new cup across the top of his desk toward Jeanne, he said, "I cannot say this is much more than watered-down espresso. And I'm afraid I can offer you some honey, but I have no milk, cream, or sugar in the office. I mostly drink mine for the caffeine, you see." The doctor sipped at his cup.

"Merci." Jeanne lifted the tiny cup and sipped at the bitter, black drink it held inside. "I don't usually add anything to my coffee either."

"Now," seemingly satisfied, the doctor settled back in his chair, "what are these questions? It has been so many years that, at my age, I hope I still have brain cells intact from that long ago." Dr. Criqui smiled modestly at Jeanne.

To steady herself, Jeanne took another sip before beginning. "Well, as you may recall, you contacted my mother's sister after my parents were, I guess, killed here during the war. My aunt and uncle - their name is Finney, by the way - took me in and raised me in the states, near Chicago."

Now that she was seated and talking with him, Jeanne felt tongue-tied and awkward in front of the doctor. It was a conversation she previously went over many times in her head, so Jeanne was surprised she was struggling to articulate her questions. She didn't want to sound accusatory and searched for the best tact to take with the physician. Dr. Criqui nodded encouragingly, so she blundered on. "But, you see, since my aunt wasn't here during the war, I'm afraid she never learned what exactly happened to my parents. I was... Well, so little that I don't have hardly any memories of that time either. So I was really hoping to find out and maybe pay my respects to them. My parents, I mean. See where they were buried and all…" Jeanne put the tiny cup to her lips and looked expectantly across the desk at the one link between her life in France and her life in America.

Dr. Criqui was silent for a few moments, and his eyes left her face to settle on a spot just over her shoulder. He then cast them around his office, contemplating his response carefully before speaking. Either, Jeanne thought, trying to remember that far back or struggling, as Jeanne was, to find the right words. He took a sip from his cup as well before starting.

"I have often wondered what became of you, Jeanne. There was much to do here in Vieux after we were liberated from German occupancy. Sadly, you were not the only orphan in this village, nor were you the only child I tried to help track down relatives or find people to take in the living casualties of that terrible time. It fills my heart to find you made it safely and found a place in this world. I prayed many nights for God to guide you." The old man's eyes were sad, but his face smiled at Jeanne. He leaned forward in his chair and put each of his elbows on the top of his desk, folding his hands together under his chin as if in prayer. The swollen joints of his knuckles popped audibly as he closed his fingers. "Do you really recall nothing? What do you remember of that time, heh?"

Jeanne sat forward in her chair, literally at the edge of her seat in anticipation, clamoring to hear each word the doctor would say. "Not much, really. The bombing, for sure. Running with my parents and others, hiding in that smelly old cavern and…" Jeanne stopped herself. She wanted to hear what the adult survivor would share with her. Afraid if she admitted what she saw her father do, it might somehow twist what this man would say some 30-plus years later. "And just being afraid, I guess," she lied. But then she finished with the truth. "To be honest, I barely even remember you. Really just from the times before the bombing. And I have no recollections at all of my time after that first day below, the day we all went down in that underground quarry together. Everything after that is gone until I got to America."

She sighed and sat back once again in her chair. "So you see, Dr.

Criqui? Can you understand why I would come back here? I want to know what happened to my parents. I want to see, if possible, the old quarry and try to find a measure of peace with it all. Can you please help me, sir?" A single, sincere tear trailed down Jeanne's face. It seemed to surprise her more than the doctor seated across the desk. She swiped at it annoyingly as one does a troublesome fly.

"Do you truly not remember your time in the quarry, Jeanne?" The doctor appeared to be shocked by this. Jeanne felt like a swarm of butterflies fluttered helplessly down in the pit of her stomach. Still worried if she admitted seeing the actions of her father, the entire truth would forever be lost to her.

"Only that first day when everyone in the village went down there…" And this was true after all.

"Do you have any idea how long you were down in the old Roman quarry?" The doctor looked oddly at her as he asked as if he were studying her.

"No, not really. I suppose a few days at least…" Dr. Criqui seemed to carefully consider his words once again before replying. Then, much like a professor giving a lecture, he recited the history of the tiny village of Vieux during the allied invasion of France.

"By the end of the day on the 6th of June 1944, everyone in Vieux still left alive made their way down into that abandoned, underground cavern outside the village. The allied bombs started to fall in France that day, and one of the targets of the attack was our neighbors in the town of Caen. But Vieux and Caen, you see, are so close together that many of the bombs meant for Caen also hit our little village as well. Vieux, I suppose, was simply considered collateral damage by both the allies and the Germans since, unlike Caen, it really held no great strategic military importance. Although also small, Caen, you see, was a central junction for many roads and even the railways. Bombing the city and destroying those lanes of travel would keep the Germans from getting reinforcements and supplies to the coast of Normandy. Cut off their links of communication and keep the Germans blind, I suppose. The allied forces also wanted Caen for the same reasons as the Germans. In fact, later, they ended up using it as a base for some of their aircraft here in France to help with the ongoing war. So the bombs fell mercilessly on Caen for days, it seemed. But after the first week or so, here in Vieux, the stray bombs meant for Caen became less and less. There was still much danger and horrible fighting all around us. But very few of the villagers of Vieux stayed underground beyond that first week or two. Oh, now, well, of course, we all made a few mad, panicked scrambles back down when we heard or saw bombing start up again nearby. But unlike our brothers in Caen, we were only underground a short time."

Jeanne nodded politely as the doctor, who survived this attack on his village, recalled vividly when the Second World War came to his doorstep. Respectfully she listened to the details that, if not directly causing, at least coincided with her family's end. She was unclear about what the specifics of it all had to do with her questions. Or why the doctor was so persistent about what she did or did not remember herself then.

"So you see, Jeanne, most everyone only hid in the old Roman quarry for maybe a week. Some a little longer and some a little less. But by the end of that first terrible week, we mostly knew, here in Vieux, who survived that awful initial barrage and who didn't make it. Many lives were lost, and a few of those did happen deep underground. Some of those injured early on had been brought below, and several died despite all of our best efforts. There were also a couple cave-ins and tunnel collapses in the quarry due to what was happening above ground. Many of those killed in the caverns were eventually recovered, but some were not. Sadly, it is not uncommon during the war for bodies to be lost to the bombs or buried by the fighting." The doctor's eyes misted over as he spoke. Untimely deaths are never easily reconciled by men of medicine. "What is important for you to understand is that, at the end of that first week, we all counted the Buttes among the lost bodies and as dead. I want to say all these losses were mourned deeply at the time. But the awful truth was that we survivors were struggling to stay alive ourselves." The old man seemed to look at Jeanne for some form of acceptance.

"I understand," she said slowly. "You are saying you have no idea what happened to my parents, then? No bodies were ever recovered?"

The doctor nodded solemnly, and Jeanne felt certain he was telling her the truth by virtue of a life spent studying other people.

"But, Jeanne, you must understand this now." He reached across the desk and cupped one of Jeanne's hands in both of his own liver-spotted ones as he spoke. "We counted all of you as dead. Marcel, Simone, and their pretty little innocent daughter, Jeanne, as well."

Confused, Jeanne shook her head and withdrew her hand before lifting both hands in front of her, palms up. "I don't understand? Why would I have been counted as dead? Obviously, I survived and was found. You helped me."

The old man, who had remained proud and sitting ramrod straight as he told the part his village and the neighboring town of Caen played in the war, now sat back again in his chair. He stared at Jeanne, and she felt his unwavering eyes boring into her as he spoke.

"Yes, Jeanne Butte, that is true. You were found, and I helped you escape this place. I did so because I feared for your life if you stayed here. You see, you were found. But not during the days we all huddled in that old quarry, scared that the world would come crashing down around us any minute. Nor were you found later when we started to leave what we thought would be our little underground sanctuary. My dear, you were not even found in that same awful month of June. You were found a full month later! Somehow not only alive but barely injured and nearly as healthy as before. You were found all alone, smeared in blood and gore, naked even. Mutely playing and dancing under a full and bright moon. All by yourself among those ancient Roman ruins at the edge of our village. Weeks after we had laid you and your parents' empty coffins to rest…"

CHAPTER
TEN

"WELL... Well, that is just impossible... I don't understand what you are saying." Jeanne, though still seated, suddenly felt lightheaded at the revelation. It seemed like all the blood had drained from her face and head simultaneously. Her voice sounded far away to her as if she heard another speak at the end of a long tunnel or pipe. Jeanne thought her words both sounded and felt hollow. She grasped at more to say to solidify it truly was her own voice talking. Finally settling on, "You must be mistaken, doctor..."

"There is no mistake," Dr. Criqui began. "When you were found, I was roused in the dead of night and came straight away. One of the villagers on the other side of Vieux was awakened by what he thought at the time was the howling of a wolf and his own dog barking loudly. When he went outside to see what the problem was, his dog took off and made a bee-line to the site of the old Roman ruins not far from his house. The man gave chase, fearful the dog heard refugees from the ongoing fighting up north or passing soldiers that might shoot the loyal old canine. But when the dog stopped running, it was at those old, broken-down pillars and white blocks that lay scattered on the ground. The villager said his dog started whining and paced back and forth along the edge of the ruins. When the man finally caught back up to his four-legged companion, he saw you, Jeanne Butte, among the crumbling stonework. At first, he did not trust his eyes and believed he was dreaming. But then, worse yet, he believed you to be a ghost! Terrified, he soon pounded on my door for help and led me to the spot where he'd seen you."

Jeanne was slowly shaking her head as the old physician recounted the story. Though his words seemed sincere, she struggled to understand what she was hearing. "So you are saying this was over a month after I'd gone missing in the quarry? And I was unclothed and all alone? A little girl of four? No adults anywhere?"

The doctor nodded. "You were all alone and singing to yourself. When I approached, though astonished, I, of course, instantly recognized you. The villager who found you was babbling superstitious gibberish and nonsense, but I was just focused on your well-being." The village physician paused, deep in thought, remembering vividly a night he knew even back then he would never forget. All these years later, that proved to be prophetic.

"I remember the night was uncomfortably warm and humid. I was already sweating in just the short, brisk walk from my house. The silver light of the moon overhead frosted the very tops of the trees surrounding that ancient area. As I said, you were covered in blood. In the moonlight and shadows, I couldn't tell where it came from or what your injuries were. You were filthy, and your hair was dark, sticky, and matted in places. Some of the blood on you was still wet and glistened in the moonlight. I remember it was so hot that summer night, yet you were so very cold to the touch. Ice cold. Your eyes were unfocused. You didn't respond to my presence or any of my questions. Up here," the doctor tapped the side of his head for emphasis, "you were not there. So I wrapped you in an old blanket I had brought along and carried you back to my house as swiftly as possible. Thinking you were in shock and hoping with more light, I could tell how serious your injuries were. Yet once I got you cleaned up, I only found minor scrapes, some bruising, and one big gash across your back. Most of the blood hadn't come from you…"

Jeanne barely registered the last few sentences of the doctor's account of that night. Part of the story seemed plausible to Jeanne. How she was found, the state of her condition, being confused, etc…

But it was the gap in time that most shocked her, and she fixated on that point. "Forgive me, Dr. Criqui, but you must have been wrong about how long I was missing." She cautiously tried to offer alternatives to the narrative. "Perhaps over the years, those days have jumbled together on you. After all, that was over 30 years ago now…"

"My dear, this was a night I have replayed in my mind a thousand times. You can either believe me or not. That is your choice. But, although I also have no rational explanation, I promise you these are the facts." The doctor pushed his chair away from his desk and suddenly stood. "I would like to show you something, my dear. In itself, it does not prove anything. But perhaps at least you can see that others, besides myself, judged your disappearance as longer than a few days or even weeks."

The doctor tugged his white coat off and slung it casually across the back of his chair. Jeanne followed him numbly as he walked out of his office and into the still-empty reception area Jeanne first entered. The doctor opened the top drawer of the empty desk in the waiting room and pulled a hat out of it. He slipped the thin, Gatsby-style cap on his bald head before stepping outside and politely holding the door open for Jeanne.

Exiting the small office building, the old physician slipped a key out of his front pocket and locked the door behind him. Together he and Jeanne crossed the street and walked past her rental car. Once more, following behind Dr. Criqui, Jeanne climbed the steps into the graveyard where she'd killed time earlier that morning. With a slow but purposeful step, the old doctor led her to a spot within the cemetery Jeanne hadn't passed earlier. A line of simple, small grey headstones jutted from the ground. The doctor walked directly to one, and Jeanne stood at his elbow as he gestured down at the plot in front of them.

Jeanne looked down at her own gravestone at her feet, between twin grave markers etched Marcel Butte and Simone Butte. The name Jeanne Butte was carved into the rock, and, like her parents' graves, the only date listed was June 7th, 1944. Reading her own name on a grave in her hometown was both unreal and fantastic at the same time. Jeanne involuntarily took a step back and, at the same time, barked out a laugh at the absurdity. For an instant, she felt certain the earth under her feet would crack wide and swallow her whole. Depositing her under the headstone that bore her name.

"Forgive me, my dear. I can only imagine the shock of seeing such a thing. But you deserve to see and know this has been here for…"

"Why did they leave it here?" Jeanne interrupted the old doctor before he finished, not taking her eyes off the grave marker. "I mean after I was found. Why not remove the headstone?"

"I may be the one you can blame for that, my dear. You see, this place has many old and odd ideas. At the time, I thought it best to leave things as they were. It is perhaps hard to explain now," the old physician smiled grimly at Jeanne. "But I endeavored to keep your resurrection as quiet as I could. Discreetly inquiring after old friends of your mother's sister, the aunt who took you in, to locate and reach out to her. There was much commotion at that time, and many people around here were coming and going constantly. Not to mention all the soldiers from Canada and the United States roaming the surrounding countryside. You were almost catatonic anyway, and I thought it best to not provoke those who lived here…"

Again, Jeanne interjected as the old man spoke. "Wait a minute, are you saying everyone still thought I was dead? Still thinks I died…" Jeanne's head was spinning as the revelations kept coming. "Was that even legal?"

"Strictly speaking, my dear," the doctor started again, "I tore up the death certificate and never filed it. So legally, you were an orphan from this village and able to become a citizen of America. You being here now is proof of that, heh?"

"But why…. I mean, how… So you kept me hidden and didn't tell anyone in Vieux. What about my friends or my parents' friends and neighbors?" Jeanne struggled to come up with any names or faces from back then. But at four, how could she be expected to remember all these years later.

"Jeanne, please. You are asking for the truth, are you not?" Jeanne bobbed her head emphatically yes. "Then let me be blunt, my dear."

"I think the time to worry about being delicate is over, Dr. Criqui.

You just showed me my grave without warning and told me my entire hometown thinks I am dead."

Dr. Criqui's lips pressed together in a tight line. "Then please do not be offended by what I now say, Jeanne. I had hoped to spare you all this. But perhaps it is no better to be safe than sorry, heh?" His face softened once again. "It may seem strange to you. But letting you leave this place and start life anew, I believed, was your best opportunity. I swear to you that everything I did was meant for your benefit. Seeing you now, a beautiful, successful young woman, is only affirmation you took advantage of that opportunity. As I had prayed you would."

"Fine, I believe your heart was in the right place." Jeanne, the one before all the counseling and therapy, was fully back in charge now and as cynical and untrusting of others as ever. Still, she was determined to hear the rest of what the doctor had to say. "But why?"

The doctor started with a question. "Have you ever heard of the French term 'épuration sauvage'?" Jeanne shook her head no. "No? Roughly translated in English, it means 'the wild purge.' Did you know, my dear, that here in France, after the war, many women were targeted by local men who considered themselves patriotic vigilantes? Women were publically humiliated, most publicly indeed. Their heads were shaved, often stripped naked, smeared with tar, and made to walk their own towns. A parade of taunting and being spat upon, rocks were thrown at them, beaten, kicked, and sometimes killed." As the doctor continued, Jeanne began to feel nauseous, a feeling that she somehow knew what was going to be said and was sick at the thought of it being spoken aloud.

"Right here," the physician motioned down to the street, "I saw a mob in front of what was left of this church. Men I knew, some who never missed a single church service. They stripped one local woman and sheared all her hair off. Dragging her back and forth across this town square and all the while…" Now visibly distraught at the memory, the doctor seemed to age in front of Jeanne's eyes as he spoke. "All the while, her two young children cowered behind her. Watching their, as you put it, neighbors and friends join the mob tormenting their mother."

Jeanne inexplicably knew the answer before she asked. "But... why? What had...? In front of a church!"

"Ah well, you see, the punishment of shaving a woman's head has biblical origins after all, so..." The look of disgust was genuine on lines that cracked across the face of the old physician. "But there were women across France accused of cooperating with the Germans during the occupation. I believe the term used was horizontal collaboration." Jeanne nodded dully in understanding, indicating the doctor should continue.

"You said earlier that you remembered everyone running and gathering in the cave that day you came to be there. But, my dear, that is not correct. Most everyone in the village and the surrounding areas came earlier that week. Or the night before your family arrived. Most of them had packed, expecting to stay underground for a long time. Do you remember what your mom and dad brought when you came?"

"They, I mean we, didn't have anything. It all happened so fast we couldn't pack because the bombs started..." Jeanne remembered the panicked running and the long climb into the old quarry. But also recalling the many things other villagers already had in the cavern when they arrived. Before now, it had never occurred to Jeanne to question how so many others had clearly packed ahead of time and must have made multiple trips back and forth. While the Buttes, on the other hand, were among the last to enter with only their clothes upon their backs.

"There was much secretive debating and questions before the bombs fell. We all knew the allies would be attacking our shores at any time. The only question was when. German forces had been putting defenses up, so we knew it would be soon. But some families, my dear, were not told this. Some families were judged as untrustworthy and secretly ostracized by the Vieux village leaders. Those men condemning their own neighbors rather than taking a chance and showing them our hiding place. But in the end, once those awful bombs started dropping, a few of us convinced all the others we could not play God. We were sentencing our neighbors and fellow countrymen to die by not telling them. That we were no better than the Nazis we were being liberated from if we left them above ground. So a few brave men returned and rescued the last of the villagers. The Butte family among them."

Again, Jeanne understood she already knew the answer to the question she asked. "But why? Why us? My dad was beloved in the village. He grew up here with many friends."

"Simone, your mother, at that time, was having an affair with a high-ranking German officer. Her indiscretions were the worst kept secret in the village. No one said anything, of course, but everyone knew. I also think many of the villagers especially feared this officer. He was a man of exceptional cruelty. When he looked at you, it was like a crocodile hiding in the water, watching a baby giraffe. He had the dead eyes of a predator…"

Jeanne felt her blood run cold, and a shiver ran up her spine that caused her to shudder involuntarily, clearly envisioning the eyes being described. "Stop! OK, just stop now… I'm sorry, I just can't hear anymore. I need time to… I don't know, process all this." Jeanne was sure she was going to faint. She had gone from possibly feeling sick to being certain she would vomit at any moment. Fleeting images assaulted her now. The underground cavern, loud tanks rolling past her in the mud, her father's face, different uniforms, her mother, men speaking German… A thousand childhood images were compressed from her time in this village.

"I am sorry, my dear. But you see why I tried to spare you? The consequences of your mother's actions would have been tough for you to escape. Then, when you suddenly appeared out of thin air, the few villagers who did know were certain the Germans had somehow brainwashed you. Or that you were in some way or another a threat. That you must be a witch as in times of old, making a deal with the devil himself. Bah!" The old man waved his arms dramatically in the air above his head. "Even a four-year-old girl scared these simple peasants. And, after what I witnessed they did with some of the other poor women of our community, I was sure there were those in the village that would come for you too. That is if they knew or found out you were alive. I feared for your life, you see? Best for them to keep thinking you were dead. Let you live a life far away from all these old superstitions and suspicions."

Jeanne needed the man to stop talking. She stumbled a step away from him and turned from the three gravestones marked Butte. Her head was spinning from all these unexpected revelations, and she felt overwhelmed. Jeanne struggled to make sense of it all and get herself back on track and back in control. She glanced down at her watch. The time change only adding to her feelings of everything being off-kilter in the world. Though it felt like she had already spent all day here in Vieux, Jeanne was surprised to see it was just now barely lunchtime.

Abruptly, she pulled herself together and faced the elderly physician once again. "I don't mean to be rude. I greatly appreciate your time, Dr. Criqui, but this is… This is just a lot for me to take in. I need to head back to my hotel and maybe lie down for a bit. Find myself something to eat too. Can you please excuse me?" The old doctor nodded his head solemnly once, and Jeanne thought she saw a look of regret on his face. She turned around and began to go back in the same direction she and the doctor had initially come. Still feeling no closer to understanding what happened to her father, Jeanne wanted out of this cemetery. To put space between herself and the garden of the dead where a stone marker memorialized her four-year-old self.

The doctor walked slowly behind her and was just at the top of the concrete steps when Jeanne reached her rented automobile. The hard chrome steel of the car door handle warmed in the sun's bright rays. The solid touch with something tangible and modern had a somewhat calming effect on her. Before opening the door, Jeanne looked back up at the doctor and apologized again for her quick departure. Asking if she could please come back and see him again once she had time to digest everything. Perhaps later this week or even tomorrow morning. The physician graciously agreed and let Jeanne know he could be found in his office all week.

Jeanne started the car and welcomed the flood of air conditioning that washed over her body. Putting the auto in reverse, she backed out of her parking space and, already feeling better, looked back to wave at Dr. Criqui. However, he'd begun to walk back down the street toward his office, his back facing Jeanne's car.

Glancing once more at the top of the stairs leading into the graveyard, Jeanne now saw a lone, hunched figure. A small old woman dressed in simple, plain clothes with long stringy white hair. Even from a distance, it was easy to see her face was wrinkled, and by the shape of her mouth, it seemed to Jeanne that the old lady's teeth must also be missing. The woman was unusual looking but in some odd way familiar to Jeanne. Had she been a neighbor or friend of her mother or aunt? Realizing she was staring and embarrassed, Jeanne raised a hand to the woman in greeting. But got no response in return. Putting the car in drive, Jeanne soon made the short drive back to Caen and her hotel.

CHAPTER
ELEVEN

WHEN JEANNE ARRIVED at her hotel, she found herself far too keyed up from her visit to Vieux to even lie down in her room. She kept replaying the morning's events repeatedly in her mind, still stunned by the shocking revelations the longtime village doctor revealed.

On the one hand, she thought, connecting with Dr. Criqui on her first day back in Vieux was more than she'd dared hope for. But the conversation had taken twists she could have never foreseen. She was hoping for revelations, and she certainly received just that. But Jeanne hadn't expected those revelations to be about her and so, frankly, unbelievable. She wasn't sure what to think after her discussion with the elderly physician. And seeing her own grave in the village cemetery! To say the least, that disturbed her greatly… With her mind buzzing, Jeanne decided to try and clear her head by sightseeing and walking the local streets of Caen.

The charming French city was rich in history. Still, much of the current tourist information and most popular destinations centered on the events of D-Day and the Second World War. Those famous landings at Normandy were several miles north of the actual city itself. Right now, Jeanne did not feel like visiting those tragic and triumphant sandy beaches. She decided to save exploration of those ocean-front sites for another day.

Caen itself, despite now being home to roughly 100,000 residents, Jeanne found awash in greenery and gorgeous flowers. Cobblestones lined the streets, and from many of the sidewalks, towering spires could be seen over the tops of the buildings near the center of town. Numerous gigantic grey churches and picturesque abbeys beckoned her attention nearly any way she turned. Jeanne made a mental note to buy more film and return later with her camera to capture some images of all the amazing architecture.

Jeanne strolled and window-shopped the quaint stores that, in many cases, sat below old gothic-looking buildings. Above many street-level shops and cafes, the buildings appeared to house apartments locals lived in. The abundant balconies above her head filled with vining plants, often with a chair or two squeezed alongside. She admired the selection of souvenirs and occasionally ducked into the tiny stores but ultimately decided to hold off on purchasing anything outside of a few postcards so soon upon arriving. There would be plenty of time for shopping later...

Wandering the curvy streets, Jeanne and other tourists were kept on their toes by the many cars that unexpectedly whizzed past startled pedestrians. The smell of cigarette smoke and fresh food filled the air, and Jeanne stopped at a small outdoor café to eat. As she dined alone outside, Jeanne enjoyed the sunshine, and, as was her habit, people watched as the residents of Caen went about their daily routine.

By the time Jeanne returned to her hotel, it was late afternoon, and the sun had begun playing peek-a-boo with the clouds rolling in. She pulled out one of the postcards she had purchased and sat at the minuscule desk in her hotel room. Addressing it and writing a few generic short sentences to Russell about her flight, arrival, and hotel. Saying only she'd visited her hometown of Vieux and expected to return there the next day again. By the time she finished, her eyes were drooping, and she found herself increasingly fighting back yawns. Jeanne was a little surprised at her weariness until she did the quick math on the time change between France and the US. Discovering if she were back home right now, it would have been the dead of night. Struggling to stay awake, Jeanne stayed in her room and ate the remainder of the lunch that she'd been unable to finish at the café. While she ate, Jeanne decided to head back into Vieux first thing in the morning again. She changed into her pajamas and pulled her heavy window drapes shut. As soon as her head hit the pillow of her bed, Jeanne was fast asleep.

————

Dreams crowded Jeanne's sleep. She soon found herself once more struggling within a blizzard of falling papers. Spying her mother, Jeanne trailed after her as always, desperate to catch up in hopes of getting answers. As explosions tore into the earth around her, Jeanne watched helplessly as her mother again dove into a black hole that split the earth.

But this time, as Jeanne sprinted after her, she saw the torn ground her mother had disappeared into was an empty grave. The bottom was visible and made up of tightly packed dark earth. Startled, Jeanne looked on either side of herself. She found she was now among a vast field of crooked tombstones and intimidating mausoleums. The usual smoke of her dream turned into a fog, thick as pea soup, which encircled the edges of her vision. Yet within the ring of the dense haze Jeanne found herself in, she could see clearly. The roar of approaching aircraft also began to dissipate. As did the usual explosions and chaos of falling bombs and crumbling buildings. A foreboding silence soon dominated the murky scene.

Jeanne looked down once more into the grave at her feet. As she did, both hands began to shake uncontrollably as if with a palsy. Her eyes, betraying her now as well, slowly rose upwards in her head bit by bit despite her best efforts to stop them. Jeanne knew she didn't want to see the tombstone at the top of this grave, certain her name would be carved therein.

But she could not stop herself.

When her terrified gaze finally fell upon the marker at the head of the hollow gravesite, the lettering stamped on the stone was not Jeanne Butte but rather a foreign script. Though it looked vaguely English, it was illegible to Jeanne. The lettering was short and tight, and as she scrutinized the marker more closely, Jeanne recognized several Roman characters among the wording. Her chest heaved in relief, and as she did, her head sagged downward. Once more, her eyes were cast deep into the burial pit at her feet. It was no longer empty. A single, well-defined, perfectly articulated white skeleton lay curled within. The bones hugging itself as if in fear. Or perhaps in a protective fetal position.

A long baying howl split the oppressive silence, startling Jeanne and causing her to flinch so hard she nearly toppled over. Barely catching herself before tumbling headlong into the open grave, a brief respite from the pervasive horror Jeanne felt. Moments later, a second wail exploded unseen in the murky gloom. The ferocity of its intent was unmistakable to Jeanne. She understood this was a terrible beast that lives undefined in the shadowy night, in the unseen spaces under your bed, in the back corner of your closet, in the black of a tomb…

Jeanne looked down again at the trench that had held a single, fleshless corpse moments before. She watched in horror as the grave erupted from within in a cascade of bones and skulls. Filling the vacant cavity in seconds and then spilling out of the pit with frightening speed. The torrent was upon Jeanne before she could move, soon threatening to bury her alive. Clawing desperately to escape, Jeanne looked around her for anything she could grab ahold of to keep from being lost in the flood of bones. With no foothold or lifeline, she cast her eyes upward, hoping to see someone coming to her rescue. But finding only the baleful stare of an awful creature without form. Coldly watching her with obvious malevolence as she thrashed violently.

The rising tide overtook and swallowed her.

———

Jeanne woke, gasping for breath in the foreign hotel room. The strange setting was unwelcoming and cheated her just wakened self even the comfort of familiarity. The nightstand next to her bed, where her red numbered digital clock usually sat at home, was empty and held no answers for her.

She kicked at the heavy blankets that surrounded her and lay twisted on top of her, desperate to feel the openness and freedom the nightmare had robbed her of. While her mind began to recall the events of the last few days, she slowly came to grips and understood her feeling of queerness in the alien place where she'd woken. Jeanne then vaulted off her bed and tore open the thick velvet curtains of her hotel window. Blessing the rays of the sun bathing her that moments ago, in her nightmare, she thought she would never see again. She drank in the warmth of the streaming early morning sun and slowly calmed both her breathing and her heart. After a few minutes of standing in the light, Jeanne walked to the bathroom and began to groggily get ready for the new day.

The intensity of the dream gradually faded as Jeanne busied herself in her room and then took the elevator down to the inn's restaurant. Before rising from the small, white linen table where she had eaten breakfast alone, she gulped several glasses of the freshly squeezed juices offered. A rare treat compared to back home in America, where near-tasteless frozen pulp concentrate mixed with tap water was the norm.

She dropped off the postcard she'd filled out the night before at the front desk to be mailed and made her way to her car. Within fifteen minutes, she was once again pulling into the village of Vieux and parked along the street both the church and Dr. Criqui's office were located. Jeanne avoided looking toward the cemetery as she walked purposefully into the local physician's medical practice. The waiting room was empty again, and she was soon seated across from the doctor in his office once more.

"Sorry for kind of running out on you yesterday, Dr. Criqui," Jeanne began. "I don't want you to think I am ungrateful for what you did all those years ago. Or the honest answers you gave me yesterday."

"My dear, it is I who must apologize. I seem to have lost my bedside manner over the years. It is unforgivable that I sprung so much on you without warning." In his admission, the old physician seemed truly troubled by his actions of the day before. "I think your sudden appearance yesterday startled me. I spilled out things I had kept bottled up and lived alone with for so long. Yet, in my head, I had rehearsed or even fantasized about telling you so often that I forgot it was all new to you. Can you please forgive me?"

"Of course, of course, doctor... But I was the one who came hunting and asking for the truth. So there is really nothing for you to be sorry about. It just was an awful lot of new information for me to take in all at once. Part of it fantastic even!"

"Then, if I am forgiven, we shall speak no more of it, my dear." The grandfatherly old man seemed genuinely relieved. "But I have told you all I know about that time and how you came to leave this village. What else can I help you with?"

Jeanne paused before continuing. She had decided on her walk yesterday what she felt like she still must do and learn before ending the search into her family's past. Yet it troubled her to say these things out loud. "Was there truly no trace of my parents ever found, Dr. Criqui? Are you absolutely positive my father was never seen or heard from again?"

"Quite certain, my dear. As I recall, the Butte farmhouse and land escaped real damage from the bombing. Eventually, the legal process went forward, and it, along with all the possessions inside, was sold. It stood much the same for years but was torn down a while ago. Maybe ten or fifteen years ago by the current owner of the property. It is now all farmland, like so much of this area. I have no doubt that if your father had somehow escaped the quarry, he would have returned home. After all, he was, like you, my dear, born in that house."

"Thank you, I suppose you are right..." Jeanne gave the doctor a small smile before continuing. "I was not completely honest with you yesterday, Dr. Criqui. I mean, when you asked me what I remembered about my time in the quarry." The old man nodded encouragingly, and Jeanne then told him everything she'd remembered during her therapy and counseling sessions back home. How she snuck after her parents deep into the labyrinth of the cavern, the argument she witnessed, and how her mother's life was ended by her father's hand. The doctor asked a few questions but, surprisingly, did not seem overly shocked by the story. By the time Jeanne was done, she was crying softly, and the physician pulled a soft white handkerchief out of his pocket for her. When Jeanne regained her composure, he spoke in calming tones.

"My dear, what a terrible tragedy for you to bare. It is no wonder when you finally surfaced from the quarry all that time later, you were troubled, heh? What men do has often baffled me, so I have no great words of comfort nor wisdom for you. The stress of that time during the war is almost unimaginable these days. I, too, saw many things I never thought I would see. Things I wished I had never seen…" He looked down briefly before continuing. "I must confess, there is also one bit of information I did not pass on to you yesterday when we spoke. It did not seem relevant at the time and still may not be. But I suppose there is no reason not to tell you now. I do not think it is necessarily related, but it has always baffled me like your reappearance back then."

"Oh! Well, please do go ahead, doctor. I came back home here for the truth. All of it. So anything, no matter how minor, could help me." Jeanne still felt desperate to learn the facts of that time.

"I wouldn't call it minor…" The old man's brow furrowed in concentration. "And please brace yourself, my dear, for more unpleas-antness." He cleared his voice before beginning once again. "I told you yesterday the village did not stay underground long, and that was true. But we ventured back to the surface so soon because all was not as we had expected below ground. Indeed, as I mentioned, we lost friends and neighbors down below. And true enough, there were a few tunnel collapses that may have been how some of those unfortunate souls met their fate. But I will tell you this now, many of us did not feel safe down there. We felt trapped or even hunted down. And not by soldiers." The old man looked down in his lap as if in shame or, Jeanne thought, perhaps to collect all his thoughts before continuing.

"When your family disappeared down in the cavern, we did search for you. Groups of men split up and combed the many manmade and natural spaces and passageways below. Two young men, good men, both strong and brave, never returned from that search. A third man, hunting with the other two for the Buttes, was found but not alive." The doctor raised his head again and faced Jeanne from across his desk. "His body had been mauled as if by a wild animal. The goring of his soft parts was unlike anything I had ever seen before or since. Whatever attacked him pulled apart his flesh in strings as if playing with him. Shards of his own bones even used to impale him in unmentionable places. I don't need to tell you how this affected the men who found his body." Jeanne thought she saw a tremor begin in the hands of the old man as he recounted his tale. She flashed back to her dream from the night before and how she'd trembled uncontrollably while in the grip of that nightmare. Involuntarily, she shuddered as the doctor went on.

"Maybe a week or so later, a young woman was found to be missing. Her bed sack, near one of the many winding tunnels below ground, looked as if it had been dragged a few feet along the ground and was empty. The soft dirt around it scattered as if there had been a struggle. She was never seen again, either. That was the day many folks left the old quarry, blaming gods of old, monsters, and myths like the Beast of Gévaudan…"

"What is the Beast of Gévaudan?" asked Jeanne. The name or tale was unfamiliar to her.

"Heh? Oh my dear, have you not yet been told about France's very own monster?" Dr. Criqui smiled vaguely. "Well, Scotland has Nessie, and England has all her ghosts. But, here in France, we have the Beast of Gévaudan. Think of it as our version of a werewolf or maybe the Wolf Man that America's Hollywood loves so much."

"The Wolf Man? Was there a Wolf Man loose in France? I thought that was Transylvania?"

The old doctor shook his head and rolled his eyes simultaneously. "Bah… Who knows where all these old tales originate from? But the truth is, France did have a creature kill over 100 people in a rural area of our country sometime in the 18th century. A so-called mystery monster nicknamed 'The Beast' ravaged the region of Gévaudan before King Louis XV had his royal hunters dispatched to kill the mad dog. And that was all it was. A big wolf that had developed a taste for man. But, despite these simple truths and explanations, the legend of our beast lives on, heh? Silly superstitions and fanciful stories of the ignorant." The doctor waved one hand dismissively before continuing.

"But as I said, we lost a few villagers, and that old quarry had also long been a source of colorful tales and speculations in the area. In the throes of war, everyone is grasping for something. Some are looking for concrete and logical answers to combat their fears. Others turn to their individual faith. But many, I have found, look for fantasy or distraction to take their minds off the harshness of what man does to man." The grandfatherly physician's eyes met Jeanne's. "You are proof of that. After all, you went years before you could face what you saw Marcel do to Simone. You had no mythical monster to pin it on, so you simply blanked it all out. Oh, and my dear, who could blame you? Four years old, no less!" Dr. Criqui shook his head sadly. "Alas, no matter how each individual deals with their own personal monsters in life, we are all much the same, yes? When we are frightened, are we ever truly anything else?"

"Well, yes, but something must have killed that man in the quarry. Possibly the others as well? What do you think happened?" Jeanne puzzled over the old physician's words. Was any of this related to the time she'd lost while below ground?

"You must remember this was during a war, my dear. No one thinks about or remembers the awful toll that has on nature. All the innocent animals slaughtered and displaced by man's quest to dominate and conquer his fellow man. Even those of God's creatures who escape man's machines of death are still prone to their own fear, diseases, or even loss of their natural prey. I think in that cave system, there may have been a ravenous wolf or perhaps even a pack of wolves just trying to survive. Or, although rarer, perhaps even a wounded or sick bear who had wandered into that underground system and was starving…" The old man looked away, and his voice trailed off.

Although hardly a nature buff and even less sure of the wild things populating France's outdoors, that seemed unlikely to Jeanne. "Perhaps… But where do you think these wolves or bears went then? I mean after the fighting ended?"

The doctor shrugged half-heartedly, and Jeanne began to doubt that even he, deep down, believed the explanation he'd told himself and was now selling her. His faith in science and medicine, his own religion that he followed faithfully, albeit blindly. "Who can know such things? Where does a cat go to have its litter? Or, when the time comes, to curl up and die, heh? In a basement? Under the stairs? There are many possible answers, I suppose…"

"Yes, I guess you are right." Jeanne decided to let the man in front of her off the hook. In a way, she supposed he really was right. Certainly, all these years later, how could anyone know what had attacked the villagers of Vieux. They may very well have, unbeknownst to them, invaded some wild creature's home or lair. She switched to another topic she hoped the doctor could help her with.

"Well, now that you know the truth about what I saw down there, I hope you can understand why it is so important for me to see it. I want to return to the quarry where my father killed my mother. After finally coming back to France all these years later and being this close, I could never forgive myself if I didn't try to get down there again. Do you know if that is possible? Are the entrances still open?"

Dr. Criqui studied Jeanne's face for a long moment before his eyes fell on a shiny letter opener lying on his desk. Picking it up, he absently twirled the small implement in his hands as he answered. "It is very strange to me. These last few weeks… I believe in science, facts, and things I can understand. Now I do, of course, go to church and have my faith. But here, in this world, I have always found the rational no matter what madness swirls about me."

"I'm not sure I am following you, doctor…"

He sighed. "I am soon to retire. In fact, I expect to close this office by the end of the summer and am no longer accepting new appointments except in emergencies. I am also still one of the village trustees and on the board here. But like my office work, that will end shortly." Jeanne remained unclear on where this conversation was heading but continued to listen passively.

"Three weeks ago, a young student from the local university came to this village. He gave a presentation to the Village Board and put in an application for a permit. This in itself has happened several times before. The University of Caen Normandy is close to Vieux, and exploring the old Roman ruins or digging around that area for more possible ruins or artifacts of that time has been done several times over the preceding decades. Even today, it is not uncommon for local farmers to turn a plow and uncover old items from medieval times. Some believe the English army of King Edward the Third once camped in this area after ransacking and pillaging Caen during the Hundred Years' War. But this young man, however, wasn't interested in any of that. He applied for and received a permit to explore the ancient quarry used by the Romans here in Vieux. He believes he can find old tools of that era and possibly learn something new about their techniques by exploring the quarry."

"Well, that is great!" exclaimed Jeanne. "Is he still working onsite? Would he give me a little tour or let me spend the day with him? What a blessing and coincidence."

"Yes, that is what troubles me, my dear. What a coincidence, indeed." Once again, the physician fell silent for a couple beats as he looked across his desk at Jeanne.

"We sealed off all the entrances down into the quarry after the war. We did it because we were afraid adventurous kids may try to explore and get lost among the decaying walls and tunnels. But there are those still in this town who would say we did it to keep whatever lurked therein imprisoned."

The old man smiled grimly. "In any case, just last week, the young man from the university finally got past those blockages. I am told he has begun exploring and mapping underground now. To my knowledge, he is the first man to go down there in over three decades. And now you, Jeanne Butte, walk out of the past from the darkest days of Vieux and into my office. Asking to venture into the very place where it would have been impossible to gain entrance a month ago. It is very strange to me, my dear...." The old doctor seemed to be studying Jeanne, making her feel uncomfortable.

"I assure you, Dr. Criqui, I had no knowledge of this student's work if that is what you are insinuating." She responded somewhat defensively.

"Oh, of that, I have no doubt, Jeanne. Outside of a few professors or students at the college and a few old men here in town, nobody knows or would even care. See that? That is what I mean. How can we explain this, heh? A mere coincidence or, as you called it, a blessing? Hmmm, but what other explanation is there? And yet..."

The village physician just shook his head before continuing. "Ah, forgive me, dear. I think I am perhaps slower to retire than I should have been. Perhaps I am more confused with each passing day." He winked and smiled at Jeanne. "Now, let's see if we can find where the young man is today, heh? Perhaps we can bribe him with a free lunch and see about that tour for you."

CHAPTER
TWELVE

WITH DR. CRIQUI GIVING DIRECTIONS, Jeanne took a paved, curvy lane leading down into a softly sloping valley. Driving herself and the old physician away from the small village of Vieux in her rented automobile. Along one side of the road was a sprawling meadow, while on the other side stood a forest so dense it was almost impossible to see into more than just a few yards, even on a bright, sun-filled morning like today.

After a little more than a mile, the doctor pointed to a weedy knoll and indicated Jeanne should pull alongside a single, light blue Datsun pickup truck parked in the grass on the side of the road. A long, rickety barrier made of thin wire fencing held aloft by old tree limbs stretched across the field in either direction. It served as a border of sorts but sagged so dramatically in places Jeanne doubted it could hold back much of anything. After they both exited the car, Dr. Criqui gingerly placed a foot across the top of one of the lowest places of the fence and pushed it entirely to the ground with his weight before crossing over. Then, with his foot still in place, he gestured that Jeanne should also follow and step across.

Walking together, the doctor pontificated about the local plants and flowers that populated the open field as he and Jeanne slowly made their way up toward the mound. The tall swishing grass rustled in the wind, and in the distance, a cluster of trees swayed in unison. The area around them reminded Jeanne of the midwestern prairies that were common across the heartland of America.

Within minutes they had made their way to the edge of the large, grassy field, and Jeanne saw to her right were multitudes of the yellow gentian flowers her papa nicknamed her after when she was a little girl. The blooms bunched together and danced in the late morning breeze as bees busied themselves across the heads of the brightly colored flowers.

The picturesque view of the French landscape and the bustling activity reminded Jeanne of her hard-working father. She felt her eyes well up again, despite the violence she witnessed when he'd murdered her mother. She could not help but miss the man whom she had loved all of her life. She missed his bushy black hair and his rich baritone voice.

Jeanne remembered fondly being held by his rough textured hands while he held hers and swung her in circles in fields much like this one. Both spun wildly until they fell down, laughing and dizzy on the ground. Then, as soon as Jeanne regained her feet without tumbling back down, she would reach her arms out once more to him, yelling, "Encore!" Both of them twirling together until her papa, finally exhausted, would eventually beg off. It saddened Jeanne to know those precious moments were, or at least now felt, all wrong. Still, the old memory made Jeanne's heartache. However, her thoughts were soon cut short as the grandfatherly physician steered her towards a line of lightly trampled weeds in the meadow that soon evolved into a path.

Jeanne fell in line behind the cautiously stepping old man as the trail made its way at a slightly downward slope before ending at the base of a small hill. The cluster of trees Jeanne saw when they first exited the car provided shade at the end of the path. The doctor stopped and greeted a young man drinking from a canteen just outside what looked like a large cave entrance to Jeanne. The man sat in the long grass under the shade of the tall tree and waved to Dr. Criqui as they approached him.

The old and young men engaged in a conversation Jeanne could not follow beyond the initial greeting of "Bonjour." As the two men continued speaking together in French, Jeanne crept closer to the mouth of the entrance under the hill. The entryway was huge, and you could have easily driven a cement truck under its high arch. Debris lay scattered along one side of the entrance, and it appeared the rock, soil, and wood that made up the pile had been recently dug out and deposited there. A few fresh timbers had been placed as supports to the side of the entrance, and Jeanne could see a small portable generator sitting silently just inside the cavern. A few hand tools were casually tossed along the ground next to a large boom box, which was waiting in silence like the gas generator. When she heard her name mentioned in the ongoing conversation, she turned to face the two men, standing side by side.

The younger man stepped forward, and Dr. Criqui introduced him as Andre, the college student he'd mentioned to Jeanne earlier. Andre was dark-complexioned, tall, and lanky with a light, wispy beard and dressed in a simple white t-shirt stained with sweat and dirt. He wore blue jeans and, like his boots, they were covered in dust. Particles of dirt also lay across the top of the dark hair that topped his head. Introductions were made, and Jeanne discovered with some prompting Andre, like almost everyone in France she had met so far, spoke English fairly fluently.

He said, "I understand you wish to see inside. We can look now if you would like?" The young man had a kind face, and he led both Jeanne and Dr. Criqui just inside the vast cave. "What you see here would have been the main entrance in and out of the quarry over a thousand years ago. But there are other smaller entrances and exits farther into the quarry. This entire underground hill and area resembles kind of the bee's honeycomb, yes?"

Now another twenty feet deeper inside, the student stopped and pointed as the light from outside faded into the recesses. "It will be a challenge here to determine the exact Roman mining techniques because very little recoverable evidence remains. Over the many preceding centuries, much was lost, and many of the tunnels farther inside collapsed. Plus, during times of war, people hid here, brought things in and out, and scavenged just about anything of value they could find."

"Yes, I'm sure Dr. Criqui told you my family was one of those that hid down here during the Second World War. That's why I am so interested in seeing inside." Jeanne took a few more steps forward and deeper into the entryway as she looked all around. "It is hard to imagine ancient men with simple tools were able to dig all this out. It's gigantic in here!"

"The Romans were experts in working underground and created many mines and quarries all over their occupied territories." Andre continued, clearly warming to the interest shown in his favorite subject. "In quarries such as this one, they would have first removed the top layer of soil to expose the rock face. Once they determined the area held what they required, the quarrymen would outline blocks of stone according to the size they needed or could handle. Then they would take iron picks and drive metal wedges in with mallets to form cracks until the stone would come loose. Or, and I think this is what they did here: they would force dried wooden wedges wrapped in cloth into the cracks. Then to make them expand, they'd add water, forcing the stone loose. If the quarrymen were lucky, a fault line might help them by acting as one of the cracks."

Dr. Criqui nodded in appreciation and commented, "The ingenuity of ancient man never ceases to amaze me…"

Jeanne asked, "What is the difference between mining and quarrying? How do we know this was a quarry?"

"The difference between mining and quarrying is simply the material sought after. Mining is done for minerals, while quarrying is done for stones. You can tell by how the rock was removed deeper inside that this quarry was originally dug a very, very long time ago." Andre gestured at something along the interior wall that looked just like the rest of the rock walls to Jeanne. But she nodded along as if she understood. "I think I can see evidence of fire-setting along in here at the beginning of the quarry as well. So I suspect they started mining but soon discovered the stone within more valuable."

"Fire-setting? Underground? What about the natural gasses? Or, for that matter, wouldn't that burn up all the oxygen?" As Dr. Criqui asked his questions, Jeanne could tell he was way more interested in this topic than she was…

"It was hazardous for a lot of reasons. But often times they would light a fire directly in front of the rock face they wanted to mine. Then cool it down immediately with cold water, quenching the rock and hoping it would crack after being weakened by the thermal shock." As Andre spoke, it became clear to Jeanne he was both very informed and passionate about the Romans' ancient knowledge and work. "Of course, as you see, this makes my work much harder. The fire-setting damages all the tools used on the rock face. So often, many of what would have been the kinds of artifacts I hope to find are lost. When I first saw the evidence of the fire setting here, I was pretty discouraged. But the deeper I go, the more I think the mining operation was abandoned early in favor of quarrying."

Trying to sound interested, Jeanne asked what she hoped wasn't a stupid question. "So, Andre, how did they get all the dirt and rock out of the way from below?"

Andre turned to Jeanne, "The loose material would have been brought up in baskets, most likely by slaves and not the artisans who cut the granite blocks. Down inside, I have found where, to avoid ladders, they dug handholds and footholds right into the shaft walls. These were used for climbing in and out and raising baskets of useless or unwanted material. Other small holes in the walls would have been used to hold oil lamps similar to those found in the Roman homes of the day."

"How far back and down does this go?" Jeanne asked the student but then turned to the elderly doctor before waiting for Andre's answer. "And where is the area all the villagers hid during the war? None of this looks like what I remember at all. I seem to recall running from the village itself and that just outside of Vieux, we used a long vertical shaft to enter the space below. But this is a long way from there."

"Andre and I were discussing that outside earlier. From what I remember, I think this main entrance is almost at the opposite end from where we huddled together. We all came out from hiding through here. But I think we tried to conceal ourselves at the far end of the quarry, and this," Dr. Criqui gestured around them, "is really the beginning. Isn't that about right, Andre?"

"It is hard to say for sure. There may be miles of tunnels and different sections of substantially sized rooms they carved out the biggest granite blocks. But I have not made it into all of the quarry yet. My partner is out of town the rest of the week, and it is unwise to explore a place such as this alone…"

Jeanne interjected brightly, "How about I be your partner for a day? I would really like to see more, and, as I am sure Dr. Criqui mentioned, I am only here briefly." Jeanne looked at Andre expectantly.

"Ah… well, not so sure that would be wise…" he began.

"And why not? Because I am a woman? Afraid I'll break a heel or twist an ankle?" Jeanne frowned at the young man, determined not to be turned away by some French student. Especially if he turned out to be a male chauvinist pig!

"Please, no, no, no. You misunderstand the danger." Andre held his hands out defensively and was smiling. "If you were to fall or be hurt, I could most likely carry you out if needed, and I would know the way. However, how would you get me back to the surface if I was injured? Or be confident of finding your way back outside and getting help?" Jeanne's thoughts first turned to the doctor. But his struggles across the field, even with a path, hardly made him a candidate for such exploration. But, the doctor seemed to have already anticipated this and offered a potential solution.

"Andre," he started, "if you had another younger and more able-bodied man than myself, would you consider giving Jeanne here a tour? She strikes me as one who is not to be denied. I fear without your help she may charge headlong into this old quarry even without your guidance." The old doctor winked at Jeanne conspiratorially. "If she were to be lost or hurt down here, you and I certainly wouldn't want that on our conscience, now would we?" Andre looked in turn at both Jeanne and Dr. Criqui. He muttered something in French Jeanne did not understand before answering in English.

"I do hate that I am at a standstill until my partner returns." Andre shrugged, "So if getting back in here means doing a little handholding…" Jeanne opened her mouth, about to jump in and say something.

Andre diffused the situation by holding his hands up defensively once more. He quickly added, "I mean, well, that was perhaps a bad choice of words. What I mean to say is, to continue working and mapping a little deeper, I can slow down long enough to show the lady around inside." He faced the doctor and nodded once, "Yes, Dr. Criqui, that would work. Should we go into town and try to recruit someone?"

Dr. Criqui smiled and, turning, winked once more at Jeanne before adding, "I think I know someone who can help us. Let's head back and grab some lunch. My treat!"

Once back in the small village of Vieux, the two men and Jeanne talked while they ate outside at the town's lone café. The doctor inquired between bites about Andre's studies, where he was from, and how long he expected to work in the old Roman quarry. As the men conversed, alternately between French and English, Jeanne's attention waned. Her eyes were soon drawn to a single woman shambling and twitching slowly down the far sidewalk toward the café. Her hair was long and white and though she faced Jeanne directly, her face was covered by the mass of unruly locks. Jeanne wondered if it was the woman she'd seen the day before at the top of the cemetery steps.

The old lady's gait had a "hiccup" in it, oddly at every third step, and it gave the elderly woman a strange sort of rhythm as she descended the sidewalk. Trying to place the reason for her awkward movement, Jeanne was appalled to see the old lady was barefoot. Her feet were filthy with caked-on dirt that seemed to run all the way up her ankles and perhaps even farther; the rest of her legs were hidden underneath a heavy wool, grey skirt. However, Jeanne's concern for the old woman's lack of hygiene was dwarfed by the dawning realization that her awkward step was caused by the woman's loss of several toes, including the big toe on her right foot. The small stumps seemed unattended and, though hard to tell over the distance between where Jeanne sat and where the limping woman walked, appeared wet.

Jeanne began to turn and ask Dr. Criqui about the crippled old lady when Andre questioned her about life in America and how she came to live there. Jeanne, in response, gave an abbreviated version of how she left France and, making it sound more like a vacation, how she had returned to see the small village where she was born. Adding, she hoped, now with Andre's help, to see where her parents were lost during the war while she was back. When she was done, Jeanne looked again for the old woman across the street. But she was no longer anywhere to be seen. Perhaps, Jeanne surmised, having ducked into one of the buildings on the far side of the street. Hopefully, getting her injuries tended.

As they finished eating, the doctor spied Father Leo, the priest Jeanne met her first morning in the village, coming down the street and waving him over to their table. Walking with the local clergyman was a fragile and petite man wearing large, wire-rimmed glasses too big for his slim face. The huge lenses sat slightly askew, and the frame was missing a nose pad. On his feet were a pair of worn-out, dirty white Chuck Taylor sneakers, and he wore blue jeans and a black t-shirt emblazoned with the American rock group Styx. He was intro-duced as Paul and someone who was currently helping out Father Leo at the church while "getting back on his feet." The priest, upon seeing Jeanne, sheepishly apologized he hadn't yet had a chance to look up the Butte family information as promised. But Jeanne explained Dr. Criqui had provided the answers she'd hoped to find and that Father Leo should no longer worry about looking. The youthful-looking cleric seemed relieved to hear this.

When the priest heard the three of them were looking for someone to help explore the stone quarry, he suggested Paul be enlisted to help. The young man, older than Andre but at least ten years younger than Jeanne, readily agreed to the adventure. Jeanne learned Paul was rela-tively new to the village and had only heard about the ancient quarry pit at the edge of town in passing. In broken English, he offered to bring with the Father's blessing some additional flashlights and rope from the church. With everyone in agreement, the three explorers decided they would meet the following morning at the large quarry entrance. Andre would gather any extra supplies needed this after-noon, and Jeanne commented she would need to return to Caen and try to find suitable clothes and boots for their underground hike.

As the group parted ways, Jeanne remarked casually to Paul about his shirt, telling the small-statured man Styx was a rock group from Chicago, a city very close to where she lived. The man appeared to not know anything about the group he advertised on the black concert t-shirt he wore. Jeanne hummed and sang some of their latest hit, "Babe," but to no avail. Paul clearly was pleased Jeanne noticed and commented about his apparel. He smiled profusely at her and awkwardly thanked her in stuttering English.

Bright and early the following day, the three met at the mouth of the quarry. Jeanne had purchased some hiking boots the day before and a button-down, long sleeve flannel shirt. But, unable to find any suitable slacks that fit her in Caen, she instead wore a pair of Jordache designer jeans she'd packed from home. Andre, admiring and taking the large square flashlight Paul brought with him from the church, was decked out in a t-shirt and a khaki-colored vest with a bright red backpack. He slung the bag across his shoulder after stashing the extra rope, water, and the flashlights he had brought.

Andre seemed anxious to get rolling and quickly took steps to get the small team organized. He gave some brief instructions regarding what to expect. Plus, he reviewed a few safety precautions before handing out the helmets he had secured for each. The white hardhats looked like typical miner helmets equipped with battery-operated lights on the top that lit up the path in front of them as they walked. Jeanne's helmet was almost too big, and Paul stepped over to help her adjust the strap under her chin, smiling at her as he did so. He was wearing the same Styx t-shirt he had on yesterday and was the only one not wearing boots, still in the same cloth high-top sneakers he'd worn the day before.

With Andre in the lead and holding the big flashlight in hand, the three began to move away from the main entrance and deeper underground. The outside sunlight vanished almost immediately as the ground sloped downward. Jeanne initially had a few moments of panic in the alien, shadow-filled cavity. Nearly losing her nerve and fleeing a mere fifty feet inside before squelching the alarms going off in her head. She gritted her teeth and clenched both fists tightly. Focusing on where she placed each step amid the loose rocks as Andre had coached until the choking anxiety slowly dissolved.

Water dripped endlessly, yet unseen. There was a feral smell in the dark Jeanne could not place, and it somehow added to the sensation of being watched or even hunted. Within minutes of starting out, a cloud of bats, startled by the unexpected intrusion, heaved themselves into the air from a separate channel above their heads. Diving and swirling among themselves as the three intruders moved past. The odd smells, sweeping artificial light, and echoing of their footsteps began to feel hauntingly familiar to Jeanne. The lights from the three hardhats and the large, wide-lensed handheld flashlight eerily illuminated the quarry's walls and ceiling. Casting long shadows that seemed to move on their own at times. The ground was scattered with broken and fallen rocks of various sizes. It would be easy to trip over them if you were not careful.

Andre traversed the familiar terrain of the ancient quarry easily. He led the small group confidently through one large cavern after another. Each space had been expertly carved out, and Andre pointed out the various marks on the walls and explained in English what could be learned from the techniques of the ancient Romans. Jeanne was pretty sure Paul could not understand much of what was being said. Jeanne herself had little interest in the topic of ancient underground Roman quarries. But it did help keep her mind occupied, and the college student's assuring voice in the darkness helped make the harsh surroundings more tolerable. Jeanne studied the winding passageways as the three moved forward, looking for anything familiar. Hoping to recognize or soon spot the area where her life changed.

CHAPTER
THIRTEEN

THEY PASSED multiple cavernous rooms as the three trekked down the long, underground corridor. All were virtually identical to each other. Time seemed to stand still for Jeanne, and when she glanced down at her watch, she was surprised to see 45 minutes had passed since the small group left the light and warmth of the sun behind. So far, the carved, winding passageway they were in appeared devoid of any human artifacts. Outside of spotting an occasional crumbling timber, there was little indication of the titanic amount of manpower and resources once employed to create this vast quarry hidden beneath the surface of the quiet French countryside.

Step after step, the bland sameness of the rounded walls, ceiling, and floors was dizzying. It reminded Jeanne of trying to walk in the large, spinning carnival rides found near the end of a funhouse at the county fairs back in Illinois. Usually, the vertigo that accompanied stepping into one of those automated, rotating, six-foot-high cylinders was minimal as long as you kept moving and looked straight ahead or down at your feet. But when you stopped or looked too closely at the round, turning walls, you were suddenly at the ride's mercy. The effect was much the same in what seemed like an endless tunnel of carved stone, where everywhere you looked was identical, featureless curvy grey walls, even without the constant movement.

Finally, Andre, who was in the lead, followed by Jeanne and Paul, slowed his pace. "At last!" he exclaimed. "I have not yet made it past this point, and I think not much farther ahead lies the area you are most interested in, Jeanne. But please watch closely where I step from here on out. Since I have not seen anything beyond here, I may stop from time to time to make a few notes for myself so that we do not get lost." Andre was clearly excited by what may lie ahead, his eyes were wide and shiny in the artificial light, and his voice was tinged with anticipation. "Is everyone OK? Would you like to stop here briefly and catch your breath?" Both Jeanne and Paul, looking at each other, shook their heads no in unison. "Water? No? Very well, then, let's keep moving. But please keep your eyes open. If you see anything out of place, please point it out to me, yes?" Andre began moving once more.

Nearing another bend and dip in the passageway, the floor under their feet grew sticky. Thick, dense clay soon caked the bottom of their shoes. Paul began walking closer to the wall, where the ground was slightly higher and drier than the middle of the tunnel. The color and consistency of the tunnel itself also began to gradually change. The hard rock walls became soft in a few places. Brown mud replaced the hard stone and, at times, dripped soppily down the sides of the enclosure around and above them.

As the three underground hikers moved past the latest curve, a wide, gaping entryway opened to their right. Slowing, Andre took one step inside the side cavern and cocked his head slightly, stopping and pulling out a small spiral notepad from his vest as he did so. Using the tiny pencil lodged in the wire spiral, he wrote briefly before tucking the pad away. Turning to leave the room, he stopped. His light was playing along the ground. Abruptly, he bent down and pulled at something sticking out of the dirt floor. It came up easily from the damp soil, and Andre held it aloft, scrutinizing his find under the light of his headlamp.

"Ah!" He exclaimed brightly, "A piece of an old iron horseshoe." Then, frowning as he turned the find over in his hand, he brushed off a few small clumps of dirt before correcting himself. "No, no, no, not a horseshoe... An ox shoe! For oxen, yes! Not Roman but very old; looks medieval, but hard to tell. I'll return this to the university and get it dated." The student smiled at Jeanne, clearly pleased with the discovery. He paused and leaned farther inside the latest room, glancing both ways. "Do you hear that? That is running water. There must be an underground river close by." Looking down at the mud plastered to all their footwear, he added, "That is likely where all this moisture is coming from. Seeping in from the rushing water."

"An underground river? Is that dangerous?" Jeanne stepped beside Andre, nearly inside the chamber, to hear the sound Andre had noted.

"No, no, not really. It is very pervasive in this area. The stream is probably one of the dozens of underground contributors to the Orne River above, which is not far from here." To Jeanne, there seemed to be something about the odd, echoing sound of the running water that gave her pause. The eerie reverberations of the unseen flow in the enclosed space hauntingly familiar. Goosebumps rose on each of her arms. The unsettling feeling showed on her face, and Andre, recognizing her concern but misunderstanding its reason, attempted to quell her unease.

"It would be a cause for worry if this was springtime or we had recently experienced heavy rains. But otherwise, no worries, see?" Andre grinned at Jeanne once more, shrugging to show his indifference. He swung the large square flashlight into and across the smoothly cut walls of the featureless chamber to help ease her worries before stepping back into the original passageway they had descended. Andre unzipped his backpack and placed the piece of iron he found in one of the inside pockets before leading the small party deeper into the ancient quarry.

The water under their feet soon began to pool in places, and Paul began to murmur under his breath behind Jeanne. She suspected he was either regretting his choice of footwear or perhaps even making this underground journey. Now, nearing the second hour of exploring the quarry, Jeanne was also beginning to feel discouraged. There had been nothing up to that point she recognized. The tunnel they were traversing was wider than she remembered. None of the rooms where the actual quarrying had taken place looked familiar or held signs of any recent human occupation. Andre seemed endlessly fascinated by what his trained eye revealed to him. Unconcerned by the slightly raised water level, he stopped to take notes and to closely examine portions of the walls. Prodding with his hands places that appeared discolored or dripped excessive water or oozed sediment.

Directly ahead and to the left, in a low spot within the tunnel, Andre's light flashed across a huge puddle some ten feet wide and five feet across. Only a narrow two-foot path of relatively dry earth and clay on the far right side of the tunnel looked like it would be passable without thoroughly soaking their feet. Jeanne thought they would have to hug the wall tightly while walking single file if they were going to successfully navigate the water obstacle standing directly in their path. Andre squatted at the pool's edge, peering into the murky liquid without explanation. Stopping entirely and waiting for him, Jeanne pointed her hat's lamp beam ahead and thought she saw, far in the distance, a small wooden structure. She started to open her mouth to tell Andre what she saw when he suddenly yelled out.

"No! Don't do that, Paul!"

Startled, Jeanne spun and saw Paul leaning casually against the cavern's wall. One shoulder pressed in tightly against the side of the concave passageway. He jolted wildly at Andre's sudden exclamation, and his wet shoes slipped on the soggy ground of the tunnel floor. His balance was lost, and Paul extended both arms against the wall he had been leaning against to try and keep himself from falling completely down. As he did so, his hands sunk deep into the soft mud beginning to give under the extra weight of his body. With both of his arms sinking quickly up to their shoulders into the side of the cavern, his face was also slammed up against the slowly disintegrating tunnel wall. His feet slipped out from under him again, and Paul began flailing. Trying desperately to claw his way out of the wall, now caving in all around him.

Andre sprung to his feet and hurtled himself at Paul, reaching the man just as he was about to be swallowed whole by the suddenly sagging side of the tunnel they were in. Andre got both hands on Paul's shirt first before reaching around him to grab one of his shoulders as it slowly disappeared into the passageway's soft mud and clay.

Pulling hard, Andre freed Paul from the rapidly expanding hole collapsing inward under the added stress of the man's weight.

Twisting and turning his body with a loud grunt, Andre tossed Paul, now splattered with muck across his entire upper body and face, roughly to the safety of the ground. But the momentum of Andre's quick movements, and the force he exerted to save Paul from the disintegrating section of the tunnel wall, caused him to lose his balance. He fell back against the same side of the cavern that just threatened to absorb Paul with an audible "thump," barely missing the newly formed hole in it.

Jeanne was frozen in place, both hands across her mouth as if holding back a secret she desperately wanted to share. The light of her helmet acting like a spotlight on a stage, illuminating the heroic act playing out in front of her. Paul, his helmet lost somewhere inside the soft wall, and lying in a heap on the ground, was spitting wet mud out of his mouth and gagging. Andre, breathless and grimacing, was still on his feet but sprawled awkwardly against the tunnel's wall, a foot from the hole that nearly encased Paul moments earlier. The large flashlight, left at the edge of the pool of water, aimed pointlessly down the passageway in the direction they had been heading.

Jeanne, with a dawning realization of the danger, just witnessed, took a step forward and reached out to Andre, wanting to help. Andre, unable to speak and still gasping for breath, waved her hand away as if to say, "Just give me a second." He took one long shuddering breath and then gave Jeanne a crooked grin. He placed his hands behind him against the side of the tunnel to steady himself and keep from slipping. He nodded down at Paul, saying a single word that had the same meaning in French and English, "Idiot." Then the entire wall and floor around him collapsed both backward and downwards in the same instant. The mudslide enveloped Andre before he could even scream.

He was gone.

A massive, wet, unoccupied mud hole - slowly dripping globs of mud and clay from above it - was all that remained where he had been leaning. Jeanne screamed and rushed forward, falling to her knees and reaching out across the fresh and hollow abyss. The light of her helmet bobbed all around but revealed nothing. She hollered his name, "Andre!!" But there was no reply or sign of him anywhere.

She scampered backward on her hands and knees to retrieve the hefty flashlight Andre had left next to the large mud puddle. Jeanne shined it frantically around the inside of the newly formed hole. The ground sagged slightly under her knees, and more mud, rock, and clay fell listlessly down the side of the fresh cavity in the cavern's tunnel. Still, there was no sign or sound of Andre. Jeanne continued calling his name and pointed the flashlight in all directions. Movement from somewhere below gave Jeanne a brief moment of hope. But as her cries after Andre subsided and she looked closer, Jeanne recognized the sight and sound of running water below her. A small river, probably the same one Andre had heard earlier, was cascading down beneath the side of the newly formed hole. Rushing past, unperturbed by Jeanne's desperate pleas.

After a few more minutes of searching and calling, Jeanne gave up. Feeling both hopeless and useless. Even if she wanted to somehow try and climb down, there were no footholds or anything solid she could have used to brace herself. All the rope the little expedition had was being carried by Andre in his backpack, and that, along with the young Frenchman, had also disappeared.

Now on his feet, Paul stood mutely behind Jeanne and looked down at her and the newly formed crater in the side of the tunnel. His glasses had been lost in the struggle, and one of the short sleeves on his black Styx concert t-shirt had been ripped and hung limply. Jeanne regained her feet slowly in the slippery mud and spoke first. "I don't understand what just happened. How did..? I mean, where did he go?" Though it sounded dumb, even as she said it, Jeanne asked, "How is he going to get out of there? Is he going to be OK?"

"He called me an idiot," was all Paul said. Jeanne turned to look at the man beside her.

Uncomprehending, all she could muster was, "What?"

Paul smiled and pointed to the wall, "Too bad he didn't realize that the water would have been slowly eroding the earth underneath and alongside this tunnel for years. Probably carving into that side a little deeper every time the waters ran high." He held his hands out and cast a sideways glance at Jeanne's way. "Oh, well. Shit happens."

Jeanne wasn't sure if she was more stunned by the callous words coming out of the man next to her or that his English was suddenly so well pronounced. Although still thick with a heavy French accent, his enunciations were utterly different from the few English words she had heard him speak. His use of American slang was even more jarring. Briefly forgetting the tragedy she had just witnessed, Jeanne's mind struggled to wrap itself around the man's sudden transformation. Her mouth hung slightly open until Paul reached out with one finger and placed it under her chin to shut it for her with a smirk.

Paul then squatted down next to the pool of muddy water that had first captured Andre's attention and began to splash it across his hands and arms. Slowly cleaning the thick mud and dirt off himself. "That was destiny, Toots. The whole time we've been hiking down here, I was trying to figure out how to get rid of the guy, and then, POW!!" Jeanne flinched at the loud and unexpected exclamation. "Problem solved." Paul, satisfied with his handwashing, stood once more and smiled at Jeanne again. "Has anyone ever told you what a great ass you have? Been watching those expensive tight jeans of yours hugging those hips this entire time. I gotta say, for an older lady, you sure take good care of yourself."

Jeanne opened her mouth and shut it again before trying a second time. "Who are you? How did...? That man may have just died saving your life, and you act like, like... What did you say to me?" The light from her helmet was even with Paul's face and lit it up brightly. A cunning intelligence was now visible inside the mud-caked man's eyes. She asked again, "Who are you?"

"Me? Just some poor, hopeless, recently paroled ex-con. My parole officer's brother is the gullible Father Leo. Didn't he tell you? He's been letting me stay at the church since I have nowhere else." Paul rolled his eyes dramatically. "I play stupid, so he doesn't expect me to do much. Did you know," the man took a step closer to Jeanne, "he feeds me and lets me sleep in a room at the back of the church for free? Sometimes, I sweep up his office, where he keeps all the donations locked up. I almost took it all after last Sunday's services, but something," the man stopped to laugh humorlessly before continuing, "maybe it was God? Anyway, something said, 'Paul, let's see what one more week brings first.' And now, look at you. Just look at what God dropped in my lap. Damn, you look good."

Jeanne stepped back away from the Jekyll and Hyde manifesting before her. The new boot on her right foot sunk into the wide mud puddle behind her. "Why are you telling me this? Right now, we need to get out of here. Go back to town. Andre may still be alive and needs help."

"Ppphhhfffttt! That guy…, that idiot is dead. The subterranean stream around us probably goes for miles and miles. It will drag his lifeless body deeper and deeper until it is buried somewhere underground in the muck. And you can forget about getting help. See, you and I will have some fun now, understand? Have a little party down here." Paul reached into his back pocket and withdrew something with a shiny handle. "When I'm done, I'll let you go try to help poor Andre. As a matter of fact, I'll shove you right down that same hole so you can follow his trail."

"What are you saying? I'd die down there!" Jeanne gasped, the threat of the man becoming crystal clear to her.

"Oh honey, you'll be dead long before I put you in that hole. You see, this hole collapsing here is obviously just a freak accident. Anyone investigating this tragic little occurrence will be able to tell what happened naturally after years and years of erosion. Such a shame that idiot Andre fell in. And you," Paul's eyes traveled up and down Jeanne's body, making her skin crawl, "you were so brave trying to save the guy. Such a shame you fell in after him. That is what I'll tell everyone after I walk back out of here anyway. But hey! You get to go out a hero, right?"

Paul advanced on Jeanne in the dark chamber. The wide-lensed flashlight on the ground cast an eerie glow and bizarrely shaped shadows across the rough floor of the tunnel. Jeanne wanted to scream for help but knew no one could hear her so deep underground.

Paul suddenly lashed out with one hand. His dirty fingernails scratched her chest's smooth, soft flesh, tearing off buttons and opening up her flannel shirt in one swift motion. With his second hand, he grasped the front of her bra and pulled viciously, ripping the straps in the process and exposing both of her breasts in the dim light. Jeanne screamed involuntarily and clutched at his arms, trying to free herself free from his grip. Her feet splashed loudly in the slippery wet mud puddle, and she stumbled backward, yanking Paul after her. She staggered once but regained her footing. Barely avoiding dragging Paul right down on top of her in the process.

Whether it was her struggles with him, her exposed breasts, or her screaming, Paul became visibly more excited. His sneer widened, and his stank breath was choppy on Jeanne's face. Reaching up with one hand, he grabbed a handful of Jeanne's hair, halting her backward momentum away from him. With terrible intent, he flicked the wrist of his other hand, and the chrome handle he had brandished moments before twirled expertly in his hand. A six-inch blade popped out from the Butterfly-style knife, and its handle fit snuggly in his grip. Paul raised the knife to eye level. Jeanne was forced to stare at the weapon as it flashed menacingly across her eyes under the bright light of her helmet.

CHAPTER
FOURTEEN

THE SUDDEN FLASH of white light reflecting off the menacing blade triggered something deep inside Jeanne. Her initial defensive posture and meager struggles against the diminutive ex-con were swallowed whole by an unexpected surge of rage bubbling within. The meek housewife who, mere moments before, felt powerless watching Andre abruptly disappear in the collapse was gone. Now, this middle-aged mother launched herself at the leering, would-be rapist. Turning the tables and erupting in a volcanic frenzy of blind savagery. Unable to bear even the notion of being touched by this man.

Violently unable.

Paul, who had tried to stroke such fear in her, was completely surprised. The modest, midwestern girl, the one her attacker expected to use and discard like trash, welled with fury. Jeanne lashed out with both her fists and her fingernails. Clawing at the astonished face of Paul and, in her ferocity, pulling herself close enough to his shocked profile to bite down on the creep's nose. Her teeth were locked in a vice-like clamp. It was as if a demon rose in her place or overcame her.

Her mind no longer her own.

Tapping into something that felt primordial, more animal than human. Yet somehow, deep inside, its release was both familiar and comforting. Jeanne let it overwhelm her…

Startled and back peddling in the slimy, shallow water of the puddle, Paul dropped his knife to the ground as he tried desperately to pull Jeanne's clenched teeth from his face with both hands. Now it was his screams unheeded in the gloom of the ancient underground quarry.

Pushing hard at Jeanne's head with his hands, the flesh of his nose gave and tore wide open. Seeing the give in the flap of skin clenched between her teeth, Jeanne twisted her head with all her might. Ripping a large chunk of Paul's nose completely off his face before spitting it to one side. The small man squealed like a stuck pig. Howling in anguish, he put both hands to his features, feeling for his ruined nose and looking down dumbly at his blood-soaked hands in disbelief. In his shock and pain, momentarily forgetting about the danger the ferocious inferno erupting in front of him still presented. Utterly astonished at the turn of events where, with a raging hard-on still between his legs mere moments before, he was certain Jeanne would submit to him with barely a whimper. Paul began to hurl obscenities at her. All but blinded by the flood of tears, choking on his own blood as it cascaded down his face and poured into his sputtering open mouth.

Jeanne glanced down for the blade the ex-con had wielded. But in the shadows, with her headlamp having fallen off her head in the attack, all she could see at first was the bright light of the large, heavy square flashlight Andre had been carrying. She bent down, scrambling for the handle until she found it, and in one fell swoop, brought it up from the ground as hard and as fast as she could. The lens shattered as it connected with Paul's chin. The force of the blow knocked him backward and completely unconscious. He collapsed soundlessly in a huff, flat on his back with only his shoulders and head outside of the dirty pool of water the pair struggled in. Paul lay sprawled, blood pouring from his shattered face, eyes rolled up in his head with the whites of each staring unseeing at the ceiling of the cavern's tunnel. Spying the tempting glint of Paul's knife lying half buried in the ground beside him, Jeanne dropped to her knees and reached for it. With adrenaline and more still in command of her, she bent over her attacker and continued the barrage.

When it was finished, Jeanne lay panting on the muddy ground. Her hard hat had come off during the assault, but miraculously, the headlamp on top was unbroken. It lay on the ground a few feet from her, now the only light fighting back the deep black of the underground. In one hand, she still held the handle of the church's large square flashlight along with half of its plastic outer casing. The lens and plastic shell were decimated, only the grip from the battery-operated torch intact in Jeanne's hand. She opened her clenched fist and let the bloody handgrip fall to the ground next to the other broken pieces. The large rectangular battery that had powered the light lay dented beside the rest of the ruined flashlight, half submerged in the muddy pool of water now stained dark red.

Jeanne stood and reached for her hard hat, squaring it on her head and clipping the plastic buckle under her chin to keep it in place again. She then refastened the three buttons remaining on her ripped flannel shirt while passively looking down at the wreck at her feet.

Paul was barely recognizable.

His acting days, either as Jekyll/Hyde or as a dumb but harmless parolee, were over. The potential theft of the funds at the church in Vieux no longer needs to concern Father Leo. Or anyone else, for that matter. Paul's skull had been caved in on one side. Small pieces of the large square flashlight are embedded at places in the exposed soft parts. The Butterfly knife Paul had so securely brought to bear was buried in his exposed left thigh. Jeanne vaguely remembered sticking it there after she had used it to cut the man's cock off to stuff down his own throat. The end of the limp member, still oozing blood, was visible in what was left of a now badly misshapen and crooked mouth.

Jeanne began to tremble uncontrollably and shook her head violently once to stop it. Reaching down, she pulled the knife out of Paul's thigh and casually tossed it down the hole Andre had fallen through in the wall. She then dragged Paul's lifeless corpse over to the same opening and shoved him over the edge of it. Watching as his body slid down, rolling over once on itself, before briefly stopping at the edge of the rushing water and slowly catching in the racing current. It turned over one final time before being carried downstream by the underground river. As it disappeared, Jeanne uttered a single French word.

"Idiot."

A part of Jeanne grimly recognized what she'd just done. Killing a man she barely knew. Acting as judge, jury, and - upon sentencing him to death - executioner. But that part, her new self so recently enlightened over the last few years by hours of therapy and counseling, now stood meekly on the sidelines. The gravity of the horror and violence silenced her.

Jeanne acknowledged these feelings of remorse, but with a practiced hand, she pushed beyond those disturbing emotions. Choosing to focus momentarily on her own, still a very real peril. Understanding she was down to just the one lamp affixed to the hardhat perched on her head. She had no idea how long the batteries in it would last. So her first instinct was to immediately start hiking back the way she'd come just as fast as she could. Jeanne turned back that way and took a few halting, measured steps towards what was likely the quickest exit out of the quarry. Jeanne felt confident that the passageway would be fairly easy to reverse engineer and could quickly get her back to the surface.

The confidence in this plan gave Jeanne time to pause, and she stopped walking to survey her surroundings again. Jeanne swung her head back the opposite way from where she, Andre, and (that idiot) Paul had come. Once again, spying the outline of the manmade wood object she had seen before the chaos of the collapsing wall and the chaos of… Well, herself, she supposed.

A slight smile played at the corners of her mouth, lifting her mood.

In the dim yellow light of her head lantern, the edge of the small wood structure appeared to be more modern than the disintegrating timbers and ancient beams Andre had been so interested in. The sharp corner of the ends was still intact despite the moisture permeating this part of the quarry. Jeanne decided she could spare a few minutes to see if the wood structure held any clues to her past. She walked gingerly towards it. Her footsteps in the wet mud made loud squishing sounds with each step in the slippery muck of the passageway. Jeanne carefully navigated the small dry path past the wide puddle in the carved rock hallway. As a precaution, walking along the opposite side of the collapsed wall.

As Jeanne approached, the manmade object was bathed in the light of her headlamp. Now fully illuminated, she saw it was simply an empty crate. Rotted, slimy, and slowly sagging on two sides. Whatever it once held years ago had disappeared. Any trace of the materials it carried was long gone, just like the writing on the wood box itself. Both relieved and discouraged, Jeanne turned once more to begin returning to the surface and out of the stone quarry.

But, as she did, Jeanne spied a small black tunnel burrowed into one of the side walls of this latest chamber. The opening was shoulder height, roughly three feet high by three feet wide, just big enough for a small adult to crawl in and out. It appeared to head away from and in the opposite direction of the rock-lined passageway she used to enter this new room where the slimy crate sat. The small passage had been partially hidden from her view by the crate itself. Still, it was actually only a few short steps behind the decaying wood box.

Most surprising, however, was the small rusted metal ladder hanging at the base of the hole and mounted into the rock wall itself. The ladder was clearly meant to gain access up and down from the tiny tunnel. It had only five rungs and looked much like the metal ladders often fixed at the deep ends of swimming pools. Its familiarity, despite its bizarre placement so deep underground, tugged at Jeanne's memory. She felt confident she'd seen or even climbed this very same ladder once before. Recalling being terrified in a dark space, crawling backward on her hands and knees in a tunnel too small for her to stand up in. Rushing breathlessly away from something terrible before feeling her legs suddenly disappear from under her. Her feet had swung desperately in the air until she had finally found the sure footing of a ladder's first rung. She had pushed herself backward the rest of the way and stepped down, one foot after another, before finally jumping off a small ladder like this. A triumphant feeling of escape and freedom so strong it was hard to imagine she had forgotten all about it until now.

Was this the same ladder?

Jeanne, now intrigued and trying hard to place that memory, stepped to the elevated tunnel on the side of the cavern. She noted the ladder's third rung was broken, and the one closest to the ground was now merely a rusted shell, already crumbling and unable to bear any weight. Yet the thick metal rivets driven into the stone wall to secure the small ladder in place seemed to be holding firm. Reaching out, she touched the cool, slimy side of the short metal ladder, squeezing it hard to see if it would crumble. When it seemed solid, she yanked hard on it once before wiping the flaking rust particles and slime from the side handrails off her hands and onto her pants. Jeanne felt satisfied the bulk of the wall-mounted ladder still held firm despite its advanced age.

The feel of the old ladder under her hands only made Jeanne's abbreviated recollection of that moment of escape seem more positive. Looking once more around the room - at the crate, the metal rungs, and the hole in the wall - she got a stronger impression she had been in this very room before.

Emboldened, Jeanne stepped onto the second rung and pulled herself up, bringing her face even with the opening of the elevated entryway. Her headlamp revealed the tunnel was not empty. A single shoe with a small metal buckle, clearly children's size, lay near the end of what turned out to be a very short passageway. The exit on the other side was only some six feet away from where Jeanne stood, peering into the small shaft. Jeanne felt sure she recognized the shoe as very similar to those from her own childhood and pulled herself up and into the tight tunnel. Her shoulders just cleared both sides with barely an inch to spare. The metal ladder screeched ominously behind her as she pushed off it with her feet to gain full entry into the narrow space.

Stretched on her belly, Jeanne wiggled completely inside and crawled forward, using her elbows and knees for leverage. Her headlamp was encouragingly bright in the tiny enclosed space. Reaching the shoe, a small sob escaped her lips, and Jeanne had to beat back tears suddenly threatening to stream out of her eyes. It was a simple shoe and not particularly ornate. Still, Jeanne felt positive she recognized it as having been one of hers. Holding it in her hand, it seemed so very small.

Involuntarily, Jeanne thought of her own son Russell when his feet had been that small. It took all her willpower to keep from crying and bolting right back out of the tightly constricted passageway. Realizing how much she missed her son for the first time since leaving home.

Silently cursing all the wasted time she could have spent with him in the past and vowing to herself to become the mother he deserved once she returned home. That is, she thought, if she ever got back to the surface and could somehow make the local authorities understand her actions and what had happened to the other two men.

Jeanne lay on her stomach in the cramped, enclosed space for several minutes until she felt she had control once again. Beginning to crawl forward, she pushed herself out of the opposite end of the small passage and found the exit on this side of the tunnel almost even with the floor of the next room. She pulled herself all the way out and stood, tucking the tiny shoe in the front pocket of her jeans.

The room had the same rock walls, ceiling, and floor as every other underground chamber. All chiseled and carved by men using hand tools, remarkably straight and uniform, dimpled and grooved manually and almost featureless. The four chamber walls appeared grey in the dull yellow light of Jeanne's headlamp. Cracks of varying width and length ran in different directions. In the sharply cut corners of the walls on the floor lay several sizes of rocks that collapsed or had fallen from the ceiling.

Yet this room, unlike any Jeanne had seen thus far, contained several manmade objects. These few Spartan furnishings, obviously of the Second World War era, immediately brought Jeanne down to her knees. A cascade of images, feelings, and memories crashed into her in a blinding rush. The remembrance was neither subtle nor gentle.

Jeanne clung to herself deep underground and remembered everything…

CHAPTER
FIFTEEN

JEANNE SAGGED *from her knees down to the floor completely. Sitting on her butt in the dirt of the cavern's floor beside the small tunnel she entered the room by. She lowered her head and bathed her body in the soft yellow light that shone brightly atop her helmet. The light provided comfort as she processed a dizzying avalanche of memories. Seeing her adult self lit up and knowing she was alone deep inside the quarry gave her the resolve she needed. Jeanne slowly allowed the long-buried memories from her time underground as a small child to surface. She opened the gate to a part of her mind she'd closed off long ago. Sifting through all that lost time. Remembering every sight, sound, and smell…*

Like a giant winged black bat, the thing that butchered her father easily swept little Jeanne off of the ground. Lifting the four-year-old effortlessly but panting hard and fast in her tiny ear. Jeanne could feel things wet, warm, and sticky on the pinching digits holding her tightly. Her head and body clamped firmly against its side as the killing machine gracefully pirouetted and rushed forward down the tight black tunnels. Eyes closed, Jeanne hung limply from its clutches like a rag doll. Her little arms and legs bounced up and down and back and forth as she was carried along at a frightening pace that never seemed to waver. She could hear the horror holding her, making guttural noises as it ran. The sound was staccato, sharp, and piercing, with a deep sense of anger or grief. Even the small child it snatched could recognize it.

Though barely aware, she still breathed - and pressed so snuggly to its side that each gasp she did draw was a struggle - Jeanne tried lifting her head. Turning it slightly to free her pinched nose and instantly inhaled the coppery smell of blood and death. Her eyelids fluttered open, but her vision was blurred in the whirlwind of motion she was caught in. Her eyes struggling to find something she could focus on. Slowly Jeanne became aware of a dim yellow light on the ground beneath her. The beam appeared to be aimed away from where she faced and pointing along the unlikely pair's path.

Still numb and unable to process all she had just witnessed, Jeanne began to cast her eyes around, oddly detached and without fear or emotion. The small girl could tell she was still deep underground in the cavern. The same chipped, rounded walls encircled them. The ground still packed with dirt littered with different-sized stones and sharp rocks that seemed to spew upwards in places. Neither of these obstacles concerned the locomotive whooshing her through the winding tunnels. Gradually, Jeanne became more aware of herself, and her dread slowly rekindled. She lifted her head higher still but tentatively. Finally, summoning the courage to turn around and see what had seized her so completely in its grip. But she was still far too disoriented to recognize this simple act as one of bravery.

The unknown "thing" rushing along with Jeanne in its arms came slowly into focus. It was a single, blond-haired man. He was carrying Jeanne in the same manner as her father often did, and because of this, it was easy for her to tell this man was much taller and bigger than her papa had been.

The large man clutched Jeanne to his side with hands dripping blood. He ran effortlessly within the carved underground channels, easily sidestepping the occasional rock piles and hurtling any small boulders in his path. Across his broad shoulders, he wore a long black trench coat slick and shiny all down its front but bone dry and dusty down the back. As he ran, the coattails spread out behind him like the billowing wings of a raven. Thick veins bulged in his neck, and when he breathed in and out, Jeanne was lifted up and down by the power of his thick chest. On his pale white face, mere inches from Jeanne's, his thick lips parted as he exhaled, revealing the straightest and whitest teeth Jeanne had ever seen. The man continued muttering between breaths, and now Jeanne recognized the occasional utterance he spat out. The words themselves were unknown to the small girl, but the language is undeniable. It was the same one used by the soldiers who lived alongside the villagers of Vieux all of Jeanne's life.

German.

Jeanne swiveled her head back around to see the path the big German man was running down. His opposite hand held a flashlight, and the tight stream of bouncing light showed they were nearing a fork in the tunnel. With a clear knowledge of the underground system, the man carrying Jeanne in his arms made a sharp right and sprinted down a much narrower channel than the previous one. The farther along they went, the more claustrophobic it became. Soon it tightened enough that it caused the man to slow to a jog and then, soon after, ducking his head slightly as he went, walking at a brisk clip.

Though still in shock from witnessing the macabre scenes and violence leveled at both her mother and her father, Jeanne gradually regained awareness. Though uncomprehending of all the ramifications, she understood what her papa had done to her mother and that the man holding her now had, in turn, slaughtered her father.

Turning back to face her papa's murderer again, Jeanne scrutinized the man more closely. She saw a sheen of sweat across his face and a deep mark or scar visible behind one ear, slightly under his short-cropped blond hair. Jeanne also recognized the red armband encircling the bicep of his large arm and the funny, twisted crosses that marked him, according to her father, as the vilest of men.

Curious, she reached out tentatively and wiped her finger across the slippery moisture splattered across the chest of the German's black leather coat. Drawing her hand close to her face, she saw her tiny finger was covered in thick blood.

Her papa's blood.

Jeanne saw once again, this time in her mind's eye, how this man pounced on top of her father as her mother lay crumpled on the dirt floor of the quarry. The light from the twin lanterns flashed white off the Nazi's knife as he plunged the long blade repeatedly into Marcel Butte, grunting with each thrust before systematically hacking her father to bits. Making and leaving behind a statement of utter contempt and horrible mutilation.

Jeanne watched the thickening blood of her beloved papa drip slowly down into the web of skin between her fingers. She looked up once again at the glossy wetness covering the entire front of the German's black trench coat and began to shriek. Shrilly screaming directly into the face of her father's killer. Jeanne struggled with all the might her four-year-old body could muster. Kicking, punching, and clawing. Desperately trying to squirm from his secure grasp and crying out over and over at the top of her lungs.

The man, dressed in black from head to toe, reacted by squeezing the little girl very tightly against his hard-muscled body. Wrapping his arm even tighter around her chest and, like a long black snake coiling around a small field mouse, crushing the girl's lungs. Depriving her chest of the space needed to inhale more air once her screams exhausted all the oxygen they held. Cutting off both her movements and breath in a powerful stranglehold. Within moments she weakened and, barely conscious, fell limp.

The Nazi, having reached his destination deep underground in the quarry, casually tossed the barely conscious little girl onto a thin, blue-striped mattress spread across the top of a small metal cot. She bounced once, and the springs of the cot squeaked as she landed. Jeanne tried to cry out and sit up but could barely raise her head. Stars and purple blotches still obscured much of her vision as oxygen slowly returned to her starved and rattled brain.

In the dim light of the room she found herself in, Jeanne watched motionlessly as the German in black crossed the room and then bent down. He unlocked and swung open the side of a large wooden crate. The slats of wood that made up the box were each spaced several inches apart, making the wood container look like a small cage. Metal hinges had been fastened on one side of the crate, creating a door held in place by a small steel plate with a hasp affixed on the outside.

Leaping out of the slated enclosure was one of the biggest dogs Jeanne had ever seen. Its ears were perfect triangles that stood erect on its large head. The dog's thick snout was all black and filled with jagged teeth. The canine was powerfully built with light brown fur except on its backside, where the fur was jet black. A heavy tail swung back and forth behind it.

The colossal dog panted and seemed to smile at its master before sensing or perhaps smelling Jeanne, the unknown newcomer. It turned towards her and emitted a deep growl as it bared its teeth, stopping only when the Nazi issued a single sharp command to the canine. The dog immediately cowered and retreated to the far corner of the rock and clay underground room. The Nazi then re-crossed the room and loomed briefly over Jeanne as she continued struggling to regain the breath he'd crushed out of her. His eyes glowed in the light of the flickering flame lamps tucked in several recessed pockets along the room's wall. The eyes were piercing blue and bore into Jeanne intensely as if searching her soul. The baleful stare chilled Jeanne, and her fear, already primed, escalated under the intense gaze of the hardened soldier.

The Nazi's hand shot out, clenching the tiny arm of the frightened four-year-old girl and yanking her roughly off the thin cot. He dragged her callously behind him in the dirt while striding purposefully back to the wood crate from which the dog had just been evicted. He casually tossed Jeanne inside and slammed the side shut again, relocking the metal hasp on the outside with a keyed, steel padlock.

Jeanne backed away from the scary man to the farthest corner of the splintery and rough textured box, hugging her knees to her chest before screaming again. The dog immediately lunged from its corner and roared at the box. Its drool and wet spittle sprayed the crate's outside as he barked ferociously at the noisy new intruder. The German watched impassively for several moments as the dog snarled mere inches from Jeanne's face. Then once more, the Nazi issued his single stern order to the bellowing dog, and it fell instantly silent.

The man squatted down and peered into the crate at Jeanne with his cold, dead stare. He pet the head of the now silent dog with his one dry hand and put a single finger from his other bloody hand to his mouth, and blew air out of his puckered lips. "Ssshhh…" The sound caused Jeanne's bladder to give out, and sobbing silently, she peed herself.

The man spoke some words Jeanne did not understand. When she did not respond, the German repeated them more softly in a slightly "sing-song" way that he may have intended to sound more comforting. However, the effect was more chilling to the little girl. The rhyming cadence, delivered by the unsmiling Nazi with his empty eyes, left her frozen in place. Silently, she stared back at the adult until turning to face the dog, who had begun to push its snout against the wood slats of the box. Sniffing more urgently after her bladder had released. Jeanne was terrified the man in all black clothing would also smell what she had done and become angry with her. Jeanne squeezed her eyes shut and bowed her head, wishing the dog away and squeezing her damp legs together tightly.

Though the dog stayed, the Nazi stood and, as he did, peeled the long black trench coat he wore off himself. Then carrying it, he walked over to where several round jugs and containers were stacked along the floor. Opening one of the ceramic jugs, he poured water onto a towel hanging from the bedrail of the cot.

He sat heavily on the portable metal bed, which sagged and groaned loudly under his weight. He methodically cleaned the blood and gore off the front of his coat and his hands using water and the towel. Dabbing delicately at his face where crimson had splattered across one cheek and ear. Periodically ringing the red water into a wooden bucket sitting on the floor beside the cot. At the sight of the bloody water running out of the towel, Jeanne turned her head. Avoiding the sight of it and both the man and the panting dog, who was still close enough that she could feel its hot breath on her neck. The little girl looked out into the room where her dad's killer had brought her.

The cavern room she was caged inside was nearly identical to the one all of the villagers had taken refuge in, only much smaller. In one corner were stacked a large number of boxes and other wooden crates of various sizes. There were words and letters stenciled on the side of many of the wood containers, but Jeanne didn't recognize any of the words. Like the language, Jeanne had not been taught to read German words. However, she had heard and seen enough of the language on signs and on the sides of vehicles to identify the dialect. She also recognized two big guns sitting with their butts in the earth of the cavern. One was very long, and the other smaller with a much shorter barrel. They both leaned ominously together in the corner beside the stacked boxes.

The room was lit by multiple lamps. Jeanne recognized a small barrel of oil for the lamps was part of the supplies stacked in the same corner as the rest of the materials and containers she had seen the man draw water from. The entrance where the man had entered the room while still carrying her was a large black and seemingly empty doorway with no door. Turning her head, she saw another black shadowed opening that could have been another entrance or exit for the room, but she couldn't tell for sure in the gloom of the darkened space.

Jeanne continued discreetly looking around the carved, rock walls of the low-ceilinged room with the dirt floor. Trying to remain motionless and move only her eyes, scared the man would be angry at her for even looking at his belongings or where she guessed he must live.

Jeanne wondered where all the other German soldiers from above were staying. Like her neighbors in Vieux, had they all come to hide far below the surface to avoid the bombs? Or had this man always lived here? Jeanne did not recognize this man in black with all his shiny metals and odd-shaped metal crosses hanging from his shirt. Although uniformed men came and went from the village often, very few stayed long or returned enough times that Jeanne remembered them.

The Nazi finished cleaning his long, black leather coat to his satisfaction. Ignoring the little girl, he stood and closely inspected the bright buttons in turn, one by one. Intensely wiping a few of them with a separate cloth he pulled from his pants pocket. He held the coat aloft next to a lantern that burned brightly from one of the shelf-like flat spaces dug into the side of the wall. Jeanne held her breath as she watched him. Eyeing every move he made for any hint of what would happen to her next. Wondering if she was allowed to speak or if he would even understand her.

Abruptly, the man finished and donned his now clean coat once more. He called the dog to him and, still without acknowledging Jeanne in any way, turned his handheld flashlight back on and strode purposefully outside the room. Heading back out the same entrance he entered when arriving with Jeanne. The large dog trailed after him obediently.

Jeanne was unsure if she should be more scared to be left alone in this strange place by the German. His presence and how he looked at her were terrifying, not to mention what he had done to her father.

But instead, her thoughts soon centered on the wall he had just stood beside as he'd put the final touches on his coat. As she had carefully watched him working beside the lantern, Jeanne recognized a third opening in this room. A small tunnel opened at the base of the wall where the German had worked. It looked like it had been made for a child to crawl in and out. Or, Jeanne thought, maybe the man had carved it out for his dog. She wondered where the tunnel led.

CHAPTER
SIXTEEN

JEANNE SAT *with her back to the wall beside the tunnel she'd crawled out of. The harsh memories of how her four-year-old self was treated jarred her. The images, sights, and sounds now incredibly clear despite how long ago it happened. Not to mention she had been so very young at the time. It was as if the pain of those days had been seared into a part of her. Never to be forgotten. Yet somehow, even as a child, she had instinctively buried what happened in a place Jeanne had not been able (or perhaps dared?) to access again until now. As Jeanne looked once more around her, turning the light on her helmet to illuminate the room, it was clear this was the same chamber she'd been held in all those years ago. A place full of terrible deeds that part of her no longer wanted to revisit. The echoes and images, freed now, scurried about her mind like crawling cockroaches in the dark. Busy laying eggs that quickly hatched and whispered of other things far worse to come.*

Jeanne drew her knees up against her chest exactly as she had when, as a four-year-old, she'd last been in this horrible room. She wrapped both arms around herself, shivering from the cool of the subterranean chamber and from the cold water and mud that earlier soaked much of her clothing. But also shaking and teeth chattering as she recalled what happened when the Nazi came back a short time later. Jeanne remembered the dog had not accompanied the German when he returned for some reason. But the man did not come back alone. God knows she wished he had… The big man had been carrying some-

thing heavy, and he had lain it softly on the cot, almost reverently. It had not been the dog or more supplies.

No, it had been her mother!

The four-year-old's tears streamed down her face as she crawled forward to the side of her wood-slatted cage. When the Nazi placed Jeanne's mother on the cot, it had been on her back. Simone's head lolled awkwardly as he lowered her, and her face was now mercifully turned away from her young daughter's disbelieving gaze. But being unable to see her mother's face twisted reality and Jeanne's emotions. Could she trust her own eyes? Was that really her mother? What was Jeanne feeling? Despair? Hope? Her mother's appearance, sprawled across the metal cot, was no different than when she would sometimes lie down for an afternoon nap. Simone was fully dressed with one leg crossed over the other in a bizarre caricature of normalcy.

This life-like appearance caused the child's heart to lurch in her chest. Jeanne began to question whether her papa had killed her mother after all. He had hurt her for sure, Jeanne knew. But perhaps her mother had just been asleep? Or maybe she had pretended and played dead to make him stop? Jeanne couldn't determine how or why, but the possibility gave her hope. She cried out to her mother, begging her to get up and help her. To come to her rescue as mothers always do for their children. To make sense of these recent events, all so jumbled in little Jeanne's mind.

The Nazi, who had been slowly shedding and hanging his long coat off of the corner of the highest stack of crates, stood mutely beside the cot. Impassively listening to the child begging for her mother. Seeming barely to register Jeanne's existence and staring oddly at only the corpse he'd retrieved. From the corner of her eye, Jeanne could see his face twitching in the dim light of the flickering oil lamps. Though scared of disobeying his earlier command of silence, Jeanne continued to plead with her mother.

The Nazi seemed to deflate briefly, and a shadow that may have been grief drew itself over his harsh features. He began talking in a low murmur, but Jeanne was unsure what he was saying. The Nazi didn't look at Jeanne as he spoke. Instead, his downward glance was still fixed on the body draped atop the cot. When his voice began to crescendo, Jeanne silenced herself. Bracing for his admonishment and fearful of his wrath and punishment. Jeanne first leaned back and then scooted herself backward in the wooden box. Her eyes moved from her mother's still form to the German man who had brought Jeanne and her mother Simone to this deep underground earthen room.

The Nazi suddenly bellowed loudly once. His voice boomed inside the small underground enclosure, eliciting an accompanying scream from the terrified four-year-old. He seemed not to hear nor care. Instead, he angrily bent down and picked up the ceramic container he had emptied of water while cleaning his coat. He threw the hollow vessel against the cavern's far wall, and it shattered into a thousand jagged pieces. His chest heaved in and out as he scowled at the unmoving figure on the bed. Moments later, he brought both hands to his face, covering a grimace Jeanne thought was one of pain. However, when his hands were withdrawn seconds later, the pain was gone from his features. The cold mask he wore earlier settled back in place. He moved to the cot and sat beside the dead body, looking at it for long minutes before lying down beside it.

Both bodies still and silent as the grave.

With no sign of the dog, movements, or sounds to capture her attention, Jeanne leaned back into the corner of her cage. Giving up on raising her mother. She listened to the steady and deep breaths coming from the Nazi that lay in the bed with her mom's corpse. Weary and exhausted from a long day of ordeals and shocks, Jeanne soon, like the German, fell asleep.

Groggily, Jeanne opened her eyes and slowly began to wake herself. She didn't feel rested and couldn't tell how long she had been asleep. But the room was darker, and she saw several lamps had burned completely out while she slept. She shivered, and, at first, Jeanne thought it must have been the cold or change in light that had woken her up. Still tired, she shifted and began to close her eyes once more when a sharp noise reached her ears. The sound was not new. Now, Jeanne dimly realized that sound was what had woken her. She lay in the near darkness, waiting for it again, trying to figure out the noise.

The cot screeched, and the metal springs protested loudly. Without looking, Jeanne recognized the sound as the same one the steel cot had made when the German man tossed her down on it. The noise came again later when the Nazi sat heavily on it next to her mother. Now the cot creaked once more. The noise came almost right on top of the previous one.

Thinking the Nazi may be waking up and climbing from the bed, Jeanne started to turn over on her side when the distinctive metal screech came yet again. Jeanne lifted her head from the wood floor of the box as the clatter came quickly once more. Then again. And again. Its pace gradually quickened. Jeanne rolled to her side and pushed herself up onto her hands and knees as the sound repeated itself over and over. Its urgency, if not reason, was made plain by the now constant squeaking of the cot's protesting springs. Jeanne crawled silently to the end of her cage and looked up at the cot, peering at shadowed movements mirroring the noise.

The four-year-old saw a dark shape silhouetted and moving up and down on the complaining cot. Jeanne could see the underside of the cot beneath the mattress nearly touching the cavern floor with every screech. Straining all of her senses, Jeanne began to make out a dull grunt falling in rhythm with the metal springs as they noisily objected under the strain. The struggling dark shadow continued moving up and down on top of the cot. The murky outline was barely visible, with only two small flickering oil lamps still lit.

Jeanne watched, fascinated and uncomprehending, trying to puzzle out what she was seeing but unable to make sense of it. But hope now surged and woke Jeanne completely. She sat up straight in the box on the ground to see more clearly. Had her mother awakened after all? Was she even now taking revenge on the man who killed papa? Or had someone else entered and was attacking the Nazi while he slept? Jeanne pressed her tiny face to the slats as the struggle continued, trying to decide whether to yell out to her rescuer. Unsure if she would be heard over the grunts and groans taking place above her.

Jeanne opened her mouth to cry out, but the exclamation died in her throat. At that moment, her mother's upside-down face suddenly appeared above Jeanne. Her mother's head fell backward from the thin mattress's edge and began to bounce rapidly. Its movement in rhythm as if mimicking the screeches of the complaining cot. Simone's long black hair spilled across the floor of the cave. Sweeping up and down and, at times, back and forth like a broom brushing over and cleaning a desperately filthy floor. Jeanne watched as her mother's head bounced in an exaggerated parody of silent agreement. Nodding her head upside down as if strongly agreeing with something. Jeanne's mouth was still wide open but completely silent. She watched as her mother's head dropped even lower to the ground, creeping slowly closer, inch by inch. Her shoulders were soon visible at the cot's edge and being pushed farther off. Jeanne could tell her mom's dress was missing or pulled down. Her bare shoulders bounced and moved across the end of the mattress.

Tearing her eyes away from her mother's dark hair and exposed soft shoulders, Jeanne looked directly into her mom's eyes. Her head hung so low off the cot that both daughter and mother were practically face to face. Though out of the four-year-old's reach, the unsmiling, upside-down face was only a few feet away from Jeanne's features. But her mother's face and blank expression were of no comfort to her now. Simone's eyes were opened, but even in the gloomy light, Jeanne could see no life there. The eyes of her mother were listless, unblinking, and grey. Cloudy and without color, dull orbs blissfully blinded and not witness to what was happening above her.

Jeanne heard one final, animalistic grunt or snarl from the cot above her. The huge shadow moving up and down on top of her mother so relentlessly earlier slowly ceased. Jeanne was left face-to-face with her dead mother. And like her mother, the little girl stayed motionless. Hearing panting slowly began to fade in the distance but paying no mind. The four-year-old left staring at her mother's cold and lifeless face. Her eyes were open but empty, still staring across at her, a mere few feet away.

A lone fly lethargically buzzed nearby in the long minutes of still and dead silence that followed. Its movement and flight gave Jeanne a reason to tear herself away from her mother's emotionless mask of death. She watched as the fly landed on the outside of the wood crate. It cleaned its back legs meticulously before considering its next move. When it retook flight, it disappeared briefly before flying low and close to Jeanne again. Landing this time inside the box. With its two over-sized red eyes, the head made quick movements, and Jeanne felt briefly elated at the new company. Happy for any distraction that diverted her mind from the horrid vision of her dead mother.

She spoke to the insect in hushed tones and slowly moved her hands close to the flying insect. Hoping to coax it into her palm where she could hold it. Jeanne was sad when it lifted itself again from the inside of the wood crate and flew off. No matter how small, the company was still a life, and it reminded Jeanne the world outside lived on. The small girl hastened to find where the fly had flown next. Playing a game with it, much like hide and seek, a game she loved playing with her mother. It delighted Jeanne when she saw the fly return and land nearby by once more. She tracked its erratic flight with her eyes.

After a few quick landings of no more than a few seconds each, the fly ended up on her mother's face momentarily before again taking flight. Jeanne lost sight of it for a few minutes and began to think it had abandoned her before she saw it had returned to her mother's face. This time it was crawling across her cheek, almost as if inspecting her skin's smooth, soft surface. The fly then walked across the dead eye of Simone, pausing briefly when the insect's legs first made contact with the unique surface of the eyeball before continuing on. Crawling its way along the upside-down face. The fly stopped next on the top of the lips that had often kissed and cooed softly when Jeanne had ever been frightened or hurt. But, as Jeanne watched in horror, the fly crawled into one of her mother's nostrils. Though the small girl watched, almost unblinking, for what felt like hours, the fly never appeared again. Eventually, Jeanne laid her head down across her folded arms. Praying for the fly to reappear before finally falling back to sleep under her mother's cold stare.

The awful clatter from earlier woke Jeanne for a second time. The groaning springs of the small metal cot calling out in a chorus of desperation. Jeanne couldn't help but look up again from the wooden box where she was imprisoned. The big shadow once more jumping or bouncing up and down on the top of the cot. But her mother's face and head were no longer in sight. Jeanne tried not to imagine the replay of what she had seen earlier. Turning away from a frenzy Jeanne could not really understand or comprehend, but it somehow still made her feel sick. As the sounds of the springs grew louder, the grunts - Jeanne now recognized were coming from the Nazi - did as well. Jeanne closed her eyes tightly and put both hands over her ears. She tried singing in her head in a desperate attempt to replace the sounds that, though muted, still were ongoing.

When the noises finally stopped for the second time, Jeanne eventually heard the man moving once more about the room. Daring to open her eyes again, she saw the Nazi fully dressed and opening several cans of food. He placed the cans on a thin wire holder of sorts that held the metal containers over an open flame he had lit on the dirt floor of the room. The small fire quickly heated the cans, and the smell and aroma soon followed, making Jeanne's mouth begin to water. Her stomach grumbled noisily, but she said nothing. While the man stirred and cooked, she peeked over at the cot. Her mother's body remained on top of it but was now mostly covered by a blanket. Jeanne was relieved to not have to see the lifeless shell again. The dead eyes, the disappearing fly, and the strange puppet-like movements she had been forced to watch were more than she could take.

Dumping the two full cans of what looked like beans onto a makeshift wood plate, the blonde man scooped the warm food up with his fingers. Noisily and greedily piling it in his mouth using three fingers, much like a spoon. Licking his long fingers up and down and slurping noisily. After eating most of the beans, he stopped and gulped down something out of a dull metal glass. He refilled the glass with water and then squatted and unlocked the side of Jeanne's crate with barely a glance down at her. He opened it as she huddled in the far corner, offering her the metal-handled cup and what remained on the makeshift plate. Sliding it across the wood slats and then slamming and locking the side again. He then grabbed a few items Jeanne didn't recognize from one of the cartons of supplies and walked out of the room. Heading through the same doorway where he'd brought Jeanne through the first time.

When Jeanne was sure he was gone, she tentatively approached the food. Hungrily finishing the scraps he left her and downing the cup of water. The beans were practically cold, and the water was mostly warm. But the starving girl finished off and emptied both of the dishes. When she was done, she sat back again in the hard wooden box that was now her home. She watched the cot and the lump hidden under the blankets she knew was her mother's body. Scared, tired, and lonely, Jeanne cried and sobbed. Curling up and cold on the floor of the underground cavern.

Locked in a wood box and alone.

CHAPTER
SEVENTEEN

JEANNE SHUDDERED *as the realization of what she had witnessed now crystallized in her head. The depraved Nazi had not only murdered her father and kidnapped Jeanne as a child. But he'd repeatedly violated her mother's dead body in the same room where he had kept the then four-year-old Jeanne. Keeping the corpse undressed and draped across the cot he slept in. Jeanne raised her head and pointed the light from her helmet at the naked, skeletal cot frame lying collapsed across the room from where she sat. She now understood why seeing the rusted remains of that small bed had impacted her so deeply when she first recognized it and this room. But Jeanne also knew murder and necrophilia were not the last of her Nazi captor's sins…*

The small girl lost all the bearings a four-year-old could have during captivity. Deep in the underground quarry, time was measured only by the meals she and the Nazi shared. Jeanne was allowed out of her wood box only when being escorted to a hole in the ground inside a nearby chamber not far from the room where her crate was kept. The blonde man with the scar behind his ear walked her briskly back and forth to the makeshift toilet each trip. Barely giving the little girl time to use it before silently walking her back again.

Jeanne discovered the German's dog was not missing after all. But instead, the dog was being kept in a separate room near where she and the Nazi slept. Like her, the gigantic dog was secured in a nearly identical empty wood crate. But, unlike Jeanne, the dog seemed content and had a dish of water she never saw empty and a large plate, often layered with pieces of bloody red meat, of its own to eat off. Scattered, dull white bones littered the area around the dog's pen. The colossal animal watched Jeanne intently every time she passed by.

Each meal the German ate, he dutifully shared a portion of his food and water with the four-year-old. This numbing routine somehow became gradually normal to Jeanne, as did her fits of crying when left alone. She remained too fearful of her captor to draw any attention to herself or even relax enough to cry when he was present. Jeanne always forced herself to hide her despair and bottle up all her emotions until he left the room. Then, once he had gone, she often could feel herself collapsing, inside and out, from the stress and strain of the bizarre arrangement.

Jeanne began to feel like one of the dolls she played with at home. She had no will of her own and was unable to do anything unless it was instigated by the blonde man dressed in black. She desperately missed her own bed, her home, and her parents. Wanting things to return as they had been before the bombs began to fall. But, she discovered, it became hard for Jeanne to remember anything about her dad without seeing her papa with his hands on her mama's throat. Or to think of her mother's loving arms around her or the kisses she gave without seeing her mama as she was on the cot. Naked and ravaged. Herself being pushed around and played with like a doll by the monster who had stolen her body.

The Nazi toyed with her mother when he wanted.

The only source of comfort the huge man gave Jeanne was the two blankets she used to sleep on and cover up with inside the crate. More and more, Jeanne began burying her face in one of them even when awake. A thick, sickly smell had started to dominate the stale air of the small room. The little girl tried not to think of where it might be coming from but recognized the awful odor was getting stronger. The Nazi seemed not to notice the foul aroma. Or that the girl had taken to often covering her face.

The man sometimes spoke when he was in the room with Jeanne and her dead mother. But his voice or words were not anything the little French girl could ever understand and were far from comforting. Often he spoke directly to the corpse of Simone, not addressing the small girl at all.

Occasionally though, Jeanne would catch the blonde man staring at her. Sometimes mumbling to himself and a few times seeming to try and speak with her. His features clouded or distorted, perhaps by the shadow of guilt stretching from where her mother lay. When this happened, Jeanne felt very exposed, powerless, and vulnerable. The German seemed to be sizing her up in some way. As if he was unsure what to make of her or perhaps to question her presence. Or her value to him. And though he never admonished Jeanne directly, the threat he presented hung heavily in the air, along with the scent of death. The little girl learned to hate the sound of his approaching footsteps echoing down the dark passageways. She dreaded his returns, which often ended with him lying with Jeanne's mother on the cot. The awful creaking of the springs and his low grunts and groans were as consistent as the meals and trips to the toilet. Jeanne wrapped and covered her entire head with the blankets whenever the German began to take his long black coat off.

It wasn't long before flies began to gather in increasing numbers where the little girl and her mother's corpse were kept. The flies sometimes clustered around Jeanne, and when she woke up with new bug bites, it scared her. The memory of the fly taking refuge in her mother's nose was one image the daughter could not shake. The little girl was terrified flies were somehow getting inside her just like they did her mama. But the additional bugs did serve as a reminder to Jeanne of the outside world somewhere above. Her papa always told Jeanne that flies only ever lived a single day. So the constant buzzing gave Jeanne hope the room was somewhere near the outside or surface. That the flies must be coming in from somewhere not too far away. Surely, Jeanne thought, flies don't live underground as worms did?

Jeanne often slept and dreamed of the sun, flowers, fresh air, and running in the rain. Fantasizing that the men in her village were searching for her family nearby, and at any moment, they would enter the chamber and discover the awful Nazi. The dreams seemed so real she sometimes awoke hopeful, straining her ears for any sounds that weren't the methodic steps of her captor or the occasional shuffle of his dog or its muted barking before losing the brief hope and listlessly falling asleep once more.

A loss of consciousness the only escape the four-year-old had.

At some point, the Nazi took Jeanne's mother's body away. She was not sure when or how long ago. Jeanne just woke one time to find it gone. With the sudden disappearance of Simone, the awful noises the cot made also ceased, and slowly the sickly smell that so dominated the small room also began to fade. The flies, however, persisted. Often gathering together in a small cloud just above the vacated cot. There was a part of the small girl that longed to see her mother once more. But deep down, Jeanne hoped her momma was now at peace and no longer being pestered by the blonde brute. Jeanne pretended her mother was buried in a lush cemetery with pretty yellow flowers. Imagining herself saying prayers over the grave. Helping her mom make it up to heaven to be with the angels.

With no way to track or measure time in a dim cavern lit only by various burning lamps, daytime and nighttime lost all meaning. Jeanne only knew that once her momma was taken out of the cavern, she had used the bathroom many times and eaten a lot of meals out of the steel cans the man pulled from his crates. (The crates seemed almost magical to Jeanne as the never-ending supply of cans kept coming). With nothing to do or play with, those meals and brief trips out of the wood crate became her playtime. Pretending she could talk with the hulking dog as she passed by it and imagined eating dinner with her family and sharing food with her parents. The little girl would often lose herself in her head, transporting herself far away and fantasizing about going to a school, making new friends, and taking long walks with her mom and dad before eventually falling back to sleep and willing her dreams to take her outside under a sunny sky.

Running across green fields where the tall grass tickled her cheeks…

The Nazi woke Jeanne abruptly by pounding his fist loudly on the top of her wooden crate. The box was shaking, and the sound like thunder was booming in her ear. Startling her out of a dream where she was running across fields of yellow flowers. Jeanne sat up in the box quickly, looking to see if she should put her buckled shoes on her feet for a trip down to the toilet. But instead, looking out from her cage, she saw the face of a young woman staring back at her. Jeanne rubbed her eyes and peered out once more from the crate. Not believing the image she saw was real but rather just a continuation of her dream.

When the woman was still there, Jeanne rushed forward in her box and reached an arm out through the space between the boards. Desperately wanting to touch this newcomer and feel something real and not hard and cold. Jeanne opened her mouth to speak when she saw the German was watching her. He had a bemused smile, but it did not touch the cold steel of his blue eyes. Jeanne withdrew her hand and arm but continued staring at the young woman before her. In silence with pleading eyes.

Jeanne did not recognize the woman, but, like Jeanne, she had clearly been snatched by the Nazi. Her mouth was gagged with a long strip of cloth pulled tight across her cheeks and tied behind her head of light brown hair. Blood discolored the cloth at the edges of her mouth as the fabric gag cut into the corners of her mouth. Her brown eyes were wide in terror and rimmed red with tears. Her hands were bound behind her back, and she laid across the dirt ground of the quarry floor on her stomach, unable to right herself even if she tried. The woman couldn't have been much out of her teens and was clearly petrified by the looming presence of Jeanne's, and now her, captor. The man was squatted beside the new woman and resting a hand on her back. He looked between her and Jeanne as if enjoying the shock the presence of each had on the other.

How he observed them both reminded Jeanne of when she had once played alongside a gurgling stream with a small group of older boys and girls. A mixture of the village's children passing the time together on a warm summer day. All of the kids' mothers were laughing and talking together close by. But, for the most part, the parents had left the children to their own devices.

The older boys had grounded several tiny black tadpoles along the shore by splashing the small river onto the rocky sides of the river-bank. Purposefully cupping handfuls of the stream where the schools of tadpoles were swimming together in the warm, shallow water near the surface. Tossing it in the air until several of the tadpoles were left stranded and squirming beside the stream. Their black bodies twisted on the hot rocks under the afternoon sun. The girls, alongside the boys, had objected and tried to rescue the slimy-looking half-frogs – half-fish, splashing water from the river themselves and trying to wash the tiny struggling creatures back into the safety of the running stream. But the two oldest boys, no more than 10 years of age, blocked the other girls' efforts. Both of them squatted down and watched as the tadpoles' mouths gaped in the air. The boys were enraptured by the real-life struggle for survival playing out before them. The look in the boys' eyes was not unlike the look of the Nazi now. Nothing seemed more important to the young boys than seeing how the tadpoles would react. When the poor creatures had finally died - their tiny tails no longer moving and mouths hung open in silent screams - the boys had stood and left without a backward glance. The amusement, mere minutes at most, was forgotten as they moved on to a new adventure.

Jeanne looked at the man in black watching her and the bound young woman struggling on the floor. In the Nazi's eyes, she watched his interest in the interaction fade and his eyes harden again. The bemused smile escaped from his lips, and his emotionless mask was soon back in place. He began to run his hand back and forth along the backside of the defenseless girl. From her neck all the way down to the back of her thighs. The German soon stood and pulled the new arrival roughly to her feet. She cried out as he hoisted the young woman up by her tightly constrained arms. Her eyes stared desperately at the unkempt little girl in front of her.

Jeanne saw the newcomer was wearing a light blue dress torn down the side. Her bound wrists and the cloth in her mouth were the same color as her dress and must have been ripped from her skirt. She had no shoes on her dirty feet. The Nazi guided the young woman over to the cot and pushed her down on top of it. When the woman hit the thin, sagging mattress, a swarm of disturbed flies hovered above the cot like the gathering of an ominous storm cloud. Buzzing angrily but not flying far. Some re-landing almost immediately on the young woman's face, crawling towards her eyes and mouth. With her hands tied, she could not fend them off beyond shaking her head violently back and forth.

Though gagged, the young woman began screaming and sobbing, struggling to move and separate herself from the dark stains left by the body of Jeanne's mother. Each struggle causing the cot to sag in a slightly different way. The tired bedsprings returned to life once more to resume the unholy chorus Jeanne had already heard too much of. The newcomer's frantic movements kept the horde of flies airborne and scattering in the air. The Nazi watched her struggle, occasionally pushing the woman in the blue dress back down onto the filthy mattress if she tried to stand or get off the cot. She continued screaming and pleading without words, twisting herself away from the big German's touch. Slowly, the Nazi began to take his long black coat off, and Jeanne looked away. Quickly shuffling deeper into the wood cage and wrapping her head tightly once more in the blankets.

The screams went on and on.

Nothing Jeanne did could block out the horrid sounds of the Nazi's brutal rape of the young woman. With both hands remaining tied securely behind her, she was easily overpowered by the sadistic man. Pinned down on the cot, the young lady cried and begged for her own death through her gag. Screaming at the child in the wood box to somehow run away and get help even as her dress was shredded from her body and left in tatters on the floor. The Nazi on top of her snarled like a mad beast. Drool and sweat ran down his face, chin, and neck.

After what seemed like an eternity, the atrocity finally ended. The newcomer lay crushed and struggling to breathe under the blue-eyed, blonde-haired mountain of spent, sweaty flesh on top of her. She whimpered softly with each breath she drew like a beaten dog without hope, motionless and wide-eyed, now covered in bruises, scratches, and welts. Blood seeping from between her legs and pooling under her.

The Nazi eventually dragged himself off his victim. Standing next to the cot, he grabbed a handful of the young woman's long brown hair and used it to wipe the clotting mixture of blood and oozing fluids between his legs. He glanced briefly down at the crate where Jeanne lay crying to herself, buried under her blankets and shaking. Showing no remorse, he bent and picked up the torn blue dress he had ripped off his rape victim. Tearing it into several long strips, tying the brown-haired woman's legs together, and binding her to the sides of the metal cot. He waved his hand in front of her unseeing eyes, barking questions but receiving no response. He reached down with one hand and, sneering, harshly pinched the nipple between his thumb and forefinger on one of her breasts. But there was still no visible reaction or anything to be read across the features of the coma-like woman. Her face was slack and empty of emotion.

Satisfied, he turned and retrieved one of the ceramic containers he periodically drew water from. Splashing it across his body and face, then drinking heavily from the simple water container. He donned his pants and slid his black boots onto his bare feet. Half-dressed, he grabbed a lantern and walked out of the room toward the toilet.

Whistling jauntily as he went.

When he was out of sight and his whistle faded in the background of the otherwise silent chamber, the girl on the cot suddenly sprang to life. She began to struggle ferociously at the bindings on both her wrists and ankles. She urgently contorted her body and twisted her arms and legs violently until finally loosening the cloth constraints enough to free one hand. Using her fingers, she pulled piece after piece of cloth loose, ripping it in places and moving other loose sections up to her mouth, desperately tearing at it with her teeth and hand until she could finally free her other hand and arm. Then reaching around to finally free herself entirely from the cot.

Sobbing and crying silently, the battered young woman sprung off the wet and bloody mattress. She limped to the crate where Jeanne was held and yanked at the metal lock. There was no give. Jeanne, who heard her struggles and had watched her free herself, pointed over the naked woman's shoulders. Terrified to speak out loud, and instead urgently pointed and gestured at where she knew the key was kept. The lady twirled, searching the room and then spying the long black coat Jeanne was motioning towards. She looked back at Jeanne, questioning her with an expression. The little girl nodded her head up and down. Hobbling over, the woman began dipping her hands inside the pockets of the Nazi's coat, trying to locate the key. At last, she pulled a small keyring out of an inside pocket. It held three keys, and she shuffled awkwardly back to Jeanne's side, glancing nervously over her shoulder for any sign of their tormentor's return.

Dropping to her knees, she shakily tried to fit the first key into the steel padlock outside the wooden crate. Jeanne's heart leaped up into her throat. The near-forgotten notion of hope, which she had nearly given up on, bubbled within. Even just tasting it made Jeanne begin to tremble in anticipation. Though she had to remain hunched over in the cramped quarters of the small box, Jeanne now stood and began to stamp her feet up and down in excitement, practically running in place. The little girl with golden hair smiled for the first time in what felt like forever.

But then, far in the distance, an eerie, almost disembodied whistled tune came out of the darkness behind the young brown-haired woman. Both captives, recognizing the owner of the haunting melody at the same time, visibly started at the sound. Eyes wide, they stared at each other in horror.

The whistle grew ever louder.

Jeanne's smile was instantly extinguished. Tears welled and then streamed down her dirty cheeks once more. The brief glimmer of hope she'd felt snuffed like a candle pointlessly lit in the middle of a dark and relentless storm. The little girl's trembling anticipation became a terrified shaking and whining. The woman rose to her feet instantly, raw fear overtaking her. She spun around several times as if looking for a hiding place. Then glanced back down at Jeanne with deep sadness, sobbing silently and choking out a whispered "Pardon" before turning to run.

Unsure where the whistling was coming from, the still bleeding woman froze after a couple steps, not darting out either of the two doorways. She seemed paralyzed, and the little girl, still locked in the box, began to back away from the side of her crate. Imagining the cruel things to come once the Nazi saw the woman had freed herself. At the last moment, the bruised and torn young woman hurled herself not out of either door. But instead dropped back down to her knees and crawled forward and into the small tunnel Jeanne had seen earlier. Her dirt-encrusted bare feet disappeared just as the blonde German re-entered the room.

Seeing the empty cot, he did not react as Jeanne expected. Instead, he smiled without humor and casually strolled over to the opposite doorway from which he entered. He looked into the black entryway and seemed satisfied with what he saw. Or perhaps didn't see. Then, casually pulling on his shirt, he walked over to his black trench coat hanging from the corner of the stacked supply boxes. Jeanne began to cry harder, sure he already knew the keyring was missing. The little girl now silently wished the lady had never taken it. But again, she was surprised as the Nazi merely pulled his flashlight from the black trench coat's pocket. Flicking it on, he strolled back out the doorway, seeming unconcerned and ready to enjoy himself in the pitch-black quarry.

As soon as he disappeared, the naked woman crawled back out of the small tunnel she'd hidden inside. Jeanne scooted forward in her crate and nearly called out. Her relief was so great. But the bleeding woman, seeing Jeanne's expression, gestured the girl should remain silent. She then noticed the two large guns resting in the corner of the room for the first time. As Jeanne watched, the young woman limped to where they sat and grabbed the biggest one. Awkwardly waving the long barrel in the air, looking the gun over, and locating the handle and trigger. As she fiddled with the weapon, the Nazi seemed to magically materialize at the doorway he had exited behind her. His silent, sudden reappearance shocked Jeanne, who saw him first.

Startling a scream of terror out of her.

The naked woman looked up from the gun. She saw the big German standing in the doorway, unmoving and silhouetted by the black of the lightless cavern behind him. She immediately raised the weapon, pointing it at him but trembling to her core. The fresh blood on her hands made wielding the heavy gun difficult. The recoil almost knocked the long-barreled firearm from her grip when she fired at him. The deafening blast sent pieces of stone from the rock wall spiraling into the air several feet from where the Nazi stood. The rock chips sprayed the side of the German, yet he remained impassive. Calmly looking at the French woman who had just tried to kill him. The smoking end of the gun still pointed his way.

The German's dog barked loudly somewhere unseen, and the blonde man cocked his head as if listening to what the canine's comments were. He then casually switched his flashlight off and began to whistle again. He stepped unhurried towards the desperate woman in front of him. She raised the weapon a second time and pulled the trigger once more.

Nothing happened.

In three strides, the Nazi was on her. Casually backhanding her as he yanked the rifle, still slippery from the woman's own wet blood, out of her hands. His blow knocked her several feet backward, and she lay flat on her back. In a mocking tone, he spewed German words at her, then casually tossed the spent and still-smoking rifle onto the cot. Towering over her, he smiled without joy. His blank eyes moved up and down her naked body before settling on the blood-streaked bush between her legs. He spoke more German at her, this time harshly, before reaching one hand down to his crotch. His dead smile broadened in the light of the oil lanterns.

The woman rolled over and lunged behind her for the second gun. The untouched shorter rifle still leaning where it had sat next to the other. Grabbing it and rising to her knees, she spun back around and leveled a gun for the second time at her rapist.

Though momentarily startled, the man coolly stood his ground. He raised both arms up to his chest and pounded it with his fists twice. Speaking words Jeanne did not understand but clearly egging the French woman on. He barked at her with disdain, showing no respect for her or the gun she pointed at him. He continued speaking to her menacingly.

By the reactions and flood of raw emotions cracking her face, it was clear to Jeanne this lady understood German and what was being said. She winced and began to wither under the savagery of his verbal assault. Hopeless tears again streaked her bloody face. His threats and taunts effectively exorcised any fighting spirit she'd clung to as her resolve waned in the gloom of the quarry's pit. The gun wavered, and her shoulders sagged. His words, whatever they were, had a profound effect. Jeanne could see the sneer on his face as he spoke. Seeing the woman weaken, the man dropped his hand again to his crotch, continuing his guttural speech as he unbuckled the belt at the top of his trousers. Slowly and meticulously, the sadistic brute tugged his belt from the loops around his pants. When the long leather belt was freed, he coiled it over once in his hands. Pulling it taught, the strap cracked loudly in his hands. The intent was clear as he spat more words out at the crying woman on her knees before him.

Without a response or a word, the brown haired-woman placed the butt of the gun in the dirt between her legs. The end of the weapon pointed up in the air. Sensing her utter surrender, the Nazi began to step towards her while raising the leather loop menacingly in his hand. His sneer became a smile, but the change in facial expression could not be called an improvement. Before he could close the gap with a second step, the woman sat up straight and placed the end of the gun in her mouth. Blood-streaked white teeth in stark contrast to the black barrel. She didn't look at the man advancing on her. She looked directly at Jeanne with eyes already as dead as her rapist's.

She pulled the trigger.

The back of her head exploded and coated the crates behind with a crimson spray. This second gunshot echoed loudly, and the dog in the neighboring cavern again barked and howled loudly in response. Jeanne barely heard the other caged animal in the quarry. She collapsed soundlessly in her own wood prison. The hope she'd briefly felt only minutes before was snuffed out by the single gunshot that still reverberated. Without sound or expression, Jeanne rolled over and crawled back into the corner of her box. Listlessly pulling a blanket over her, she closed her eyes and fell into the only escape available.

Sleep.

CHAPTER
EIGHTEEN

JEANNE REGAINED *her feet and stood in the near pitch-black cavern room of the old Roman quarry. The battery-operated light on her head pierced the darkness and exposed the crumbling objects that had rested untouched for over 30 years. She gingerly walked over to the corner of the chiseled room where the young woman chose to, on her own terms at least, end her life. Sad and crumbled wood crates, soft and rotted like the few contents they still held, all that was left. Just a pile of useless rubble.*

The memories of her time imprisoned were all returning with amazing clarity. The images and her perceptions of that experience were now being run through the filter of adulthood and a life decades in the making. Had she known back then what the Nazi did to her mom and that poor unfortunate French woman? How had a four-year-old reconciled, or even processed, the mix of brutality and sex being witnessed? Jeanne could visualize all this so clearly now. She recognized the implications behind the Nazi's actions. His pleasure at hurting the woman and the joy at the power he held, completely unchecked, here underground. Had he purposefully talked the young woman into killing herself? Maybe convinced her there was no escape in the winding subterranean labyrinth? Or had the woman already known she could not live with what she'd seen and what the Nazi had already subjected her to?

Jeanne's eyes burned with tears for the little girl she had been. Captured and treated like an animal. A pet even. How had she kept from going mad?

Had she…?

When Jeanne next opened her eyes, the headless body had, mercifully, disappeared. The German was nowhere to be seen, and the dog was either with him or still caged, like Jeanne, in one of the cavern rooms down the tunnel. But despite these absences, when Jeanne woke up, she found she was not alone.

"There's my brave little girl," said Jeanne's mother. "I was hoping you would wake up before Gunther returned." Simone then turned to the brown-eyed, brown-haired young woman next to her. "See Louise? I told you we would have time." Both women smiled at each other. Louise then shifted to where Jeanne sat.

"Honey, I am so sorry that I couldn't get you out of that crate before he returned. I really tried. I think I just got scared…" The woman, Louise, appeared very sincere and troubled by her admission.

"Aw… That's alright. I know you tried." Jeanne looked at the pretty young woman kneeling down beside her. Her hair was soft and tied loosely in the back with a white bow. She wore the blue dress the Nazi had torn to ribbons and used to bind her. Confused at what she saw and unsure what to say, the little girl added, "I like your dress."

"Oh! Well, thank you, Jeanne." The lady who Jeanne last saw putting the gun barrel in her mouth and pulling the trigger seemed pleased at the compliment. She smiled at the four-year-old.

"How did you get back here? Aren't you hurt? I saw him hurting you." Jeanne felt a little dizzy and was having trouble talking. Her speech sounded funny, and her tongue felt too thick for her mouth. She added, "I don't understand…"

Louise gave Jeanne a sympathetic smile, "Here," she nodded in the direction of Jeanne's mother, "let's have your mom explain all that." She smiled again, and then Simone replaced her, sitting close and smiling at her daughter. Simone was wearing the same green dress she wore when the Butte family made its mad dash across the fields and down into the quarry. Only now, it was not torn or stained with the black soot that had fallen from the fires.

Jeanne reached out to her mother, but Simone sat just out of her reach. The little girl pressed her face against the scratchy wood surface of her cage. She stretched her arms out as far as she could, and her fingers clenched and unclenched repeatedly. Trying to reach out and touch her mother once more, desperate to feel her comfort. But Simone stayed motionless where she was, with a sad smile as she looked down at her daughter. "Oh, baby, I so want to hold you right now. To take you in my arms and just make all this go away. But you have to believe that right now, I can't. No matter how much I want that and you want that. There are some things that just… Well, they just can never be again." Simone looked up at Louise, who was now beside her, and Louise nodded in a silent but sympathetic agreement. Simone went on, "I know this is going to be hard to understand, Jeanne, but I need you to listen closely to me now."

Jeanne stopped stretching her arms out and sat back slightly from the wood-slatted wall separating her and her mother. But she never took her eyes off her momma's kind face. She was afraid to blink and lose her again. Jeanne nodded yes and strained to hear her mother's soft voice as she spoke. "You see, this is a very, very old place, Jeanne. This place was forged as much from pain as from the hard labor it took to make all this." Simone gestured in the air around her. "The people who worked to carve this out are all long gone now. Gone and forgotten… Do you understand, Jeanne?" The little girl did not really understand, but she nodded again in agreement. Not wanting to disappoint her mother, only wanting her to continue talking. She hadn't realized how much she missed her mother's voice. Or even a simple conversation. Her mother's words soothed Jeanne, seeming like music in her head. She hung on to everything said as Simone continued.

"This is a place like no other. I know it is hard to see from where you are now, but there are so many down here. All around us." Simone raised her head and smiled at Louise, who remained at her side. Both women looked around them, nodding as if addressing a packed room.

When Jeanne's mother next spoke, she had moved and was now directly in front of the wood crate. Louise had taken Simone's place beside the girl, both tantalizingly close yet still out of reach. "But this is no home, and there is no comfort to be found here. For anyone. We are not alone down here, Jeanne. There is something very old and very wrong down here. And what is wrong down here will never be right or satisfied. It hungers, it uses, and it lies, sweetie. But you and I get to be the ones who finally change things down here for good. We are going to end this once and for all. We will open eyes and let everyone see they are not powerless. They do not have to stay walled inside this big, cold void. That this place, though very full, is actually empty. It will always be hollow and feel empty. And that there is another place waiting for us." Simone looked up, casting her glance around once more. "For all of us." Then focusing once more on Jeanne, she said, "Another place if we could just find the key…"

Jeanne's mother raised her arm and pointed as she said this. A single lone finger wavered in the air, and Jeanne had difficulty focusing on where the blurry image was pointing. At last, her vision cleared enough to see her mama pointing at the ground just outside the crate. Where half buried in the dirt lay the keyring the brown-haired and brown-eyed woman Louise had taken earlier from the Nazi's long black trench coat. Surprised at the discovery, the four-year-old immediately reached out of her box for it.

"No, Jeanne! NO!!" Louise stopped Jeanne, her voice gravelly, commanding, and loud. Scaring the little girl, who quickly pulled her hand back inside her cage as if touched by fire. Briefly, Louise appeared as Jeanne had last seen her. Headless, with only a bloody, jagged stump rising up and out from between her shoulders, her naked body was once again ravaged and torn. The image wavered once before the girl could even cry out and then was whole once again. Louise's pretty face frowning but dressed once more in blue, and her long hair tied behind her head in a bow. She spoke again almost apologetically, "Not yet, Jeanne. It must stay where it is to keep you safe."

"But I want to leave here, momma," the little girl looked once more for her mother. But she was now kneeling next to Louise on the other side of the crate by the keyring. When Jeanne looked at her, she could see both women side by side for the first time. The twin images seemed to almost blend together, and Jeanne shook her head to try and clear her vision, still feeling dizzy and woozy as she did so. Jeanne continued talking as she tried to refocus again on her mother's beautiful face. "How can the key keep me safe if I don't have it to get out of here?"

"The most important keys have a time and a place when they work best. And sometimes what you think you want the most is better left as a prayer unanswered. I understand all this so much clearer now than ever before..." Simone's face showed a deep sadness for the first time, and its sorrow troubled the confused little girl. "Did you know you were the key to my happiness? And your daddy's too. But I took that key and twisted it all out of shape. I got what I wanted most and unlocked the door to my paradise. But I didn't understand or appreciate that. And instead of walking through the door that bringing you into the world unlocked for me, truly enjoying the riches inside, I just went on looking for other keys. I didn't understand that as exciting as discovering a new key was, by itself, the key alone was not the treasure. It is just the first step, like a leap of faith. And, if you truly believe, then the second step, the treasure itself, can be profound. Real riches are wanting what you have, not longing for more. Can you understand that, sweetie?" Jeanne didn't understand at all. But unlike before, she couldn't hide her confusion or just pretend. It felt like what her mother was saying was so very important. Yet she didn't understand her at all. The little girl began to cry and felt ashamed.

"Oh, sweetie, please don't cry. It's unfair that one so young should carry this burden. But you, my darling, you have to believe, are oh so very important, and you must get out of here. You are the key, Jeanne. You will be the reason this quarry will stop being a prison. What you do later will release all the shame and the pain that gives this place such power. But for right now, it remains not yet the time or place. You have more time to carry, and time will help carry you and us along. After all, time is really the only currency down here."

Louise, who had briefly drifted out of Jeanne's eyesight, became clearer. She tugged at Simone and said, "We must hurry now. He is coming." Simone nodded and turned once more to her daughter. Though the light remained low in the room of the cavern, Jeanne's mother seemed to crystalize and glow when she next spoke.

"My dear little girl, you must stay strong now. Gunther, the man who brought you here, is not what he appears or who he used to be.

You see, that old and wrong thing I told you about is a parasite down here, like the leeches and ticks living outside in the meadows. Remember when daddy had that long black leech on his leg from swimming in the river? How it latched on and twitched but wouldn't let go? Or when we found that tick in your hair? We couldn't get it off, could we? Not until we found the key to making it let go. Remember? We burned a needle real hot and placed the hot steel on the tick's back, and when we did, the tick let go of you, and you were finally free of it. Well, sweetie, down here is the biggest and worst kind of parasite ever. He won't let go until we find the key to getting away. So until then, it is still in charge down here. And when it has a hold of someone, it can make them act in ways that otherwise most of them never would. Losing themselves in the process. So, Gunther, I'm afraid he may try to scare or hurt you. But you listen to your momma now." Jeanne nodded, but her eyes were filling once more with tears. Simone and Louise seemed to waver in the dim light of the cavern. It felt like her mother was about to leave her again, and deep inside, that made Jeanne feel broken.

"Remember what I told you after we walked together to use the toilet when we first arrived down here? I told you I would not ever let anything get you. That I would beat back hell itself if I needed. Remember?" Jeanne nodded once more, remembering that day. Though no longer sure how long ago that had been. In one way, it felt like forever ago, but in another, since it had been the last time she was held by her mother, it seemed close, like just yesterday. Jeanne could still feel her touch, the smell of her hair, and how they held hands as she fell asleep that last night. The tears were streaming down her face as she looked at the shimmering face in front of her, now so close.

"I remember, momma," she finally croaked out.

"So you must trust me now. It will be scary, and, at times, Gunther may seem like he will start hurting you. But if he ever truly does, I promise to be there. I'll be there, and you won't be alone. And Jeanne, I made some new and surprising friends down here. When I need them, they will come to help us too. They trust me that you are the key. They know. So you hold on and always remember I am close by."

"Are you…Are you leaving me now, momma? Where is daddy?

Why did daddy hurt you, momma? Did one of those ticks or leech things make him do that?" Jeanne felt like she was being abandoned again. She tried to be brave but could feel her mother slipping away. She didn't want to be alone again. She kept asking questions, trying to keep her momma with her. "Why do you have to go?"

But then Louise spoke next, replacing her mother's face in the young girl's eyes. "Jeanne," she said. "I want you to do something for me. Can you do that?" Jeanne nodded as she wiped the tears from her face. Everything seemed so blurry to her that it was hard for Jeanne to focus on who was saying what. Both women's faces seemed to blend at times. Jeanne thought fleetingly that she had not noticed how closely they resembled each other. "Good girl. Now listen, if Gunther gets too close to you and makes you uncomfortable, I want you to run away up here." Louise pointed to her head. "You may not be able to get away down here," again she gestured, this time at her body. "But in your mind, you can get away. You can think of nice things. Take yourself out of your body. Maybe imagine yourself floating away like a big puffy white cloud. Or be like the snowflakes spinning and falling down? Can you do that? Think of another one, Jeanne. What would you like to pretend to be?"

"I could… I mean, can I be yellow flowers in the field? When it is windy, and they dance together?"

"Oh! That is a good one, Jeanne. Like your daddy's little flower." Now it was Simone's face again in front of Jeanne and speaking. Louise was no longer there. "I know another one. Do you remember the dandelions? How would we find them and blow the fluffy white seeds off their stems?"

Jeanne nodded, "I can be dandelions blown in the summer sky." The little girl grinned as she remembered the fields she would play in near her home.

"And remember," once more, it was Louise who had taken her mother's place. "If he touches you and it makes you feel bad, you run away from him and go to this place in your mind."

"And know that I am coming, sweetie. Momma won't let him hurt you, I promise." Again it was Simone replacing Louise now, speaking softly to Jeanne. "You just become a butterfly. You fly away. Like a crow is chasing you. You fly away and dart and dip in the wind." Jeanne's mother smiled at her daughter. "Now, one more thing, and then I have to leave. Gunther will be here again soon. See down here? Where the keys are?" She pointed once more at the keyring half buried in the dirt of the cavern floor. "Bend down here and lay on your stomach, sweetie." Jeanne lowered herself to her stomach, resting her chin on her hands and looking directly at the shiny keyring. Her mother continued talking to her. "That's right. Now, Jeanne, I want you to blow really hard. I want you to blow all this loose dirt over to the keys." The little girl puckered her lips and blew as hard as she could. "Good job! Now keep blowing, sweetie. It might make you dizzy but keep blowing and blowing. Cover up that key ring. Keep blowing. There you go… A little more…. Blow, just keep blowing…"

Jeanne kept at it. It was hard, but slowly the ends of the ring and the unburied keys got covered with the soft dirt and dust surrounding it. Jeanne thought as she blew with all her might how smart her mother was. But also that all this blowing did make her dizzy. And sleepy, so sleepy. Jeanne kept at it until she had fallen back asleep. Dreaming of wavy fields of flowers, butterflies, and busy bees.

CHAPTER
NINETEEN

JEANNE DREW *in a long and quivering breath. For the first time since she'd entered this room, some 30-plus years after leaving it, she felt very vulnerable. And uncomfortable. She pulled off her helmet and inspected the light. Was it her imagination, or had it begun to grow dim? How long had she been underground now? She knew if the batteries in her headlamp were to go out, she would be stuck wandering blindly in the pitch black of this subterranean maze. Forever lost... She cleaned the dust off the lens of the light, and the extra illumination comforted her slightly. She placed the helmet back on top of her head and turned for one last look at this room that had once been her prison. The decrepit items left to rot haunted her.*

Haunted... What had she seen? Who had she been talking with? It seemed so real, but surely it had been only a dream. Or perhaps a version of "imaginary friends" kids sometimes play when alone. Had she conjured up the two women in her mind to keep her company? But if so, she remembered when Gunther returned just a short time later, he had been all too real.

The enormous black and brown dog trotted into the room alongside his master, whom Jeanne now learned had a name: Gunther. But for the first time, as it entered, the big dog took no notice of Jeanne still locked inside the wood crate. The dog instead stopped just inside the cavern room doorway and sat on its haunches, whining slightly and staring fixedly up at the far corner of the stone-carved chamber. Its ears laid flat against its head and, unmoving, appeared transfixed by something Jeanne could not see.

The Nazi, dressed again in his horrible black coat, did not notice the dog's odd behavior. Instead, he was distractedly searching the pockets of his long coat before turning and rummaging along the tops of the stacked wood supply boxes in the corner of the room. Still coming up empty, he took off his long black coat and hung it from the top corner of one of the crates. He then dropped to his knees and looked under and around the small cot before moving over to the area where he usually changed in and out of his clothing. Eventually, he stood again, grabbed his flashlight, switched it on, and exited back out of the room, calling the still-immobile dog to him.

When Gunther returned a short time later, it was clear to Jeanne he was becoming increasingly agitated. The dog was no longer by his side, and the Nazi turned the thin, blood-stained, and moist mattress over, upsetting the remaining flies still lingering in the room. Finding nothing, he dropped to his knees again. He shined his flashlight into the shadowy, small tunnel Louise had briefly hidden inside. His bulky, wide shoulders barely squeezed inside the constraints of the narrow ground-level shaft. When his head came back out of the hole, he was red-faced and panting. His short blonde hair was disheveled, and the knees of his trousers were soiled.

Not bothering to stand, the German crawled on his hands and knees the several feet between the narrow shaft and where Jeanne sat imprisoned, watching him wide-eyed and soundless from her box. Gunther pressed his face close to the wood slats and smiled hideously at Jeanne before speaking to her. The German words still meant nothing to the small girl. Frustrated, Gunther mimed the turning of a key in the lock still fastened tightly at the end of the crate. His expression was questioning, and his meaning was clear. Where was the key?

Jeanne did her best to look into his cold, blue eyes without emotion. Shaking her head and turning her hands up. For good measure and to keep from looking at the ground where she knew the keys lay buried, she stood, hunched over, and looked around the floor of her crate.

Hoping she appeared to be helping him search. Jeanne even pulled her threadbare blankets up as if the keys might be hidden therein.

Gunther studied the 4-year-old for several long seconds before abruptly standing once again. He lashed out with his foot, striking the wood crate where Jeanne was caged. His black boot loudly kicked the side and solicited the little girl's startled scream. As Jeanne turned to scramble into the corner farthest away from the increasingly angry Nazi, the box shook once more. Then again. Each time Jeanne screamed and, as her eyes filled with tears, Gunther barked loudly at her as his foot connected with the wood crate repeatedly. In response, the four-year-old kept shaking her head, too scared to meet his dead eyes. Jeanne buried her head between her upturned knees as she trembled in the corner.

The German stopped striking the wood box when the dog re-entered the room and woofed once loudly. The unexpected noise and intrusion caused the Nazi to jump slightly. Gunther turned his growing frustration at the hulking animal, commanding the dog harshly and marching over to where it stood, grabbing the thick leather collar hanging around its neck and half dragging the big dog back outside the room. Jeanne poked her head up and, seeing she was alone, peered at the spot where the missing keyring was buried. The dirt around and on top of it remained undisturbed.

The keys still lost to her Nazi captor.

When Gunther reentered the room again a short time later, he was breathing hard as if he had just completed running a race. He stopped momentarily just inside the doorway, looking again at Jeanne as she sat silently in her crate. The German shook his head with a sneer before moving forward once more.

Making his way to the stack of crates, he proceeded to open two new cans of food and cook himself a meal in the usual way. But, for the first time since snatching Jeanne, he did not offer the little girl any of the food he made. Nor did he give her any of the water he greedily slurped as he ate. Instead, he talked to himself and gestured in a taunting manner in her general direction. Jeanne didn't move or respond, scared he may be testing her somehow or just waiting for a reason to explode again.

When he finished eating, the dog once more appeared in the room. Trotting casually inside the doorway and sitting a few feet away from where the man sat on the cot's edge. Its reappearance infuriated the blonde German. He issued no single, stern command this time. But instead roared at the large dog, who no longer seemed intimidated by its master. The canine merely cocked its head and barked once in response. This verbal rebellion upset the Nazi even more, and he launched himself off the squeaking cot.

At this, the dog turned and ran back outside the door. Gunther yelled and gave chase as Jeanne watched the near-comical events unfold. Though she remained stone-faced, inside the little girl cheered the dog on as the angry German dashed after his suddenly unruly companion. She wondered if, while Gunther was distracted, the time for her to reach for the key and make her escape had come. But she hesitated, unsure what she would do or where she would go if she gained her freedom from the box. Moments later, Gunther reappeared again, panting and still looking very frustrated. For the first time, the little girl recognized new and different emotions etched on the man's face. Doubt for sure and, perhaps, even a little fear.

Gunther gulped down the remaining drinking water from his cup and then pulled a tall glass bottle out from inside one of the crates of supplies. He pulled off the tan cork on top and tossed it on the ground before pouring some murky brown liquid into the cup. He grimaced slightly when he took a drink, and Jeanne wondered why he would drink something he clearly didn't like. But Gunther, despite how he reacted when he drank what was in the bottle, seemed unfazed by the taste and soon emptied his glass. He poured more into the cup several times. Nearly filling it with each pour before placing the open glass container at the top of the wood crates stacked in the corner by the cot.

As Jeanne looked on, the Nazi took several more drinks out of the cup while slowly unbuttoning his shirt and removing it before slug- gishly pulling his boots off one by one. Settling himself and laying down on top of the soiled mattress. It wasn't long before she recog- nized he had fallen asleep, breathing deeply and regularly. As her racing heart slowly began to calm, Jeanne soon followed. Dozing as the light given off by the oil lamps grew dimmer.

BANG!!

The loud, unexpected boom woke Jeanne, and her wood prison shuttered around her. Scared and disoriented, she turned over from her side, where she lay slumbering, and flipped herself onto her back. Searching the darkness desperately with her eyes, flinching from the noise.

BANG!!

Both the sound and the tremor repeat. Now wide awake and staring out into the darkened cavern room, Jeanne makes out the silhouette of an ominous dark shadow looming above her box. It lunges at the outside door of her wood cage, and once more, an ear-shattering bang replaces the tomb-like silence of the quarry. The last bang was followed by an almost equally loud crack: the unmistakable sound of splitting wood. Jeanne screams as the swinging door of the crate suddenly springs wide open. The menacing presence reached inside and grabbed hold of her. Tugging at the little girl by her ankles and pulling her out of the wood-slatted crate.

Jeanne clutches desperately at the sides of the wood crate. But her hands and arms lacked the strength to stop the momentum, and her tiny fingers and fingernails were left torn and bleeding. Despite all her efforts, Jeanne continued to be dragged on her back across the bottom of her cage.

Still screaming, Jeanne's dirty dress gets rolled up and caught on the rough wood underneath her. The cloth tears on a splintered and jagged piece of plank sticking up from the bottom of the crate as she is yanked out of the wood prison. The thin material of the well-worn and stained dress first bunches up, caught under the piece of split wood. Momentarily stopping her from being hauled completely out. But then, frustrated, the hands holding her wrenched roughly at Jeanne's ankles. Ripping the girl right out of her dress as it tore down the seam. In the process, opening up a jagged cut across the bare skin of the little girl's back as she is wrestled out from the crate.

Kicking and screaming the entire way.

Only two lanterns remained lit. But, even in the dim light, there is no mistaking what pulled Jeanne out. Gunther, shirtless and swaying slightly, towers over the scared little girl. In his hand, he held the longer of the two rifles. The wood handle of the weapon was now dented and scratched, where it repeatedly made contact with the steel lock and hasp on the outside of the crate. The Nazi tossed the gun on the ground of the cavern now that it served its purpose. The weapon landed next to the broken metal hardware and the tightly clamped lock he had busted off to gain entry.

Jeanne was also lying on the dirt floor, naked, except for her small buckled shoes. Shrieking in terror. The deep, bleeding scratch across her back barely even registered with her. Gunther reached down for Jeanne and pulled the little girl to her feet before him. Wrapping her in a suffocating hug.

The Nazi turned and stumbled backward, clutching the child tightly to his chest. Slurring, he shushed her as he staggered several steps toward the metal cot. His gait faltered when he reached the edge of the small bed, and his shin made painful contact with the metal frame. He exclaimed loudly in German before slowly tumbling onto the filthy and smelly mattress, crushing the four-year-old girl under his entire body weight. The familiar and horrible sound of the cot's metal springs screeching loudly again. That sound was now nearly as debilitating to Jeanne as Gunther's overwhelming size.

The wind was knocked completely out of Jeanne as the big man landed on top of her, cutting off her screams instantly. Leaving the last cries to echo alone and unheeded off the rock walls of the cavern room before slowly fading away.

The little girl struggled under the Nazi, wiggling her head from side to side in a panicked search for air. Finally, finding a small opening to the far side, big enough that she could just squeeze her face out from under him. Her tiny features found precious breathing room under his arm and gasping in, open-mouthed, his foul body odor but also getting a mouthful of his wiry armpit hair at the same time. Frantic, she inhaled anyway, breathing, gagging, and coughing simultaneously. The rank, coarse hair filled the inside of her mouth as she desperately breathed air in.

When Jeanne finally caught her breath, she continued screaming and struggling. But her feeble attempts to move were hopeless. She was drowning under the large German man and could feel a growing wetness pooling under her wounded bareback. Sticky moisture oozed up and out of the thin cloth mattress. Spreading… The Nazi did not move. He didn't have to. The little girl was trapped and lacked the strength to even budge him. Gunther breathed in and out heavily, almost contently. He mumbled and continued shushing the little girl trapped below him. His eyes closed, and he had a slight smile on his face.

As Jeanne wiggled back and forth, pinned and feeling her strength fade and weaken, she felt something beginning to grow hard against her belly. The more she struggled, the more pronounced it became. It felt hot and was pressing down tightly against her, enlarging.

As she lay there powerless, Jeanne felt Gunther take several deep breaths. Each time he inhaled, it seemed to crush more life out of her. But he turned slightly, and Jeanne felt some cool cavern air briefly wash across one arm and parts of her exposed stomach and chest. The sensation was wonderful but short-lived. In another moment, she felt one of the German's sweaty hands lay across her cheek, covering part of her mouth and further making each desperate breath she tried to draw a struggle.

Worse yet, down below, Jeanne felt Gunther's other hand slowly sliding up and down her leg. His hand, rough textured, was large and sticky against her smooth bare skin. She struggled as she felt his hand moving, utterly trapped and unable to escape, a desperate panic rising from deep inside herself. His hand pawed at her, hot as fever. So big compared to her tiny body. Jeanne, barely able to breathe, could no longer even cry out. She thought of her mother, praying for her to come to rescue her. She thought of what she'd seen the Nazi do to Louise and what Louise had, in turn, told her to do if Gunther ever really scared or tried to hurt her.

The little girl began to float away in her mind. Leaving everything far behind, feeling her light fade as his sickness darkened everything about her.…

CHAPTER
TWENTY

WOOF!! Jeanne was hurtled back to reality before she barely had begun to drift. The Nazi, startled at the unexpected intrusion, rolled off her, and the little girl drew in a deep breath. The first not fouled by the German's stench since being ripped out of the wood crate. Looking to her left, Jeanne saw the big dog had again returned and faced the cot. Rigid with intensity, hackles raised, baring its teeth, hostile and growling. Staring intently at its master, who, surprised as he had rolled off of Jeanne, ended up on the cavern floor on his hands and knees. Face to face with the big dog menacing him. Confusion and fear contorted his face. Still trying to catch her breath, Jeanne froze where she was on the cot. The bulky beast was a terrifying threat. Its deadly intent dominated the small room.

Beside the intimidating dog stood a new figure. A lone and ancient woman with long white hair hung in disarray about her shoulders, barefoot and wearing what could best be described as a gunny sack. The material was featureless and shapeless, tied around the middle of her waist by a single frayed cord. Her two arms were bare and coming out of holes cut into the side of the rough material. Her face was scarred and lined, and though she was hunched and feeble looking, there was a fight in her eyes. It was Laurent. The wraith-like old woman who had warned Jeanne and the other intruding villagers of Vieux when they first descended into the ancient Roman quarry.

WOOF!!

The large head of the dog bobbed forward as it barked loudly once more. Its snout, filled with long yellow teeth, was within inches of Gunther's twisted face of fear. Foam pooled at the corners of the canine's black lips as it looked sideways at the shirtless Nazi. A low growl emanated from somewhere deep inside.

Gunther stayed completely still and softly addressed the looming dog, trying to regain a measure of control. When the dog did not respond or back away, the German peered up at the strange old woman for the first time, addressing her directly. But she, like the hulking dog beside her, did not react. When Gunther tried to speak with her a second time, he discreetly moved the hand and knee on the right side of his body backward. Attempting to put some space between himself and his one-time canine companion. The move was a success. He then cautiously did the same with his other hand and knee, moving nearly a foot away from the massive animal. Jeanne remained motionless on the top of the cot, studying the face of the old woman who dared challenge the Nazi.

As Gunther continued to slowly retreat, his self-assurance grew despite the bizarre situation. He spoke soothingly to his dog and questioningly at the haggard, disheveled white-haired lady. But she either, like Jeanne, did not understand the German language or chose to remain silent. Tension filled the small cavern of the quarry. With every movement farther away, the shock and fear displayed by Gunther slowly receded. Replaced by a slow burn that soon began to bubble up. Now a yard away from the pair, he stopped addressing the snarling dog and gradually raised his voice, still trying to communicate with the fearless woman who invaded his space. His words became harsher. The phrases turned from questioning to orders or commands that he spat out at her as he slowly gained his feet and his confidence.

The dog remained motionless, and though it watched his master's every move, it periodically panted. Giving the beast a brief look of normalcy and, visibly anyway, diminishing the threat. Its head followed Gunther as he took tentative steps that brought him around to the cot's other side, placing both Jeanne and the small bed between himself and the still tensely crouching canine.

Now that he stood and had some distance and a barrier separating him from both the old woman and the dog, the large man's swagger swelled once again to the surface. The sneer beneath his dead eyes, a look Jeanne considered his true face, returned. As his shadow fell over her, Jeanne began to tremble. Sure that just like the previous would-be rescuer Louise had failed, this tiny odd woman surely would as well. But before Gunther got any closer to Jeanne, the old woman spoke to the little girl in French.

"Jeanne, do not fear this magnificent animal beside me! It has been a monstrous tool. But like all weapons, how it was used was not a choice. Its soul is pure, I assure you. My name is Laurent. Come over to me now, and we will leave this place together." Surprised to hear the woman's gravelly voice, the small girl turned to look at her as she spoke. But like the massive dog beside her, the diminutive white-haired woman never took her eyes off Gunther. Jeanne began to do as she was told. Still, as she started to turn and push herself from the sticky mattress, Gunther forcefully spoke the one German word she recognized.

"Nein!!"

The Nazi reached across and into his black trench coat hanging off the corner of the supply crates stacked beside the cot. Swiftly withdrawing the long steel blade he used to carve up Jeanne's father. He brandished the weapon expertly, feeling his command of the room was restored. Jeanne, who had stopped, unsure of his order, was still seated at the edge of the mattress. Her back to the Nazi murderer. Looking directly at the dog and the old woman, neither of them moved.

Out of the corner of her eye, Jeanne saw a small flicker of blurry movement like the heat waves coming off of a tin roof on a scorching summer day. Or radiating off the many armored vehicles sometimes parked all day under the hot sun in her village. The heat baking them and distorting their outlines, making what you see with your own eyes a false reality. Now, in this room, the small movement or ripple seemed to alter the air around the stack of supply crates as Gunther stretched out his arm to restrain Jeanne.

The next moment, the nearly full glass bottle of brown liquid tipped off the same high crate where Gunther had placed it earlier. Perhaps having been bumped when he hastily retrieved his deadly knife, it wobbled for long seconds before finally tipping over. But as it fell, the amber fluid splashed out forcefully. Spraying as if under pressure, coating the entire side of the blonde man's face and flooding his hair, neck, and features. Nearly emptying the entire contents of the bottle in one fell swoop.

Shocked and surprised, the Nazi turned, yelling and raising his empty hand to his head. Quickly wiping at his soaked skin and hair. Swiping at his face and, in the process, flinging the excess alcohol into the air, trying to quickly get it off of him. But in his haste to get the whiskey out of his blinded and stinging eyes, his wet hand hit one of the two open flamed oil lamps still lit inside the room. The liquor instantly ignited as it made contact with the flame, and the fire jumped from the lamp onto his dripping hand. Blue flames licking his fingers and singeing the hairs on his arm. Gunther cried out and waved his flaming hand next to his face. Not believing what he was seeing, his eyes wide and his mouth a perfect "O" of disbelief.

The flame from his lit hand leaped with an audible "whoosh" to the dripping alcohol still running down his face. Half of his face, including his open, steel-blue eyes, were burning in mere seconds. The Nazi screamed much like the little girl whom he had terrorized the last several weeks. And just like a scared little girl, Gunther pissed himself.

The huge dog was spooked by the erupting fire, frantic actions, and smell of the German's burning hair and flesh. It howled and barked loudly. The flames were a danger any animal knew well. But in less than ten seconds, the fire spent all of its meager fuel. The alcohol burned both very quickly and very hotly. During the commotion, Jeanne jumped from the cot and stood behind the dog and the old woman. Together they watched first the flaming and then the flailing man as he battled the fire enveloping his face.

Gunther threw himself onto the mattress and buried his scorched head in the material. Rolling and suffocating the last of the flames even as they died out. He sobbed in agony. When he raised his head at last, much of the blonde hair was missing from the side of his head. Smoke smoldered off of him, and his face was varying shades of red. His ear was an angry bright pink, and one of his eyes - the eyelid on it curled up and burned away - exposed a black bubble that slowly oozed and hung like melted wax from the ruined eye's orbit.

Gunther regained his feet. His one good eye focused on the old lady, who evenly and calmly returned his glare. Raging, the smoldering Nazi launched himself at Laurent from the far side of the cot. Stretching forward and stabbing down at her with the knife he still held in hand despite his burns and agony. But, still feeling the effects of the alcohol inside his body and outside, his shins banged gracelessly against the side of the metal cot. Gunther sprawled awkwardly across the top of the small bed as he fell. His attack was far short of the intended mark. The blade's arc instead plunged down towards the cavern floor, eventually sinking into the bare foot of the strange white-haired lady. Severing the big toe and the one next to it completely before the blade was buried halfway into the dirt.

Laurent grimaced and backed away in pain but barely uttered a sound despite her gruesome injury. She staggered once and caught herself, putting a withered, petite hand against the rock wall of the room for balance. She looked down at her wounded foot as blood pumped and spurted from where the digits had been. Laurent seemed more annoyed than hurt. Across her face flashed anger instead of fear.

The dog meanwhile pounced on top of the German. It began brutally shredding the ruined face of the Nazi as the man struggled to right himself and regain his footing. The huge canine growled and pulled at the soft flesh it sunk its teeth into. Gunther cursed and screamed as he tried to separate himself from the attacking beast. But the powerful dog dragged the Nazi head-first off the cot, pulling him closer to where Jeanne and Laurent stood watching the man be savaged. The once domesticated and trained pet gave in to the blood-lust, igniting the wild animal deep within. The dog ripped out chunks of flesh, jerking his large head back and forth viciously and spraying blood across the room. Splattering Jeanne in the Nazi's gore as the life and death struggle played out between her, Laurent, and the doorway closest to them.

In response to the violence, Laurent turned and dropped to her hands and knees. Beckoning Jeanne to follow, she crawled forward and into the small tunnel dug into the side of the wall. Though scared, Jeanne first ran to where the keyring lay buried and grabbed it before following the wounded old woman. Crawling on top of the trail of blood left by Laurent's bare feet as she entered the dark tunnel.

As Jeanne scampered after Laurent halfway into the shaft, she felt something grab her ankle. Turning and flipping herself over onto her back in the small passageway, she saw the ruined face of Gunther filling the enclosure behind her. His bulk blocked out much of the light as he scrambled after them, still trying to fight off the snarling dog behind him. Jeanne could hear the animal tearing into the German.

But still, Gunther came.

The Nazi held one of her ankles and pulled the little girl towards him. Jeanne screamed loudly for help. But behind her, she could no longer see any sign of Laurent, who had continued on. Jeanne kicked wildly at the raw and bloody face of the Nazi with both her feet. The small heel of her buckled shoe made contact with the ruined eye socket and forced a full-throttled yell out of her kidnapper.

The sound seemed to shake the walls of the small enclosure they were fighting inside, leaving Jeanne's ears ringing. She kicked again, and the toe of her shoe lodged itself in Gunther's open mouth, briefly cutting off his curses and howls of pain. Angered and surprised but unable to fit his second arm or shoulder into the small passage, the German bit down hard on the tiny leather shoe. Now holding the small girl by both feet. One in his mouth and one in the single hand he'd managed to squeeze inside the narrow tunnel.

But behind him, his body convulsed as the dog continued its vicious attack. The pain distracted the Nazi enough that Jeanne could push herself up from her elbows, lean forward in the small passageway, and sit up. Face to face with her captor, she reached out with her hands to rake and claw her fingers across his wounded, tender, and inflamed face. With the long keys still clutched desperately in her hand, Jeanne repeatedly stabbed at the bloody face. Screaming and raging back at him until she finally pulled her barefoot out of the shoe, still clenched in the man's mouth. Her attack surprised the Nazi enough that she could pull her other foot from his startled grasp as well. The small buckled shoe came off in his hand, which he looked down at dumbly with his one remaining eye before dropping it onto the floor of the constricted passageway as he was suddenly jerked backward. Cursing while being gnawed and dragged away by the beast he once mastered.

Jeanne stared at the empty tunnel he had just disappeared from. Fearful that, like some horrible jack-in-the-box, the Nazi would jump back into the opening. So she backed up, never once taking her eyes off the dimly lit entrance, ready to defend herself and crawling backward on her hands and knees. Gunther's cries of anguished desperation echoed all around her in the small tunnel.

Jeanne continued scuttling backward as quickly as she could until she felt her feet and knees disappear from under her. She cried out in surprise, unsure if she should keep going. Kicking out with her feet, fearful she was about to plunge out of the black tunnel and fall to her death when suddenly her foot was guided by a steady hand. It gently placed her flailing barefoot on something cold and hard that supported it. Jeanne backed up a little more with one foot secure until her second foot found the same spot. When she stepped back down again, she found a second, lower metal rung and crawled down. One bare foot after the other until she was out of the small passageway. Carefully grabbing onto and holding the sides of what she now recognized as a small steel ladder until her feet made contact with the ground of the next room. She turned around and found Laurent waiting on her. A lit candle in one of her hands. She beckoned Jeanne to follow her, leaving the carnage and sounds of the Nazi being torn apart behind them.

CHAPTER
TWENTY-ONE

JEANNE BENT *down and let the light from her helmet illuminate the small opening carved into the wall. Empty. She squeezed herself back into the tight passageway and once again used her hands and knees to wiggle and push herself on her belly back through the narrow tunnel. The small ladder's rusted remains practically crumbled in her hands when she pulled herself out the other side. The long-ago sounds of the final death throes of the Nazi still reverberated in her mind.*

Standing, Jeanne brushed the dust and dirt off of the front of her jeans and half-buttoned, torn flannel shirt. She reached into the front pocket of her pants where she'd stuck the tiny buckled shoe from her childhood. Pulling it out, she examined it again, amazed that the tiny leather thing had lasted so long in the old quarry. She brushed some dirt off it and then tenderly stuck it down deep in the front pocket of her jeans again. The single souvenir she would reclaim from this dark and terrible place. Then moving forward, Jeanne began to retrace her steps. Determined to make it back to the surface just as she had done in the past. She thought again of the strange old lady who came to her rescue. Laurent…

Laurent did not speak as she moved slowly but methodically within the tunnels. The path she walked - lit by only the single candle within the otherwise pitch-black ancient Roman quarry – was steady and confident. The old woman limped but otherwise ignored her bleeding foot and new injury. Jeanne, completely naked, covered in blood, and, like Laurent, without shoes on her feet, stayed close behind her savior. Stumbling at times as she navigated the uneven dirt floor in the near dark. Occasionally crying out when she would step on one of the many sharp rocks littering the passage. But otherwise, kept her eyes trained on the small flame of the candle as it danced within the black channels they walked down. The keyring, nearly forgotten now, was slippery and wet in her right hand. Their steps were silent, and the only sounds came from behind them. Baying howls and terrible screams echoed eerily until a calm and empty stillness finally settled in place. The sound of silence was only broken by the echoes of dripping water, unseen but all around them.

Gradually the slope of the underground passage changed, and Jeanne could tell they were beginning to trudge upwards. Higher and higher within the underground labyrinth. But the exposed, scared little four-year-old girl was far too terrified to yet feel hope. The utter black around her was suffocating and disorientating.

Entering a vast cavern, Laurent veered slightly left to avoid running into a dark shape that loomed ahead of them in the near dark-ness. Jeanne glanced up at the obstacle as they circled around it. Carved of stone, it was a giant wolf-like statue crumbling with age lying half buried in the ground. Several pieces of the grim totem had cracked and split over time and lay around it in bunches, including the massive head of the statue. The candle in Laurent's hand illuminated a chiseled snout full of ravenous teeth and piercing eyes. A dark visage of unmistakable power and awful wrath meant to be feared and avoided. As they passed it, the wavering candlelight in Laurent's hand threw shadows that seemed to animate the expressive features. But the center of the stone-cold dead eyes, much like Gunther's, remained blank and emotionless. Jeanne quickly turned her face away and plodded on.

Mechanically, Jeanne focused on putting one foot in front of the other. She felt frail, and her breathing came in starts and fits, very irregular. Shivering in the cool of the shaft and teeth chattering but otherwise numb. Her ashen skin was clammy to the touch, and her blue lips, though hidden within the black of the concourse, would typically have been a cause for alarm. Every few steps she took, a wave of nausea would come over her, and Jeanne felt certain she would be sick. But still, she shuffled on, following behind the hobbled old woman.

As the pair walked, Jeanne began to see other things out of the corner of her eyes. At first, she ignored them, too weak to even muster the courage to question her eyes and too dazed to fear them. Eventually, she came to believe she was seeing many strange faces she didn't recognize. Subtly appearing along the sides of the seemingly endless passageway Jeanne and Laurent were inside of. The wavering faces appeared dully luminescent, visible outside the lone candle's meager light. Men, women, and children seemed to hover briefly near the two walkers, but only at the edges of Jeanne's vision. None of the faces were smiling or frowning. They watched the solemn procession like silent spectators at the smallest of parades. They seemed to be clustered at times but then would break apart for the pair when they drew near. There was no malevolence or threat, but the sheer number of them, an endless stream, intimidated Jeanne. Laurent, if she saw the faces, paid them no mind. She continued to climb the subtle incline, candle gripped in her hand, looking down at her wounded, marching feet.

When Jeanne got bold and tried to turn and look directly at the faces or focus on any of them, their features seemed to fade back into the black. The little girl left with only an impression of their image in her otherwise blank world of darkness. It was like looking into the bright sun and then closing your eyes: a colored halo remains behind the eyelids, but the defined edges soon drift and bleed together. Jeanne began to doubt her own eyes in the black of the quarry. Wondering, as she walked, if she was dreaming or imagining the hazy figures. Or if the candle's flickering light was playing tricks and creating dancing shadows and figures where nothing really existed. Jeanne soon bowed her head, looking only at the ground under each step. Ignoring everything else. Including what she thought was the defining feature shared and imprinted on each face.

A desperate hope.

Eventually, Laurent stopped before a fork in the long passageway, and Jeanne bumped into the back of the old woman. "Pardon," mumbled Jeanne, barely raising her eyes and so exhausted she nearly toppled backward as she made contact. When she tentatively looked up, the little girl found the images of the faces she thought had been traveling alongside them were all gone. But in their place, Jeanne saw a shaft of meager, almost less believable light. The light was pale and seemed to be coming up ahead of them in the passage on the right side of the fork in the rock corridor.

"You have the key, yes?" Laurent's dry voice came out like a hoarse whisper. After so much silence, the sound was shocking as an expletive shouted in a cathedral. "There is a lock, and you must have the key to leave here." Jeanne looked down at her hand, tiny fingers still wrapped around the sticky keyring. The keys were forgotten by her during the long hike. But now, the little girl extended her pale arm triumphantly, holding them aloft for Laurent to see. "Then you go," Laurent nodded down the passage to their right. "Go to the light, and you will see."

Jeanne turned and started down the channel. After a few steps, the light streaming into the passageway got brighter. Moonlight! She was sure of it. A slight breeze, warmer than the cavern's air, surprised her. A flicker of hope stirred excitement in the little girl's belly. The fresh air was intoxicating and full of wonderful aromas already barely remembered. Jeanne started to run towards the increasing light and fresh air before stopping briefly. Turning around to share her discovery with the old woman. However, the narrow, rock-lined pathway behind her was now empty. No sign of Laurent or the candle Jeanne followed up from the Nazi's room. Jeanne, realizing she was alone, nearly called out, afraid and unsure of herself.

"There's my little girl," said Simone, suddenly beside her daughter. "Shall we go outside and play again?" She smiled down at Jeanne before turning and gliding towards the opening.

"Momma!" Jeanne ran after her, but the small sharp rocks that lined the floor slowed her down. She trailed behind her mother the rest of the way, catching up just as the narrow opening appeared. Then, excitedly, Jeanne rushed past her mother to reach where the light and breeze flowed in. The hot, humid air instantly bathed the little girl's body in its comfort and warmth. The bright moonlight hurt Jeanne's eyes to even look at it. "Oh, momma! Look, look outside! I can see the tall grass waving… And the moon!" Not only the moonbeams lit up Jeanne's face, but the little girl's smile radiated as well. This feeling, Jeanne thought, was better than any holiday or birthday she had ever experienced.

The opening was a simple human-sized hole dug into the soft earth between two boulders. A small piece of metal gating kept anyone or anything from going in or out of the discreet entrance. A single padlock hung from the gate, secured to a metal plate bolted directly into the side of one of the big rocks. The other side of the gate was wedged into a natural crack running the length of the second large rock bordering the entryway.

Jeanne smiled as she held the bloodstained keyring up in the moonlight. The keys glinted in the bright light, and the little girl lifted and twisted the padlock, trying the first key. Though the key slid inside the lock, Jeanne could not turn it. The padlock hung stubbornly, still blocking her escape to the outside. Disappointed but undeterred, Jeanne tried the second key. It slid in and turned easily. The lock popped open with a sudden click. Its quick surrender startled Jeanne. The padlock, keyring still stuck inside it, fell to the ground at her feet. Unlocked. Jeanne could hardly believe her eyes and turned to smile at her mother. Simone smiled back. "Good job, sweetie. Can you pull the little gate out of there? Does it move for you?"

Jeanne turned back towards the opening. Her pink tongue stuck out of the side of her mouth as she grabbed both sides of the gate. Pulling and pushing at it with all her might. For several long seconds, it would not move. Before finally, Jeanne, wiggling it back and forth several times, dislodged it from the side of the rock. She shoved it to the side, and the barrier landed on the ground outside the small entrance with a soft "thud."

Jeanne crawled out and stood in the sultry summer night. Letting the air warm her and looking up at the bright, full moon overhead. When Jeanne turned and looked at the surrounding landscape, she saw a familiar sight. The ancient Roman ruins were just a short way in the distance, down from the small hill where she had just emerged. The white marble almost glowed under the moon's light puncturing a hole in the night sky. Jeanne knew her house was just beyond the far side of the field where the broken pillars lay tumbled and broken.

Her mother stood beside Jeanne and pointed at the moonlit countryside around them. "Isn't it lovely, Jeanne? Shall we go play down there? Just you and me?" The little girl looked up at her mother and nodded with a genuine smile before taking off and running down the side of the grassy hill. Stopping when she reached the first of the broken monuments and reaching up. Swaying and spinning among the crumbling white marble, dancing and getting lost in the songs her mother sang in her ear. Paying no mind to the long, lonely, mournful howls rising from the side of the hill she had just run down. Nor seeing the white hair and yellow flowers blowing nearby in the warm breeze.

CHAPTER
TWENTY-TWO

JEANNE ADJUSTED the headlamp on top of her helmet once more. She raised it slightly so she could better see the passageway as it stretched before her. She made her way carefully around the water, still standing near the gaping hole in the tunnel wall. The collapsed opening snapped Jeanne back to reality, pulling her out of those dark childhood days. Reminding her of the tragedy that took Andre's life and forcing Jeanne to remember what she'd done to Paul.

Paul, the idiot....

Passing the scene where both men died, Jeanne continued the way she had hiked before the accident. Positive she could backtrack what had been a relatively straight shot from the outside entrance down into the depths of the ancient quarry. The three sets of tracks left in the mud only increased her confidence. Jeanne looked down periodically as she hurried along. The presence of the footprints was more an affirmation than anything else. The bright light from her helmet illuminated the circular rock channel as she returned to the surface.

As she picked her way along, Jeanne began to contemplate everything she had uncovered buried in her memories. (Or "compartmental-ized," as her therapist liked to say.) She questioned what had been real and what was imagined. There was no question in her mind she had found what she had hoped for when she'd made the trip. Which was the truth regarding both of her parents' deaths. She also felt she could put aside her more recent concerns over whether her father had somehow escaped punishment or justice for the murder of her mother. But, for all those questions answered, her trip back into the past also raised several new ones. Again, she thought, what was real and what had just been a fantasy concocted by the active imagination of her four-year-old self?

Finding her shoe from childhood and revisiting that horrible chamber had clearly brought out long-lost and deep-seated memories. The clarity of which was so intense and startling. The smells, the sounds, and the things she witnessed were all undeniably real. But what of the conversations with Louise, who she watched kill herself? Or with her dead mom? Who had shared the suicide victim's name with Jeanne? Were they all just, as a young child, how she had coped with what was happening to her? A version of the "drifting away" Louise had been trying to explain to her four-year-old self as a strategy to deal with the trauma she was witnessing? Or was Louise just her subconscious helping Jeanne through what a four-year-old's mind could not possibly comprehend or deal with?

But if all that were true, then how could Jeanne possibly have learned not just the name of Louise but also the name of her Nazi kidnapper Gunther? Of course, Jeanne thought as she hiked on, there was no way to know Louise's or the Nazi's name. For all she knew, the German could have been Hans, Claus, or Dieter. But if it had all been simply her subconscious, how had she known to carry those keys to the surface? Unless those conversations were actually real? And if they were real, what does that mean? Jeanne kept going round and round in her mind. Unsure of what to believe, she slowly shakes her head…

A face!

Jeanne twisted her head quickly, looking where she thought she saw a man's face staring at her. But nothing was there. Just a trick of the light from her headlamp. The shadows down here stretched and contorted things, making even the boring rocks seem to come alive. Jeanne said aloud, "Get a hold of yourself." The "self, elf, el" echoed off in the distance. Again out loud but murmuring softly, Jeanne talked to herself a second time. "Well, that sure sounds creepy…" The echo muted. Jeanne nervously chuckles to herself before beginning to walk again. The light in front of her bobbed up and down with each step.

"Idiot."

Jeanne twirled once more, her heart pounding. She strained her eyes, moving her head back and forth. The swirling light in the otherwise black passage made her dizzy. "Idiot," the sound came again. Loud enough to hear but not enough to locate where it was coming from. "Hel...Hello." Jeanne spoke without thinking and instantly felt stupid, like an idiot. She strained her ears, and the sound came again. Struggling to catch the fleeting repetitive sound.

Is it

Divot

Idiot

Did it

Ticket

Idiot

Drip it

Dripped

Drip

"Oh, my god!" Jeanne exclaimed. Her heart was about to burst from her chest, and her hands shook. She barked out a small nervous laugh.

Drip

Drip

Drip

The sound was just ahead of her, and she could see what was causing it. The rock ceiling nearby was damp. Moisture from the ground far above traveled down and seeped into the cavern. The naturally filtered water slowly dripped and splashed onto the floor below it. The sound reverberated off the walls each time the heavy drops struck the rock beneath. Distorting the sound and sending it echoing around the empty chamber. Jeanne stood still and watched the natural occurrence developing in front of her, trying to calm the rocketing of her pulse. The sound of dripping water was so clear and obvious now that she could lay eyes on the cause. Yet unseen, her mind had turned the ambiguous sound into words. Well, she thought, one word anyway, idiot… Jeanne laughed at herself without feeling any humor. Despite the cool of the underground quarry, she felt the sweat under her armpits trickle down the back of her ribcage. Jeanne wiped her damp palms across the tatters of her flannel shirt, happy to see her hands were no longer shaking. Then she turned and began walking once more. Her eyes were wide in the black of the tunnel, and the pace of her step was quickening.

Jeanne could see multiple passageways to both her left and to her right. She thought to herself, each leading to nowhere, then puzzled at her negativity. She reset her mind. Thinking again about the openings and deciding it was more likely they each led off into rooms. Rooms where men once labored within the confines of this ancient quarry. Many were chained and slaved away until they eventually died down here, alone and far away from their families. Jeanne stopped walking. She thought of her own family. Her little Russell. She caught herself stifling a sob. Such sadness came over her, hitting her like the undertow of an ocean, pulling her in deep. Pressing down on her, depressing her.

Depressed…

Jeanne snapped her head up. What was happening to her? Why was she thinking such dark thoughts? Men or slaves being beaten down here? Chained and dying? Jeanne felt panic strike. She decided she could no longer wait to leave this awful place.

Picking up her pace once more until she was nearly jogging, she looked down at her feet. The last thing she could afford was to fall or twist an ankle. Jeanne forced herself to slow once more and scoured the ground she walked. Looking for the three sets of footprints she'd been following. But she kept on looking. Before finally stopping completely and aiming her headlamp directly down at the ground before her. Where were they?

The footprints were gone!

She spun and looked behind her. Only one lone set of prints, hers, was all she could see where she had just walked. Looking up, she again saw the many black holes on either side of her. Skewed doorways, each a separate tunnel or room. But, she pondered, there were far too many of them. Jeanne could not recall passing this many clustered together when Andre had led her and Paul. In fact, Andre had stopped to look inside the few single doorways they did pass. Especially once they got deeper into the quarry where Jeanne was now. Jeanne twirled again. Her feet twisted in the soft dirt. Panic now threatening to overtake her.

She was lost.

"Get a grip here, Jeanne. Just slow down and think." Jeanne spoke to herself in whispers. Hushed tones that didn't echo and add to her unease. Hearing her own voice somehow made her feel less alone. She closed her eyes and tried to mentally reset. What should she do? Thinking it through, the answer became obvious. She would simply retrace her own new footsteps. Go back to the point where she must have gotten off-track and pick the trail back up again. Simple. Opening her eyes, Jeanne began to head back the way she'd come. Following the prints she had just made in the soft earth on the floor of the long-abandoned quarry.

Tense and focused, Jeanne hurried back. Her eyes scanned the ground as she moved. At certain points, the tracks were very light and hard to see. The ground was rocky or hard, dry-packed earth in patches. But each time she thought she had lost her trail, a small indentation would lead her back onto the right path. Eventually, the small indentations grew deeper once more, and Jeanne breathed a sigh of relief. Moving more confidently, the lamp perched on her head, still brightly lighting her way. Her eyes trained on the ground directly in front of her. Watching for the three sets of footprints to suddenly reappear.

Cresting a small rise in the tunnel floor, the beam from her head-lamp reflected off something shiny just a few feet in front of her. Jeanne stooped down, thinking she must be close to where she had lost the trail earlier and getting close to the surface. A metal, manmade object was clearly a good sign in a long abandoned underground quarry. Perhaps something Andre or his partner had dropped during a previous exploration.

Reaching out, she picked up what her light had drawn to her attention and stood, bringing the item to her face and letting the light play across it. It was the handle of a huge knife. Its single blade, though, was much longer than it appeared when lying half-buried in the ground once it was pulled off the dirt floor. It was heavy in her hand, clearly well-made but very old. Jeanne wondered if it was Roman but doubted it. She was no archeologist, but somehow this weapon seemed newer, more like the swords she had seen on display in museums from the time of kings and queens with noble knights who served them. It looked to her like a badly corroded medieval sword. She swung it back and forth in front of her, wondering if she dared risk carrying it out with her or if she should just leave it where she'd found it. But as she swung the weapon, the light from her head-lamp flashed off the blade. The bright light briefly blinded her, just as Paul's knife did when he had first withdrawn and threatened her with it.

Jeanne staggered as if struck. She dropped the heavy sword on the ground where she found it. Backing up a single step, "Oh my god! I have got to get out of here…"

"Nein!"

Jeanne spun and came face to face with the Nazi who had snatched her as a child. He was impossibly close, long black trench coat covering a sunken torso and hanging low over his thighs. Not a day older than when she last saw him as a child, Gunther glared at her with his one good eye. The other socket was an empty black hole squirming with tiny white worms. Patchy blonde hair stood awkwardly on one side of his head and in places along the top. Flaps of torn, bloodless skin dangled off his face, and one ear was missing completely, exposing a second empty hole in his head that oozed something grey and thick. Bright, white teeth, both top and bottom rows clenched tightly, visible where a cheek should have been. Long lines of sinewy strings stretched and pulled at his throat when he moved. The dog's butchery of the man was far worse than Jeanne could ever have imagined.

Though utterly without lips, Gunther somehow smiled. His lone eye dilated, yet, his stare was just as dead as it had been all those years before. His right arm reached up (Jeanne dimly recognized his left arm was missing), and the four fingers remaining on that hand began to unbutton the top of his trench coat. One button at a time, slowly, as if in seduction. A dark drool began to dribble out of the side of his face, and his mouth parted. A black tongue ran itself out and over his white front teeth.

Jeanne screamed…

Turning and sprinting the opposite way, Jeanne made it ten steps before she saw Paul. He stood hunched over, and his head was lumpy and badly misshapen like a rotten pumpkin. His severed dick still hung from his open mouth where Jeanne had shoved it. The flaccid member was pale and soft in the light of her headlamp. As Jeanne veered to avoid running headfirst into him, Paul spit his own cock out at her. She stopped and ducked her head to avoid letting it land on her. When she paused, Paul called out to her. "You can't leave here. Don't be an idiot."

Jeanne barely heard the words as she turned and ran desperately once more. Though her headlamp still lit up the path before her, she ran blindly. Her screams filled the cavern until her feet suddenly dropped from under her. The ground disappearing below. Jeanne was flying, nothing around or under her, hair whipping in the air. The light of her headlamp showed her nothing but emptiness on all sides. Her feet and arms pinwheeling wildly. She fell down and down for what seemed like an eternity. But Jeanne did not really have anything to measure the currency of time. Or understand the absolute desolation of eternity.

Yet…

Jeanne landed feet first on something hard, which gave slightly under her. Separating enough from the force of her long fall, her entire body and head slipped just below what she had fallen into. But at impact, as she landed, Jeanne had felt herself break deep inside. When she first made contact, it felt as if the wind was knocked out of her. And once her downward momentum stopped, every breath she drew was a struggle, each one accompanied by searing agony running up her side.

When her feet first hit, a sharp pain more significant than she had ever felt before, even during childbirth, exploded in the middle of her back. But then the pain had gone, instantaneously, as fast as it came. Still struggling to catch her breath, Jeanne tried to take stock of her injuries. Her side was extremely tender, and she located a dull ache in her shoulder when she tried to move her arm, but otherwise, she felt nothing else.

After a few moments, the initial shock from her abrupt fall faded, replaced by the horrors she was running from. She struggled to look around her and gain her bearings, trying to see where she was and what had happened. Fearful Gunther or Paul was somehow close behind. Soon to come after her once more. But she couldn't really see anything. Whatever she fell into was all around her. Pressing hard against her face, constricting her body and making the movement of her arms a struggle. Each move she did manage made more things collapse and fall against her anguished face. Small pieces, hard like rocks or sand, sometimes even landed in her open, gasping mouth. Jeanne tried to place what she was mired in. It felt like a gravel pit of sorts. Heavy, hard, and loose material crowded in on her every side. She moved her head slightly and tried again to see where she was.

The lens and reflective material covering and surrounding the light-bulb on top of her helmet all had shattered. The naked bulb, still lit, was now dull and yellow. A soft, meager light covered mainly by the cascade of material Jeanne found herself swimming in. Though nearly drowning, Jeanne knew she hadn't landed in water or mud. Eventually, realizing what she was in was also not dirt, gravel, or any other waste that might have come from the quarry dug so long ago. No, she was swimming in bones. Big, small, sharp, dull, and all around her. Dry, dusty, and fleshless. All she could see everywhere she looked were bones

Lots of bones.

Panicking, Jeanne tried to pull herself back up and out of the pile she had fallen into. Her unfeeling legs pinned and immobile, she reached above her and pulled. Grabbing anything big enough to gain her any leverage. She struggled mightily to gain just inches, pulling and crawling upwards desperately. Clutching at the bones spilling all around, swimming up using only her arms. Willing herself on until she was finally able to break the surface. Gasping and spitting out, struggling to support herself amongst the constantly sliding and shifting bones.

It was not an improvement when she finally stabilized herself enough to begin to see where she was. Her head bobbed barely above the surface of a charnel chamber of thousands and thousands of bones all dumped together. She turned to her left and saw a human skull sitting sideways, inches from her face. Freeing one arm, she looked down at what she had been using as leverage to pull herself upwards. It was clearly a human thigh bone. Jeanne was stuck in the middle of a massive pile of human bones.

She looked up and could just make out where she had fallen from. Dirt and dust still swirling and tumbling almost casually from where her feet last touched a solid surface. The edge of the pit she had fallen into - the meager light from her broken helmet barely able to reach that far - was at least twenty feet above her head. Once more, she tried to right herself and gain some traction. But only her arms were working and obeying her. The gravity of the situation became direr with every movement.

Her legs were dead to her.

She felt nothing below her waist. Jeanne spit again and looked at what she kept spitting out. It was blood. Her own blood. She was barely able to move, her light dimming with each passing minute. Twenty feet from solid ground and pinned in a deep hole of human bones torn asunder. Defeated with no reason to scream or cry out. Fearful if she did, somehow the horrid vision of Gunther and Paul would return. She cried…

"Oh, sweetie, please don't cry." Jeanne looked up wearily, already knowing what she would see. Simone, her long-dead mother, was peering over the pit's edge and looking down at her. "I know it doesn't seem fair right now. But this is right where you need to be." She was smiling down at Jeanne, and the sight of her made Jeanne cry harder. She could feel her breathing slowing. Her lungs seemed heavy, and each breath was more of a struggle than the previous one. Nearing the end of her strength, she clawed a little farther out of the pit of bones she was buried in. Exposing everything from the waist up before collapsing forward. Utterly spent and exhausted, her paralyzed legs were still buried under the thousands of bones she had fallen into. She looked up at her momma, spitting more thick blood and still crying. Jeanne sucked in a breath as deeply as she could.

"Why…" The single word was all she could manage, and even that, barely a whisper.

"Oh, sweetie, it's just like I told you. You are the key. You are the reason this place will finally rest. You were always meant to be right here at this time and place." Jeanne continued looking up and out of the pit she had fallen into. The light on her helmet began winking in and out. Becoming a weak strobe light as it, like Jeanne, neared the end of its usefulness. But, even as everything faded, Jeanne could see another now standing next to her mother. It was Laurent. Her white hair was like a wild crown around her head.

"But… But I'll die now... Can't you go…? I'm dying…Go…" Jeanne began to see more and more faces all around her. Beside her and all around the ring of the pit. Every one of them was smiling. Using the last of her energy, she pleaded one last time. "But I'll die here…" It was Laurent who spoke the last word Jeanne would ever hear.

"Exactly."

CHAPTER
TWENTY-THREE
PRESENT DAY

RUSSELL SWITCHED his turn signal on and moved into the right lane. The exit for Kankakee, the town he'd been born and raised in, came into view, and the nursing home West Willow Acres was just minutes away. He rolled down his window as he waited at the exit's stoplight and ran a hand through his little-too-long-for-his-age greying hair, enjoying the fresh air and comfortable breeze of the near picturesque mid-April day. Wearing faded jeans and a black concert t-shirt from the group Disturbed, he reached for his insulated travel mug and downed the last swallow of coffee before wiping a hand across his bushy white mustache. His other arm thickly muscled with a full array of vibrant tattoos covering it with color, dangled casually out the driver's side window of his Jeep. As he waited for the light to change, Stander sang along with the satellite radio's classic rock station as it blared Cheap Trick's "Dream Police."

Russell Stander, aka Stander, as almost everyone except his dad referred to him, had made good time on his drive down. Traveling from his home in Marquette, a small town of only 20,000 but still the largest city in the Upper Peninsula of Michigan, the drive down to see his father had taken him a little less than seven hours. The route one he dutifully did once a month unless his best friend, retired Michigan state detective Tom Secrist, couldn't watch Frazier for him. Frazier, a boxer/pit-bull mix and Stander's only roommate, had always seemed to prefer the company of humans over other dogs. So Stander never had the heart to ever actually board him. Instead, he'd drafted Secrist to be Frazier's personal dog sitter for a few days every month. Deep down, Stander thought it actually did both Secrist and Frazier some good. At least Frazier wasn't alone.

The nursing home his father, the long-retired Dr. Timothy Stander, lived in came into view as Russell hit the outskirts of Kankakee. Sparing Stander from having to drive into the city itself and finally giving him a reprieve from the Chicago area traffic and its array of endless vehicles. Most, he thought, apparently without fucking turn signals or the ability to discern what speed should be driven when cruising in the far left lane.

Idiots…

As he pulled into the parking lot of the sprawling complex, Stander hurried to get inside and then made a beeline for the public bathroom in the nursing home lobby. Trying to appear nonchalant and unhurried, he fell in line behind a group of well-dressed, slow-moving old ladies. Tinted, prim hair puffed and bright, colorful makeup, jangling bracelets, and gaudy earrings clinking as they walked together in a cloud of almost overpowering and competing perfumes left in their wake. Most were pushing walkers and conversing casually - time no longer a concern - as they rolled towards their wing. Stander smiled and nodded as the group meandered across the carpeted floor, gossiping and chatting. He finally reached the restroom door and burst into the single bathroom after spending the last hour emptying his coffee travel mug, the unlocked door and unoccupied toilet a most welcome sight.

After washing his hands and checking himself in the mirror, Stander exited the bathroom and returned across the lobby. As always, any staff he encountered smiled and greeted him. Despite the facility's grand size and many residents, they knew him and his father by sight. Two large TV's hung from the lobby walls: one with golf playing and the other tuned to a 24-hour news channel. Both of them were silent and unwatched at the moment. Stander passed the empty dining room, where equally pleasant staff vacuumed and wiped down the wood tables and padded chairs. Bright chandeliers and muted but colorful walls made the residents' eating area resemble a fancy restaurant instead of the cafeteria it really was.

As he made his way down the long hallway to his father's room, he counted eight framed pictures, all with slightly different prints of flowers. Most of the residents also decorated their doors in some fashion, and many of the doors had wreaths or crafts with artificial flowers and greenery adorning them. All the bright flowers, fake or framed, reminded Stander of a funeral home. And, since here at the West Willow Acres, two or three elderly residents died each month, that association was not far off.

The retired Dr. Stander's door was unlocked as usual, but Russell knocked before opening the heavy brown door. His dad had lived in this same apartment for over three years now, and on the outside of the front door, as it had since the second day his dad moved in, hung a single 8X10 framed color picture. A family photo taken when Stander was a small boy. He smiled out from it. Gap-toothed, sunburned, blonde hair bleached almost white by the sun, sitting between his dad and his mom. The picture was taken the summer before his mother died, even though Russell's parents were divorced by then. It was the last photograph the three of them ever took together.

Russell's mother and his dad's second wife, Jeanne, died when he was just ten. His half-sister, Sherry, had been murdered when he was just eight years old. Her fate and body were finally uncovered only just last year. Stander was now over 50 years old, his father was over 90, and slowly but surely, both his dad's mind and body were beginning to break down. Without any living grandparents, aunts, uncles, or, of course, cousins, Russell always told people he had a "micro" family. Though he had been married in his twenties and had one day hoped for a family of his own, he had ended up widowed at 26 when his pregnant wife's car had swerved to avoid an animal and skidded off the road. Landing upside down in a ravine and instantly killing her and Russell's unborn child.

He never remarried.

"Hey, dad! It's Russell. Where you at?" The entrance opened into the tiny kitchen of the two-bedroom assisted living apartment.

Although, you could see right into the living room as well. It was clean and neat, as always. The TV in the room was turned on, but the recliner where his dad usually sat was empty. "I brought the stuff you asked me to pick up." He closed the door behind him and moved to the kitchen counter, perusing the mail and ensuring no new notices or unexpected bills had arrived since last month's visit. The old doctor still insisted on doing his own bills. Still, Stander tried closely monitor everything coming in. He knew his dad was becoming increasingly forgetful. He heard the bathroom toilet flush, so he sat down on the couch to wait for his dad.

"Well, right on time…" The elderly man, hunched over but otherwise appearing in good physical health for his age, made his way slowly back into the living room. He opened the blinds running across the large window that dominated one wall. The sunshine streamed in and instantly brightened the white-painted room. He picked up the remote to turn off the TV and sat beside his lone son. Upon sitting, the two men embraced briefly, and the old man pulled his glasses down from where they had been sitting on top of his bald, shiny head.

"Right on time? Was I supposed to be here for something?"

"No, no… I meant my bowel movement. Right on time. Now I don't have to worry about it." The old man's eyes sparkled mischievously as he spoke. "Nothing would be worse than being unable to make it to the wine tasting this afternoon because you might soil yourself."

"Oh, well, great. Thanks for sharing. I'm… uh… I am happy for you." Then, to keep his dad from heading down the rabbit hole that was his latest toileting adventures, he quickly changed the subject. "I put those batteries for your hearing aid on the kitchen table. I also grabbed another book of stamps like you asked me. They are both sitting there together."

"Stamps? Did I say I needed stamps?"

"Yes."

"Hmmm… Well, good thing you brought them, then."

Stander, smiling at his dad, nodded in agreement. The question another example of his dad's slipping memory. "I also finally got back the results from the DNA test we did together. I brought the papers down here with me today. Do you remember when we did that?"

"Sure, sure… That was at Christmas, right? A Christmas present we could do together." The older man paused before adding, "You made me spit in that little tube."

"Well, I didn't make you. That is just how they get the DNA. From our saliva samples. We spit in our own separate tubes, and I mailed them into the company for analysis."

"Amazing, just amazing what they can do nowadays, isn't it?" Stander nodded his head in agreement with his father, who continued on. "But I still think that was a waste of your money, Russell. After all, despite his surname, my dad was a proud, full-blooded Frenchmen from way back, and so was my mom. That makes me French through and through. Even though I was born here in America. And your mom was actually born in France. Never even lost all of her accent even though she came to the United States so young. And both of her parents were childhood sweethearts from the same little French village. So you, Russell Nicholas Stander, like it or not, are of one hundred percent French heritage. A Frenchie!" The old man cackled lively, recounting once again to Stander the same story he'd told on Christmas day when he first opened the gift his son purchased for both of them.

"Oh I remember, dad. We even pulled out all the pictures of your family so you could show me."

"That's right, that's right. I remember that…" But the look on his dad's face betrayed he probably didn't actually remember that part of Christmas day, now some four months before.

"So here is the thing, dad. The data came back, and with a tiny bit of Danish variance, you are right. You are pretty much all French." Stander pulled out the results he'd printed off from the company's email. Showing the papers to his dad and explaining the various graphs and areas on the provided map showing where his father's family originated from near Paris. Though the elderly doctor was slipping in his old age, he had always been one of the most brilliant men Stander ever knew. As a physician who had run his own very successful private practice, it didn't take much explanation or time for him to grasp what the documents showed. Together they trailed the results back in time and forward to the present day, ending with the DNA passed to a single heir, his son Russell Stander. Since everything coincided with what the retired doctor always believed, there was no convincing needed.

"Here, though," started Stander, pulling out some different papers, "is the results from my DNA test." Again the two men poured over the documents together, although Stander had already seen everything. He waited for his father to reach the same conclusion without any prompting. It didn't take long.

"It says you are almost 20% German, Russell. How can that be if you are my son?" The older man's eyes showed his puzzlement and doubt. Stander quickly explained.

"First off, there is absolutely no fucking question—I am your son. All this only validates that." Stander was relieved to see his dad reassured, so he went on. "See this? I looked everything up and cross-verified a couple things. But it boils down to mom probably having one parent who was almost all of the Germanic descent. That makes me part German, and really, if you think about it, it was obvious with mom's blonde hair and blue eyes. She even passed those two traits down to me, her offspring, as well."

"But how can that be if her parents were French and from the same village?" Though clear-eyed and brow furrowed in concentration, the obvious answer still alluded the elderly man. A man raised in the '30s and '40s by an affluent family in America, in many ways, a sheltered environment.

"When was mom born? The end of 1940, right?" He was trying to help his dad put the pieces together without just springing the answer on him. His dad nodded his head. "And when did the Germans invade France during the Second World War?" He didn't wait for the answer, "Early in 1940."

The old man's eyes lit up in instant recognition. "Oh my! And your mother never knew… Oh no! And she had loved her father so much. I mean, that is until…" It was the old man who, this time, didn't wait for a response or question from his son. "You know, I often sit and wonder what I have and have not shared with you. All for good reasons, I assure you. But maybe it's time I quit procrastinating. Put pen to paper once and for all. Try to explain myself and share a few tidbits before it's too late. Things you deserve to know… After all, look at me! So old I can barely remember where I put the TV remote anymore." The old man smiled warmly at his son. "But there will be time for all that later. For now, why don't you go make us some coffee? No reason not to share a little family secret from my brief time with your mother. Not sure it is directly related to all this," he waved his age-spotted hands across the papers Stander had printed, "but it might be. Kind of makes some sense when I stop to think about it…"

Intrigued, Stander got up and quickly brewed a couple cups of coffee. Although he barely touched his after downing so much on the last hour of his drive that day. Instead, he sat and listened. He listened and heard details he'd never been told about his own parents' divorce over 40 years before. The counseling sessions and what his mother thought she had seen her dad, or whom she thought had been her dad, do.

Murder her mother.

CHAPTER
TWENTY-FOUR

FOR THE FIRST TIME, Stander heard the entire story behind his parents' divorce. The events leading up to it as well as the aftermath. When his dad was done speaking, Stander sat very still. Contemplating the additional facts his father shared. The new information didn't fundamentally change what he was always told and had understood about what happened. But the insight into his mother's past was very enlightening, to say the least.

It also helped explain some of his mother's odd behavior that, as a kid at the time, he just accepted. But later, as an adult, had always looked back and wondered about. The coldness and distance that, as a small child, he hadn't recognized wasn't normal, mother-like behavior. To Stander, it seemed she never truly grasped love herself, so she expected her son to go without it as well. Of course, he now knew this odd relationship with his mom, as short as it was, shaped him in ways he probably still did not completely understand.

To Stander, his mother had always been an enigma.

"So, let me get this straight. Mom never knew or remembered this until she started marriage counseling with you? Or later on, when she began seeing her own professional head shrink? Was she put under hypnosis or something?" Stander, who thought he would be the one shocking his father by sharing a family secret, had been, in turn, far more shocked by what his father was now telling him.

"I don't really remember any talk of hypnosis. You have to remember this was back in the 70's. There was plenty of hypnosis on TV shows and movies back then, but not many doctors actually practiced it. Or were good at it anyway..." The older man looked out the window of his living room. Lost in the remembrances of the time shortly before his second wife disappeared.

"My impression was your mother suppressed the event. At four years old, how could such a small child otherwise have dealt with witnessing such a thing?" He turned back and faced his son once more. "I always thought I fell in love with your mother at first sight, in a romantic, predetermined destiny of some sort. I know, I know... Such an old-fashioned notion nowadays." His father smiled as he recalled first meeting Jeanne. "She was, of course, beautiful. But also just smart as a whip! However, there was always something else underneath. Deep down. A brooding she couldn't always hide. You don't need me to tell you she could sometimes be aloof. Standoffish and not always very loving or affectionate. But even back when I first met her, I could see there was more." Stander shifted uncomfortably in his chair. The subject of his mother still touchy all these years later. A woman he had very complicated and mixed feelings about.

His father asked, "Do you remember when you found that black cat under the porch of your mother's house? After she moved into town?"

"Samson? Sure, he became the fattest cat I have ever seen." Stander smiled at the fond memory of his first real pet.

"Sure, you are probably right about that. Your mom spoiled him, I think... But anyway, when you found him, he had been hit by a car or something and had a big gash on his back leg. When we pulled him out from under that old wood porch, he tried hard to get away, scratched, and hissed at us. Clawed me pretty well, as I recall." The old man smiled, his memories from long ago still rock solid despite his difficulties in the short term. "But you, no, you were not to be deterred. Even though that cat acted mean and scratched you a few times, you kept after it, petting and talking to it, trying to pick him up and get him to come inside. Do you remember?" Stander nodded. He loved that cat once it finally accepted him. "You knew that cat wasn't mean or trying to hurt you. It was just that something bad happened to it, and he was hurt. Underneath all its bluster, that cat was just a scared little kitten. You saw that and gave it all your love; sure enough, you were right. That cat Samson became a regular part of the family, didn't he?"

"He lived with mom until she died. Then he came and stayed with us. I think he spent most of his time in my room and my bed, mostly purring and trying to get me to pet him. Unless he was hungry, anyway."

The retired doctor chuckled, smiling again at his son. "Yes, sir. A most contented creature unless he was hungry, which seemed often, as I recall." He reached out and affectionately put his hand on his son's tatted-up arm. "What you saw in that cat was what I saw in your mom. In her eyes was a hurt. That hurt made her defensive, distrustful even. She kept her guard up and never really let people in. But just like you, I kept at it. Gave her my unconditional love, and eventually, she came around too. I know we divorced and all that. And who knows what might have happened had she lived. But if nothing else, I think I, we really, you and I, we gave her peace. Gave her a foundation, something solid under her feet. Gave her strength to face whatever demons were down below. And with some professional help, she did get better. She did face things for the first time. Became warmer and more open. That was why she went back to France, you know. To finally face what maybe had been holding her back."

Stander stood up and walked into the kitchen, dumping most of his coffee cup out into the sink. Talking and thinking about his mother always made him anxious. He said over his shoulder as he rinsed the mug, "That didn't exactly work out, though, did it? She went back to face those demons, as you put it, but she never fucking came back." He was stunned to feel his eyes welling with tears. He shut them down by switching the topic of the conversation slightly. "So how did she die, dad? What really happened to her?" When he felt composed again, he walked back into the living room, sitting by his dad once more. "All I really knew was that she had an accident in France. Was there anything else?"

"No, nothing much else to tell from what you already know. I never lied to you or held anything back concerning any of that. I just never shared what she went through and saw as a little girl. Or why it had been so important to her that she return home. Maybe that was why she acted the way she did when you were…" Stander cut him off.

"So she just fell into an underground river in a cave? Was her body washed away? That was it? How do you know since she was alone in a foreign country?"

"You may be too young to remember. But when I got the call from the local authorities about the accident, I flew right over. Not that it did me much good." The old man frowned and seemed to shrivel slightly in his easy chair. "She had found the quarry where the people of her village hid during the war. That was, well, that was where she thought she saw her father kill her mother. She had wanted to go back and see it again, I guess. Give herself some closure, as they say. Your mother hiked into the quarry with a local villager and a student excavating the site."

"Excavating? Why?" Again, Stander heard more new details he did not recall ever being told. His father continued.

"The quarry itself was originally mined by the Romans and was centuries and centuries old. Maybe over a thousand years old. Who knows? There must have been old artifacts or something. I don't recall exactly what the student's interest in it was. But anyway, your mother and the two other guys got caught in a tunnel collapse down there. Part of the quarry caved in from natural erosion caused by a nearby river. All three of them perished."

"But how do you know? Mom's body was never found, right?" Stander was focused now. This conversation and some of these questions had burned inside him for years. He knew if he had ever really pursued the entire story or asked him these questions before, his dad would have told him earlier than this. But in the past, it had seemed pointless. Stander usually just pushed past the questions about his mother's death. It all happened so long ago. What had it really mattered? His mom abandoned him, period. He'd never forgotten or forgiven. Always told himself he didn't care anyway. But now, once and for all, he wanted to hear everything. To understand her story.

"Her body, my lovely Jeanne, was never found. That is sadly true... When I got to France a few days later, I couldn't go down into the quarry itself. They said it was flooding in places and very dangerous. Parts of it were still collapsing. I guess one of the first men from the village who tried to find the group when they didn't return also got killed. His body was lost as well. So they shut everything back up. Out of concern for public safety and all. Closed the quarry for good. But before they did that, some volunteer searchers found the spot where the collapse happened. They said a portion of the tunnel wall had caved in and, leading up to it, were three sets of footprints. They also found pieces of a flashlight they showed me that had been damaged and broken apart when the wall collapsed. There was enough of the flashlight left that it could be identified as having been carried by one of the men. Plus, I guess there was blood where it looked like one of them may have been hurt in the accident. Or, the authorities also surmised, the blood may have come from an injury that occurred as they tried to fight their way back out of the cave-in."

"But no bodies? All three just disappeared?" To Stander, it all seemed incredible, possibly too convenient. One woman alone with two men? Who knows what could have happened down there. How competent or trusted could the authorities in such a small village actually be?

"By the time I flew in and arrived, one body had been recovered. It was the student, and his body was found on a riverbank above ground a few miles away downstream. There is some large river that runs by the village - I don't recall the name of it - but anyway, the body was positively identified as the archeology student who was leading the exploration. They could tell, by the lungs, that he'd drowned. I met the student's family, and they were just as devastated as I was. It was all just a terrible and sad tragedy." Stander could tell it was painful for his father to revisit this old memory. There had never been any doubt in his mind that his father had truly loved his mom.

The old doctor sighed once and continued. "A few years later, I got another call from the French authorities again. They wanted me to know they'd found more human remains a long way downriver from the quarry. It was only a skull and some bones after all that time. Had to be identified by dental records, but it had definitely been the second man from the group. Of course, there was no way to tell how he had died after all that time. But again, everything was consistent, with all three having been caught and drowned down in that quarry. That god damned quarry..." Stander was startled by the cursing. Personally, he swore like a sailor on leave but rarely had, if ever, heard his father swear.

"But mom's body was never recovered?" His dad just shook his head.

"But she still haunts me. Still haunts my dreams." Once more, the elderly man gazed out his living room window before continuing. "What could have been? I loved her, warts and all as they say..." Stander nodded. The memory of his mom haunted him as well. But in a completely different way.

The father and son eventually moved on to other, more mundane topics. Before long, it was time for the wine tasting in the facilities lobby. Though invited by his father and the West Willow Acres staff, Stander begged off, citing his earlier long drive that day and desire to get to the local hotel where he stayed overnight each visit. Soon he was walking back to his parked vehicle. Driving himself across town and thinking about his mom.

Alone.

CHAPTER
TWENTY-FIVE

DR. TIMOTHY STANDER died peacefully in his sleep some three months later. There was no actual warning ahead of time. But, having just celebrated his 91st birthday the month before, it was hardly unexpected. Stander had braced himself for this inevitable event for the last year or two, but it still hit him hard. The "micro" family could no longer really be called a family. It was now just Stander. Always a loner and now truly alone.

The funeral came and went drama-free. But completing and filing of the various legal forms - all setup, prepared, and signed well in advance by the retired physician – proved to be a bit more unsettling. Stander's father, as was his nature, had taken care of everything. The real stunner, however, was the total amount of land and wealth his father's family had accumulated over the years and was now left to him, the last sole heir. Stander was not surprised to learn he was inheriting a lot of money. But he was surprised that he would never need to be concerned about his finances again.

Ever.

With his father's death, Stander learned he was now the sole Trustee of a family trust fund titled "Noviodunum Suessiones" that had apparently spanned generations and generations of family before him. The family trust and its presumed French origin were previously unknown to Stander. His father had never mentioned any specifics about his financial status or holdings, and Stander never pressed the issue. His father's often repeated comment when the subject of money came up was always the same. That money only bought one thing of value. The ability to not have to worry about it anymore. Anything else it bought was worrying. The group of lawyers from the prestigious law firm presiding over the paperwork transfer seemed to know little beyond the vast value of the trust. Puzzled by the many files of land deeds, funds, and resources just as much as Stander was. But they assured him that if he wanted a full review as the new Trustee, they would assign someone from their office to painstakingly list all the holdings and research the history of the trust. Not knowing what else to do, Stander agreed to the audit, if only to put off dealing with the unexpected responsibility.

In the meantime, Stander continued working and running his bar in Marquette as before. Mostly because he didn't yet know what else to do with himself. Staying busy in the day-to-day routine of his work and life. But, checking in at his dentist's office later that month, he caught a fleeting glimpse of a seemingly familiar face under a tussle of blonde hair. "Liz?" Stander whispered under his breath as his heart lurched in his chest. The woman, as if hearing, glanced briefly up at him without recognition from where she sat across the waiting room from him. Though her green eyes matched Liz's (Stander could never forget those radiant orbs), the fellow dental patient was, however, not Liz.

"Ellie?" The young woman looked up a second time as the dental hygienist called out her name. "How are you doing today? Ready for that night guard fitting?" The young woman nodded and tossed a well-thumbed magazine down on the seat beside her before rising and starting to follow the hygienist down the hallway toward the back of the dental office. She smiled pleasantly and commented at Stander as she walked past him.

"I'm done with that magazine if you are looking for something interesting to read while waiting." Suddenly realizing he was staring at her, Stander stammered out thanks. He finished checking in with the receptionist before numbly taking her place in the same waiting room chair. He shook his head and thought to himself, "get a grip," as he began absently scrolling through his phone. Minutes later, bored as he waited for his turn, Stander slid his phone into his pocket and picked up the worn magazine the young woman had left behind. Distractedly flipping its pages until suddenly spying an article titled, "Quarries and Caves in France Hid Thousands of Locals at D-Day." Stander quickly sat up straight and started reading in earnest. The story began by recounting the amazing survival rate among the citizens of Caen, France, during the D-Day invasion of 1944. Though the bombing had nearly leveled the city, the casualties of its citizens were minor by comparison. The reason? Many residents hid deep inside an old, nearby quarry.

Stander was stunned.

It was the same story his father told him about his mother's childhood war experience. And now here it was, worldwide news! The writer said the quarry in Caen was later turned into a brewery but had ceased operations sometime in the mid-60s. After that, the old quarry was forgotten, unused, and abandoned for the most part before recently being rediscovered and now celebrated. But what caught Stander's eye was learning that local French cavers and spelunkers were also actively looking for similar caves and quarries in that same part of France. Quarries that were used as bomb shelters during the 1944 battle of Normandy. The article added that scores of professional and amateur archaeologists and amateur cave enthusiasts were rediscovering quarries largely undisturbed and frozen in time. Local adventurers even headed into areas previously off-limits to try and document survivors' stories.

Stander, alone in the waiting room and about to be called back for a teeth cleaning, looked around him. With no one seeming to be paying him any attention, he muttered to himself, "Oh, fuck it," before discretely ripping the two-page article out of the three-month-old, dog-eared magazine and shoving it in his back pocket. When his routine dental checkup was completed, he raced back home. Searching for and finding the faded and well-worn postcard from 1979 his mom had sent him from France. It was the last message he ever received from her. The written phrases were generic, to the point, and held little warmth or affection, just like his mother. But Stander, having read the postcard thousands of times, still remembered what it had shown and said.

On one side was a picture of the city of Caen! And on the back, his mom references the small village nearby she was born and visited: Vieux. The second to last line tells little Russell she will be returning to Vieux again the next day. As it turned out, that was the day she died. The tight cursive script ended. The fading blue ink was hard to decipher at the curled edges of the card but it read, "Remember that I love you, little Russell. Love, mom." The words stung his eyes and filled them with tears even 40 years later. She had given almost nothing, but it was all he had.

Stander could count on one hand how many times his mom told him she loved him when she was alive. He was never sure why he had kept this postcard all these years, but deep down, he suspected it was so he had proof she really had loved him. Even though she rarely showed it and said it even less. Before one day, out of the blue, announcing she was taking a trip overseas. Going away without him and, as it turned out, never to return. This postcard was the only bridge left between then and now.

Until today…

Inspired by the news article and armed with the name of the tiny village where his mother was born and later made her fateful trip down into its quarry, Stander went online. He had no idea where the city of Caen was in relation to Paris or the sea (the only two geographic landmarks he knew of in France). Or where the tiny village of Vieux might be or if there was any information available yet about its quarry. So he spent time the next week doing his own research on that area of France, the part it played during the war, and the groups currently researching the old bomb shelters nearby.

Stander found several other news articles similar to what he stumbled upon at his dentist's office. Some of the reporting included pictures and accounts of the quarry in Caen. But frustratingly, there were few specifics about any other quarries mentioned being discovered or mapped. Though he followed link after link, by the end of the week, Stander decided all of the information he could find online was really only about the one quarry used for shelter by the residents of

Caen. He wondered why, with so much interest and obvious news coverage, no one locally identified the neighboring village of Vieux and its very similar history.

Perhaps, he thought, it was just one of many old mines and quarries and not very unique. But deep down, he doubted that. Once again, Stander's earlier suspicions when his dad relayed the story of his mother's accident returned to him. It seemed to him his dad may have been a little too trusting back then. No body recovered and not allowed to enter the quarry? Even though just days before, students, or at least one student, had been working inside it? The whole story just seemed fishy to him. Stander may not have many fond memories of his mother, but she was his mom. He knew his father had loved her and, after all, she was part of Stander's "micro" family. If not him, who else would ever bother to find out what might have happened to her all those years before.

Having traveled internationally in the past, Stander already had a valid passport. With money no longer a concern, the decision, if somewhat impulsive, was easy to make. He would fly over to France and retrace his mom's final footsteps. See if he could hook up with some of the amateur groups mentioned in the articles he'd just read. Maybe even try to look up the archeologist quoted and named in that first news story he found. Find out if the quarry near Vieux has been discovered yet, and if so, explore it. Or if not, maybe he would help those groups discover something new.

He contacted a travel agent he'd used several times in the past. The agent was able to put everything together for his trip in just a few short days. Plus, using local French travel resources to ask questions, Stander's agent provided him with a contact in Caen. A man who did professional city tours said he knew many of the locals involved in the ongoing cave and quarry explorations. The man would give Stander (as long as he paid for it) a tour of the city and put him in contact with a local archeologist he knew. Reserving and paying for everything with his credit card, and lining up Secrist to keep an eye on his dog, Frazier, while he was away, Stander soon was all set. Less than two weeks after stumbling across the magazine article, he was landing in France.

The local travel guide met Stander at his hotel the morning after his flight arrived. The walking tour of the city of Caen was fascinating, and Stander learned firsthand the town's storied history long before it became famous for the beaches of Normandy. The many cathedrals, abbeys, and castles were endless and gorgeous. Stander felt a little conspicuous having his own personal tour guide while most of the other groups seeing many of the same attractions had anywhere from 10-20 tourists being led by a single guide. He felt the eyes of a few fellow tourists and other visitors to Caen appraising him. Undoubtedly wondering how he, dressed in scuffed boots, old jeans, and a faded REO Speedwagon concert t-shirt, could afford a personal guided tour. But Stander shrugged off the occasional stare and concentrated on what his knowledgeable tour guide was saying. The three-hour tour ended at a small restaurant where the guide had arranged for the local archeologist to meet them.

The bearded archeologist Dr. Lucas Chanet, born in France, was raised and educated in America. He had long black hair tied back in a ponytail, wore wire-rimmed glasses, and was directly involved in the search for local caves and quarries. Working on his own time with other enthusiasts to document where their fellow French countrymen once huddled together under an onslaught of artillery shells and bombing. The three men, all English speaking, ate a pleasant meal together that Stander paid for. The guide excused himself when the meal was over, saying he had another tour to conduct, leaving the two men alone.

Though it was touched on during the meal, Stander explained to Lucas in greater detail what brought him over to France. The article he'd seen and that his mother had emigrated from this area to the United States after surviving D-Day as a child by hiding in a local quarry. He gave the archeologist a brief synopsis of his mother's return trip back in 1979 and the accident that claimed her life. Emphasizing that, as her son, he was very motivated to explore the quarry in Vieux and, if it was unknown, he would like to help locate it. Financially or otherwise.

Lucas listened thoughtfully, affirming that he'd heard talk of a quarry near Vieux. Still, among the locals, the quarry itself was described as very small, with much of it collapsed. The local archeologist went on to say that with so many other safer and potentially more compelling options, the rumored one near Vieux would likely never be one his little team of volunteers would have otherwise actively pursued or explored.

However, Stander's story compelled him enough that he promised to do a bit more research and see what he could find out about it. Additionally, if a student from the University of Caen Normandy back in 1979 was authorized to excavate the quarry, his interest was definitely piqued. Speculating if, in the '70s, the quarry was known and explored, the university would have answers and, more than likely, maps showing its exact location and perhaps even the original entrance. When Stander explained he was told it was sealed off, Lucas did not appear phased by that or surprised. Many of the local quarries and caves were blocked off at different times for different reasons over the years, but rarely had that ever proven to be an insurmountable obstacle. Before parting, Lucas took down Stander's cell number and the hotel he was booked in. When he left, the two men shook hands, and the archeologist promised to be back in touch soon.

Stander spent his time relaxing as a vacationing tourist for the next two days. Appreciating all the sites in and around Caen, enjoying good food, and spending one full day at the beaches of Normandy. Seeing for himself firsthand the valor and courage of the men who had sacrificed so much during the Second World War. At the end of the second day, Lucas contacted him, and the two men made arrangements to meet at the bar next door to Stander's hotel that same evening.

Once they had taken their outdoor seats under the sun slowly setting in the distance, the two men ordered their drinks, and Lucas began to share what he had learned. "I have to tell you, there isn't much documentation regarding the quarry itself in Vieux," Lucas began. "But I found there have been several, various-sized excavations over the years at the site of the Roman ruins nearby. Most of what I found about the quarry was just brief mentions among the paperwork filed or papers written about those ruins."

"I did see online when I was planning for this trip something about Roman structures visible in Vieux. It kind of looked like a lame-ass tourist spot, to be honest, but there really wasn't much detail. Were they important?" Stander hadn't paid very close attention to what he saw on the internet regarding the ancient works. "What were they?"

"That's where it starts to get a little interesting. And where they might tie in with the nearby quarry. I'll try to summarize the conclusions of a couple theories based on the limited evidence unearthed over several different excavations. But I must warn you that most everything I found was purely speculative." Stander settled back into his seat and made himself comfortable as Lucas took a sip of his red wine before continuing.

"The Roman era ruins in Vieux date back to when the area was a settlement called Araegenve. It even appeared on the Roman map Tabula Peutingeriana. What you still see above ground today was most likely once part of a temple. That much is pretty clear, and it seems the one point those who worked the site in the past all agreed upon. But what the temple was built for and what gods were worshipped in it is less clear. One of the more interesting theories an early archeologist came up with was it was built by the followers of Mithras. The religion itself was called Mithraism, and its followers were an underground Roman religious group that worshipped a pagan deity named, not surprisingly, Mithras. What's fascinating is even though it was considered a secret sect, the covert religion was once so widespread that some historians considered it an early rival of, or even a sister religion, to Christianity. But little is actually known for certain about it."

"Well, I suppose Christianity was an underground religion at first, too..." Stander countered.

"So true, so true. You are right there," continued Lucas, "but Mithraism certainly pre-dated Christianity."

"Predated? Really? By how much?"

"That is where the real mystery truly begins. Even the very name of the pagan god and religion is shrouded in questions. Some ancient Romans believed Mithras was originally based on an even older god. Most likely Persian. Others in ancient writings said Mithraism was a star cult with strong ties to astrotheology, where stars and other heavenly bodies are worshipped as deities. There were also a smattering of other Roman sites and temples unearthed over the years, with zodiac symbols hinting heavily at the cult's connections with the celestial world. Though what exactly those connections entailed is still a conundrum."

Stander found the topic interesting but wondered why Lucas shared these details with him. "At least the Romans wrote stuff down, huh?" Lucas nodded and chuckled as he took another drink of his wine. "But what the fuck does this have to do with the quarry? You said some papers mentioned the quarry by the guys trying to figure out the Roman ruins. What was this tie-in, as you put it?"

"Yeah, see, here is the thing: Mithraism did have temples, but as far as we know, they were always underground. I know I said earlier the religion was an underground religion. That is true, but all their meetings were also underground operations. Members gathered in dark, underground temples, sometimes built inside caves but often using parts of mines and quarries. They would gather for feasts, rituals, and worship within windowless walls adorned with religious artwork. These dark caverns usually contained scenes from Mithras's story, such as the god feasting upon the souls of the dead or a youthful Mithras being born or emerging from a radiant rock. Which most think was meant to show him being born from the inside of the earth. Or maybe born from another planet or star."

"A glowing rock, huh?" Stander shook his head contemplatively. "I don't suppose this Mithras was a female god, was she?"

"Not sure. I never read anything specifically calling out Mithras's gender, but it could be. Why?"

"Never mind…" Stander took a deep drink of wine from his glass. He briefly recalled his recent discovery of a sometimes glowing rock that he'd locked safely away in the basement of his bar back in Marquette. He'd hidden it away after witnessing and feeling the power it wielded. A relict he'd uncovered near a landmark in Michigan ominously nicknamed Skull Rock. "So anyway, this god Mithras is depicted in believer's art as coming up and out of the ground. Anything else?"

"Usually, those depictions are accompanied by an assortment of other images. Typically a huge dog or wolf-like creature. Sometimes scorpions, snakes, and even ravens. But in ruins without these animal-like images, we always find stars and other figures from the zodiac.

Cryptic celestial images and symbols are abundant throughout the interior of the temples. On all the walls and even adorning the ceilings. Usually, there are also remnants and sculpture pieces of Sol, the god of the sun, and Luna, the goddess of the moon."

"So I don't understand what you are saying. If all these old-time archeologists thought this was a temple to Mithras, why would it be outside?" Stander leaned forward, taking another sip from his glass.

"Not sure, really. But one of the theories I read said this was a secretive group. Its members were only fully welcomed after completing seven harrowing initiation levels linked to the planets. Previously it was thought they had to complete these initiations to be a cult member. But one archeologist's hypothesis, after excavating the ruins in Vieux, was that the seven initiations had to be completed each time before worshippers were allowed down into the underground temple itself. So what we see above ground today in Vieux was perhaps where those rites were carried out. Each member proving themselves and more than likely only able to do that during certain lunar cycles. Or when planets or stars were aligned in some way. Therefore to do that, it had to be done above ground. Under the stars instead of in the darkness of the temple, where any natural stray light would be forbidden to penetrate the ancient cave. Or, in this case, quarry."

"So you are saying the Roman ruins were like a temple outbuilding or something? But the actual temple itself was underground? Maybe part of the quarry?" It sounded incredible to him, but ancient Roman or Greek history was never a subject he'd found interesting enough to delve deeply into.

"I'm not saying anything. I'm just telling you what some of my peers have theorized over the years. And without proof, that's all that is. Theories." Lucas drained his glass and waved down the waitress for a refill. Stander took the opportunity to order a second drink as well.

"Well, that is all really interesting, I guess. But were you able to locate any specific details about the quarry itself? Like maybe a key to the front fucking door?" Stander laughed.

Lucas smiled back before answering. "Not the front door, no. But I did find where the back door was. Or at least one of them. And I have to tell you, after reading all these various Roman theories, I personally am now very interested in getting inside this old quarry. So what do you say? Want to do some underground hiking tomorrow?"

Stander felt his heart leap in his chest, excited at the prospect. "Are you kidding?! I flew across an ocean with a suitcase full of ridiculously expensive fucking hiking gear to do just that! You only need to tell me where and when…"

"Great! I have already contacted my team. We will pick you up tomorrow morning at 8:00 AM in the lobby." As the second round of drinks arrived, the two men toasted themselves under the light of the full moon rising in the clear sky above their heads.

CHAPTER
TWENTY-SIX

STANDER MET Lucas in the bustling lobby of his hotel early that following day. The two men were joined by Dr. Chanet's team of three energetic and agreeable sorts. All locals with ties to the area. Two of the three turned out to be a middle-aged married couple. The woman, with hair, dyed bright red, was a gregarious, short, plump history professor and colleague of Dr. Chanet's at the university in Caen. Her husband, a tall, lanky man with a shaved and shiny bald head, told Stander he'd been roped into helping with the search. But the friendly couple, the Cerdans, both clearly enjoyed the sense of adventure their travels back in time hunting for old bomb shelters on the weekends afforded them.

The third member joining Stander and Lucas was a university student of Dr. Chanet's named Christophe, who was currently working on his doctorate in archeology at The University of Caen Normandy. After a few introductions and brief pleasantries, the five underground searchers piled into two vehicles already loaded with the equipment needed for the exploration. Stander rode shotgun in a white cargo van with Lucas and the grad student. At the same time, the second car, carrying the married couple, followed close behind. The short drive, in the bright and brisk morning air, from Caen to their destination was uneventful, and soon both cars were parked near the Roman ruins of Vieux.

The four experienced explorers gathered and readied their gear. Stander, outfitted in boots, cargo pants, and a newly purchased bright yellow all-weather jacket, looked on anxiously. It felt surreal to be moments away from entering the quarry where his mother had lost her life. He fiddled with the buckles on his new jacket as the team members, obviously having worked together often in the past, readied everything for the descent.

Stander looked out over the Roman ruins they'd parked alongside. The modest outcropping of squared-off grey pits and white pillar bases were oddly out of place among the green fields dominating the land-scape around them. A modern, wide staircase led visitors into the ruins, which sat low inside a mini-valley between several small hills on two sides. Stander, who had seen pictures of the area online, expected something more grandiose and was surprised at the modest size of the site. On the drive over, Lucas promised to give him a full tour of the ruins, suggesting since the group packed food that, perhaps over lunch would be the best opportunity.

The group donned their lighted, protective headgear and headed up the nearest hill's side. Walking for less than ten minutes without a path, thigh-high dewy weeds and thick grass swishing against their legs before halting in front of several large, granite boulders.

In the gap between two huge rocks was a shadowy, upside down "V" shaped opening that split widest at the base of both stones. This "backdoor entrance," as Lucas called it, was sealed but only halfheart-edly. A piece of metal fencing had been laid across the ground-level-manhole-sized opening. The discolored, rickety steel barrier was secured to the large boulders on either side; the ends bolted into the rock. Two rusted padlocks held both sagging pieces of metal together in the middle. But if anyone really wanted to gain entrance, without much effort at all, they could. However, judging by the high weeds and multiple spider webs decorating the cracks and opening, it appeared to hold no interest locally.

Almost as if it was shunned.

There was no evidence of anyone recently trying to force their way in. Nor any sign of the typical bored teenage graffiti or carvings in the trees or various big rocks scattered about. The place was either entirely forgotten or clearly avoided. If he had not personally been so interested in the quarry, Stander wondered if it ever would have been rediscovered and explored…

Lucas, who lugged a large bolt cutter with him on the brief hike, used it now to snap off each padlock. He tossed the broken locks and bolt cutter on the ground in front of the small entrance, which was out in the open and clearly visible should anyone approach the area while they were exploring. After removing his backpack, he clicked on his headlamp, dropped to his knees, and crawled inside the opening without hesitation, dragging his pack behind him. Each of the explorers followed suit one by one, with Stander taking a deep breath before bringing up the rear. Within minutes all five were standing inside the quarry, backpacks in place, lighting up a straight, long tunnel ahead of them.

"If everyone is set, let's make our way forward," said Lucas. Then beginning to walk, he added over his shoulder, "Christophe, will you please do the mapping, so we don't get lost?" The young man nodded, already writing in his waterproof notebook.

"I would have figured these days you wouldn't need to manually draw or map things. Don't you use some kind of fancy-ass underground radar?" Stander's voice sounded loud and echoed hollowly around him. He chuckled nervously. Ever since childhood, he'd avoided underground places like this. It always seemed, below the surface, anything could be concealing itself.

Anything trying to avoid light.

"Sorry, good question. I should have told you outside." Lucas stopped and unclipped a small handheld unit hanging from his backpack. He held it up for Stander to see, as did Mrs. Cerdan, who had a similar device in her hand. "Three of us have what are basically just glorified GPS units. But they each are called 'DGPS-ready,' which stands for Differential Global Positioning Systems. So, in theory, they are capable of receiving DGPS corrections and will pick up satellite positioning while at the same time also tracking where we have been so you can backtrack later if needed. But the problem is, if we descend very deep underground, they sometimes don't work well, and different manufacturers' models seem to work more effectively in different environments than others. And until you actually get inside a new cave, you never know which model will work best. Plus, you are battling high humidity, constant dripping water, narrow tunnels, etc… All these environmental obstacles can negatively affect the devices too. So anyway, we always have a couple different models with us and create a handwritten map as we go. Believe me, our safety is number one, and the last thing I want to do is get lost down here…" Lucas looked around him, "It is easy to get spooked and lose your cool once you get below ground. Best to have a couple backups in place."

Christophe nodded and chimed in as well. His English was thick with a French accent, "We also have a couple air quality meters that will alarm if we come across heavy CO_2 or methane pockets." Then he held up what looked to Stander like a walkie-talkie and clicked it on and off. "Regular walkie-talkies don't work very well underground. But these are very low-frequency cave-in radios that transmit through most rock walls. If something does happen, and when we get split up, we can still stay in contact."

Stander nodded sheepishly, "Sorry, guys. Going underground like this just freaks me the fuck out…"

"Nothing to be sorry about. If anything makes you feel uncomfortable, just let us know. And please, do keep asking questions. This is your find, after all!" Lucas, smiling, reached out and squeezed Stander's thick shoulder. "Now, let's go see where this leads. Hopefully, we won't get blocked a few feet in and just have to turn back around! Wouldn't be the first time that's happened to us." The others chuckled and nodded in agreement with him.

Lucas started walking again and led the group down a slight incline, moving deeper inside the quarry. The five halogen headlamps brightly illuminated the path ahead of them. They reached a fork in the tunnel, and almost automatically, with little communication or fanfare, the Cerdans took the passageway to the right. Leaving Lucas, Stander, and Christophe to continue descending the carved channel ahead of them. The weeping stone walls led them ever deeper into the quarry.

Their path was gradual and steady. The three men stopped periodically to allow Christophe to update his map, take notes, and occasionally measure their progress.

After another 30 minutes of hiking inside the chiseled, subterranean hallway, the men entered a vast chamber. Their previously constricted lights expanded in the open space, filling the darkness but failing to reach the outer limits of the giant underground room. Lucas and Christophe pulled out larger, handheld tube lights resembling small fluorescent lightbulbs, which were much brighter. Battery operated and, when lit, even one of them easily doubled the output of all their combined headlamps. In the additional light, two things were immediately revealed. One was a steep drop-off ahead of them, roughly 50 yards from where they had entered the interior cavern room. The second looked to Stander, at first, like a rudimentary cluster of large stones lying on the ground of the vast open space.

The anomaly, some ten feet away from where they stood, fell between themselves and the drop-off. All three men were magnetically drawn to the jagged shapes. One piece loomed large and stood starkly out of place against the backdrop of the otherwise featureless dirt floor. The trio huddled around the object, all standing first before Christophe and Lucas eventually knelt down for a closer look. Stander soon followed, and he squatted nearby, watching anxiously. Lucas examined the object closely, reaching his handheld light out to see it more clearly. He blew across the exposed top and fanned away the cloud of dust he unsettled with one hand. Immediately revealing the object to be engraved and obviously manmade. A carved image emerged suddenly from out of the swirling particles, and the apparent likeness struck all three men simultaneously. They were looking at the snarling image of a giant wolf's head. The sculptured features appeared animated under the disturbed dirt and sweeping lights of the archeologists as they pondered the find. It was a fearsome effigy, a stone sculpture carved as much out of nightmares as it was rock.

Unprompted, the three men glanced nervously around the cavern in unison.

Lucas and Christophe then refocused on the other pieces of the huge broken statue. Continuing to clear more of the sediment collected over an incalculable amount of time. Then, once all the exposed pieces were bathed in bright light, it became clear what they had found. Originally one piece, it was a toppled and very aged statue. The base of it was either still sunk or buried deep in layers and layers of accumulated quarry dust and dirt. Much of what remained above ground had cracked and crumbled over time. Several broken pieces, like the disturbing wolf head, lay scattered around the largest piece remaining: the base or the stand of it. The carvings and barely visible markings on the ancient stone pieces were very faded and had smoothed out over time. Making an immediate identification of who may have initially chiseled the image impossible within the confines of the black quarry. However, it was obvious the monolith was dated almost beyond measure. But, beyond the obvious antiquity, how ancient was guesswork at this point.

Lucas continued to gingerly blow and fan the excess dirt away. His brow furrowed in concentration. Christophe pulled a small brush from his backpack, pointing and whispering simple adjectives as he worked with the older archeologist. "Wow," "beau," and "sapristi" chief among them. Stander stood once more and nodded appreciatively as he looked down upon it, about to speak and add his own commentary. But the words died in his throat when he saw an old lady standing twenty feet away. She stared at him, holding a single flickering candle in her hand. The flame created peculiar shadows that scrambled around her like rats deserting a doomed vessel or sinking ship.

The woman, it seemed to Stander, was ridiculously aged. Her skin weathered and cracked. Thick, matted long white hair barely parted enough to reveal the craggy features of her face. Her expression was one of deep suffering and long with sorrow. Deep lines crisscrossed her forehead, and her nose was misshapen and scarred. Her skinny arms were bare and poked out from a drab, box-like garment hanging unflatteringly off her narrow shoulders. The single ornament of her dress was a threadbare cord knotted tightly against her thin hips and stomach. When Stander stood, the artificial light from his headlamp fully exposed the ancient woman. The illumination only accentuated her bizarre appearance. Her feet were filthy and bare. A gruesome wound on one foot, wet and weeping where several toes should have been.

She spoke to Stander in a raspy voice filled with gravel. "You have finally made it. Following the seeds I have sewn for more years than any not a god could count." The archaic woman beckoned Stander to her, raising a gnarled hand that quivered as she extended it out, gesturing him forward. As he took small, hesitant steps to close the gap between them, she continued speaking. "You are the last of our line. The last root from which my life bloomed, such as our ruined family tree could have ever been considered life." The woman seemed to wither even as she spoke each word. Her voice grew fragile. The sound, just like the old woman—shriveled.

"Last of your line? Do I know you?" Stander continued to shuffle forward, moving tentatively in the quarry. His footfalls were hollow on the stony floor, dust around his feet swirling.

"My name is Laurent," began the woman once more. "I have stood guardian of this place as countless generations of my blood waned. The well of life they sprung from was poisoned by my actions centuries before most were conceived. I seek and deserve no pity, but I am a woman long tormented and cursed by those I once betrayed. Vexed continually by them still and, worse yet, by the knowledge of my long-ago selfish deeds. I have existed in purgatory, never able to leave this area and damned to live without even the smallest of plea-sure. Food without taste, air without fragrance, sleep without rest, and touch without feeling. Alone without peers, compassion, or love. Haunted by thousands of souls and companion to those I damned to their own eternity of servitude."

Stander tried to form words, but his tongue grew thick. He heard himself panting, and the inside of his mouth was dry as a bone. Thinking of his mother, who, like him, had ventured down here to search for answers about her parents, Stander's mind raced with a million questions he wanted to ask this strange hag. But he continued his approach in numb and mute silence. Though his feet moved steadily, the space between him and the white-haired woman never seemed to close. Her voice sounded once more as if reading his unspoken thoughts and questions. Stander noticed her mouth was no longer moving, and the cracks about her face had deepened.

Somehow, still, she spoke to him…

"I was born a foundling without parents, embarrassed by my gypsy blood and the dark skin of those who took me in. A people I was grateful for but thought far too simple for one such as myself. Yet, as if born out of step with my time, I also hated the citizens of Caen, where I lived too. The endless teasing, the men who took advantage of us, and the French women who despised me out of petty jealousy. For I was once young and beautiful. Oh yes. So much so that I fell in love with myself and thought only of my desires. Letting pleasure of the flesh, the wine, and man's riches rule all my actions. I longed for more than I had, and even as a young child, I was seduced by the majesty of the neighboring power of my time, the English. So, when given a chance and without hesitation, I betrayed them all. The nomadic gypsies who had harbored me, and the French citizens of Caen who scorned me."

"I used my beauty and youthful energy to gain influence with two powerful local counts. These lords owned the grandest castles and ruled the most men in Caen. I went from one to the other, delivering children by both. Waiting to see which one would join with the English rumored to be threatening our shores. When neither of the French nobles bent to my wishes, I began to court favor among the visiting English dignitaries. All the while learning the two French counts' plans and defenses as the English drew near Caen. When at last the English arrived, I made sure I was part of the emissary of Caen able to meet, not King Edward himself, but his son Edward the Black Prince. With him, I stayed unashamed, allowing him wickedness others would withhold. I used every moment to entertain and pleasure him until I was certain he had fallen in love with me. So certain was I that he would make me his wife…" The old woman continued to wilt as she spoke these lines, her eyes dulling inside her head.

"So I confided in him all I knew. Betraying my people, my blood, and my country. Spying for him and sharing what was learned. The people's defenses, and the numbers of armored and trained fighting men. Where our city's riches were kept and where we were most vulnerable. With this knowledge and advantage, the English could carefully strategize before rushing upon our shores. Continuing to wage their never-ending war that had now finally reached France. It was less a battle than it was a massacre. King Edward the Third and his son, with my treachery, caught the citizens of Caen by complete surprise. Pouring into and overwhelming the weakest barriers, taking anything and anyone they wanted. Burning the entire town to the ground, hauling away incalculable wealth for themselves while killing half the population. The half unable to run away… More than 3,000 citizens of Caen were slaughtered in a matter of days. When it was over, the streets ran red with crimson blood. The English left nothing in their wake."

"Their men's total bloodlust and diabolical deeds laid Caen to waste. So much so that King Edward and his son hastened to hide the brutal carnage they had overseen. Asking of me where they could most easily dispose of the innocent villagers' corpses. The piles and piles of the dead. How they could best rid themselves of the taint their butchery left. How to cleanse their tongues and wipe the taste left in their mouths by the burning flesh. How to wash their hands of the spilled blood they had squeezed. I, oh I, knew just the place. I brought them here. I knew in this place, Romans once enslaved scores of ancestors of these very same people. A place long hoped for and, perhaps, pretended to be forgotten by most. But nonetheless, a place where whispers and dark rumors still swirled. The place was said to be of long ago sacrifice and worship. Where wicked Pagan Roman soldiers once did their darkest bidding to their god, Mithras. I thought it was perfect and even poetic. The Romans had enslaved our people and worse. Only to get away with it. Leaving only a scarred, black void here deep in the earth. So why shouldn't our new English king as well?"

Stander had not stopped his steady progress, feet shuffling along the floor. Yet this woman, Laurent, never got closer even as she continued speaking to him. He could not tear his eyes from her face nor fail to hear a single word she said. As if she spoke directly into his ear.

"All the dead and nearly dead, unable to escape, were gathered and brought to this place. An endless line of carts, all filled with the stinking and dripping bodies of Caen citizens, dumped one load after another down into the dark pit you see here now. The wounded and living witnesses were treated no differently than the dead witnesses. Lazy English soldiers did not bother to raise their weapons once more to kill those tossed into the pit yet still alive. Instead, interring every citizen of Caen unable to flee from them together in one mass grave. Filling what I thought was simply an empty Roman quarry, previously filled with only silly superstitions."

"So I urged them on, desiring to leave these shores and start my new life as a princess in England. I showed Edward the Black Prince the route you now took here, the path crossing both the old Roman ruins outside and this blasphemous underground temple where centurions once worshipped Mithras. But when the dark task was done, and their deeds and sins were well hidden, I found I was just as disposable to Edward the Black Prince as the corpses he had filled this ancient and unholy place with. For he had understood the strategy I had played better than I did. Upending my hollow game and mocking the emptiness where I should have been most human."

"The Black Prince imprisoned me down here. Chained me to a long-forgotten statue of a beast, a hideous wolf-like creature said to be Mithras incarnate. There I was raped over and over again by a multitude of faceless English soldiers, so many I lost count and consciousness, one after another after another. Bent over and made to watch as the last of the men, women, children, and, indeed, entire families were brought in and dumped. Most were dead by then, but some were not so fortunate. Those who yet lived moaned out loud, cursing me with their last breaths. Knowing it was I that had sold out the people. And right here, where we are now, is when I finally learned what true power was. Deserted by my lover, the English prince, left alone to bear witness to the final agonized wails of the citizens of Caen. A suffering that lasted for days. I stood in utter blackness, hearing their dying prayers and curses of me. Feeling the strength of their hatred and what it fed." The haggard face laughed without joy. "Real power, you see, is not military might, looted riches, or the command of mortal man. All things once plied in ancient times by the Romans and then later, in my time, by the English. Down here in these profane stone walls was true, ageless power."

The voice had remained steady, never rising with emotion and never wholly fading. It was oddly hypnotic, yet Stander likened it to background noise. The static of an old TV powered on but not tuned to a station or receiving a signal. A white noise. Somewhere in the distance, he heard yelling, someone shouting his name maybe... But he ignored that bothersome clatter and focused again on the words of Laurent.

"That power was stirred and summoned by those praying for vengeance as they took their last breaths. They called back in time to the long-dormant pagan god Mithras once worshipped here in hiding. Deep underground. Rousing and bringing it forth with their curses of me even as they struggled under the weight of the rotting dead around them. Buried alive and yet using the last of their strength to curse me. I was damned to never die. I was damned to never live. Cursed to never forget and to never leave. Held responsible for each and every dead soul who had ever been and ever would be brought here and buried in the black of this hell I had reignited. The agony of each sufferer is engraved deep in my mind and soul. With an eternity ahead of me, I soon began to guard this evil place. Hiding this quarry, helping the memory of it fade, and spreading false rumors among the surrounding countryside and villagers. Keeping all those who lived for generations upon generations away from here. I stood as sentry, not daring add even one more soul to my eternal torment."

"I was cursed to remain alone, unworthy of even death until every branch, root, and leaf of my family tree was ended. Judged by Mithras so worthless that every drop of my bloodline was destined to suffer. I stood by and watched the corrosion of my surviving family. Each generation that followed was worse than the last. Each one less caring of their own, more damaged. Falling into their selfish lust just as I had. Until finally, the last to be born on these cursed lands came. Your mother, Jeanne, was the key. She saw the last of the carnage."

"For again, in your mother's time, soldiers had invaded this country once more. They uncovered this unholy place, these men from a faraway land. They would not be swayed by the superstitions or by my warnings. Like the Black Prince, their leaders had been evil and soulless people who worshipped their own ruler as a god. All demons in their own way. They broke in here, finding this place and stirring Mithras again with their twisted ideology. Men who wore black both inside and out. Their cruel acts pleased Mithras here in his ancient temple. Atrocities it could once more actively participate in on a whim."

"Little Jeanne, your mother, watched as did I, the woman who had birthed and raised her, murdered right before her eyes. Watching the one she had loved most as a child do the terrible deed. But it was not really her beloved papa in control. It was Mithras that pulled the strings. Then later, still unsatisfied, Mithras forced her and me to endure the rape and desecration of her mother's hollow corpse. By her own blood-father no less! He was possessed and manipulated by the hungry thing brought back by the men in black's foul deeds. Soon this most wicked soldier turned on your mother. Driven by Mithras, he very nearly raped his own daughter. An act that would have endangered, if not ruined, her chance to later produce the last heir needed. The one destined to finally set us all free."

"But these last abominations finally roused all the souls trapped down here for countless centuries. Those who were fed on by Mithras finally rallied, finding the strength to act as one. All of us are rising to save your mother and preserve her destiny. Enabling her to be freed and get far enough away that Mithras's long grasp could not reach her. Until you, the final and last leaf of my twisted family tree made it here. You are the end of the line. The one who will finally reveal these long-lost souls. Uncovering this place and, at long last, removing each body ever placed here, returning them all to the light. All of man has finally found the wisdom, tools, and passion for doing this. To uncover this place. To free us all, your mother and even me, from Mithras."

"I don't... But I don't understand. Why was this place so evil? So cursed and damned? How could this Mithras be so powerful yet remain stuck here?" Stander dimly recognized he was approaching the ledge of an endless drop-off, nearing the end of ground he could walk on. Yet Laurent remained the same distance away. Floating in the air— her bare feet dangling and touching nothing.

"The Romans dug into this pit, using the stars to guide them. Pulling out and unearthing evil older than time itself. This is home to Mithras, the ancient one. He who fell from the sky and shuns the light. Never able to quench his hunger. A keeper of the very souls of man. Those who cursed me had their prayers answered by him. But in exchange, Mithras used them. All of them, ever lying dead in here. Keeping them as pets and feeding off their misery until he drains their very souls dry."

"But what happens when we take his toys away? What will he do then?" Stander barely got these last words out before being flung roughly to the ground from behind. He landed face first, and the front of his helmet and forehead was smashed into the cavern's floor.

When Stander raised his head and opened his eyes moments later, his vision was tinged pink. His own blood cascaded down his face and clouded his eyesight. He blinked several times and rubbed an arm groggily across his face, clearing his vision slightly. The light on his helmet hung askew but remained working, providing just enough light to see what was directly in front and below him.

Stander was mere inches from the steep drop-off they had first seen upon entering the room. He tried to push himself up from the ground with his hands, but they were so close to the pit's edge that the ground under them crumbled and collapsed. Sending a smattering of dirt and small rocks to clatter downward and fall helplessly below him. Dust reflected in his headlamp, spiraling gracefully out and down into the emptiness in front of his face. His head still spinning, he pulled his hands back slightly and braced himself again before finally looking out over the ledge. A massive pit of bones stretched out endlessly below him. As far as he could see, the jumbled remains extended out on either side.

The number of dead immeasurable.

His headlamp was not bright enough to expose the far sides of the infinite abyss below him. But the illuminated pile of the dead he could see were all bare bones with just one exception. A single corpse adorned in more modern clothing. A faded and torn threadbare flannel shirt barely visible, a pair of jeans hanging loosely from its legs. The hollowed skull grinned up at him from under a few remaining strands of blonde hair. Stander instantly knew it was Jeanne, his mother. Little Russell had found his mama. He started to cry while his head dripped. Consciousness left him like murky water swirling down a dark drain. Laurent's last words filled his bloody head, answering his last question.

"Mithras will endure. He is eternal, and he will find a way. Mithras will be born again..."

EPILOGUE

THE VEHICLE'S tires crunched on the white gravel as it turned into the newly created temporary parking lot. The automobile pulled up and stopped next to a handful of other cars parked and sitting together in a cluster under the cloudless French sky.

Russell Stander rose from the driver's side seat of this newest arrival and swung the door on the rental car shut behind him. Smiling in the warm morning sun, he weaved his way between the parked cars and began walking up the new rock-lined path leading to the ancient quarry's entrance. He nodded to a team of workers signing in and being handed their tools for the day's work. Brushes of various sizes, hand trowels, buckets, and small tape measures made up most of the instruments. Stander waved at Lucas, who spoke with a small team of local archeologists from the University of Caen Normandy. The hastily assembled group of seasoned excavators, who had just recently begun the preliminary work of cataloging what had been found deep inside the quarry, broke apart as Stander approached them. The conversation ended, and a couple of them smiled and waved amiably at the American who had almost literally fallen into what was a find of massive importance for them. Left alone as the team dispersed, Lucas called out to Stander.

"Hey there, boss man! Nice to see you back out here among the living. Everything go alright?" Stander made his way up to where Lucas was standing. As he walked, he self-consciously reached up and fingered the fresh bandage affixed to his forehead just that morning. One that covered the gash where his stitches had been removed the previous afternoon. It still stung him a bit, especially when he had inadvertently let shampoo get in the wound when showering that morning.

"Yup, nothing new to report. They put a few butterfly stitches over it that I am supposed to leave on for the rest of the week. But other-wise, I shouldn't have to worry about it anymore. They said it would probably leave a scar, but I don't give a fuck about that. I have plenty of other scars, inside and out, to make it feel right at home." The two men shook hands, and Stander continued. "The doctor did warn me to not let you tackle me anymore…"

Lucas laughed, "Well if I didn't, you would have walked right off that ledge. And it would have taken more than a few stitches to patch you up if that had happened."

"Yeah, hard to imagine I didn't recognize where I was headed. I still don't remember much of anything after entering the quarry. The doc said concussions sometimes do that. Just wipe out stretches of time right before the blow." Stander shrugged.

"Not surprised," stated Lucas. "I still think you must have gotten a whiff of some bad gas. You were talking to yourself, just a bunch of gibberish, as you wandered away from Christophe and me. Who knows what might have been rising up out of that charnel pit? They," he pointed after his fellow archeologists who were making their way back into the quarry, "still haven't come close to reaching the bottom of it yet. Or really have even begun to tell how many bodies were dumped in there…"

"Kind of like trying to count snowflakes in a blizzard, huh?" Stander glanced over at the newly expanded and stabilized entrance of the quarry. "Speaking of the pit, anything come up these last few days I should be aware of?" He felt himself involuntarily bracing inside as Lucas answered his question.

"Nope. Outside of your mom, the group from the university is saying every other body they've examined so far appears to likely date back to the 14th century. They say it keeps looking increasingly like this was the site of that long-fabled mass burial pit from the 1346 Battle of Caen. Why the English would have brought all those bodies here, some eight miles from Caen, still makes no sense to me. Or them. Hopefully, they'll find more clues when they truly start to excavate."

"They still mired in all that bureaucratic BS?" Stander watched as the team of archeologists disappeared into the opening of the quarry that led down to the gruesome depository.

"That's what I was talking with them about. They admitted even once they get the green light to go full steam ahead, it will be years before they can start to make sense of it all. But they sure appreciate that the gracious land owner donated all this so they could start the preliminary work." Lucas gave Stander an exaggerated wink.

"And the government and university bureaucrats never questioned where we drew the boundary? Or why we kept the land directly adjacent to the quarry for ourselves?" Stander was relieved to hear the nonchalance in Lucas' reply.

"Nope. I think they are all still amazed you turned out to be such a generous benefactor. Plus, they never asked to see more of the carefully cropped images we gave them from the deep underground scans we commissioned earlier. What is that old American saying? Don't look a gift horse in the mouth? Is that it?" Lucas smiled conspiratorially. "They have no reason to think there is anything of note on the part of this property still tied up in your trust. Much less suspect the donor of lying to them or holding any information back."

"Good. Then if you are wrong about what you think is buried over there, no harm-no foul." Stander gave Lucas a discreet "thumbs up" sign.

Lucas turned and began walking farther away from the bustling activity outside the quarry's entrance. He lowered his voice as Stander joined him, both men walking together closely, just beyond the border of the official government-sponsored archeological dig of the ancient quarry. "But I'm not wrong, Stander. Based on what we found doing those underground scans of the entire area, that charnel pit you stumbled into was a place of sacrificial offerings made to what is actually buried under our feet."

"That giant skull, huh?" Stander shook his head wryly. "Thought I was done fucking around with giant skulls…"

"Skull? Head? Monolithic statue? Who knows? Hard to tell from the scans what exactly is buried so deep down there. But I'm sure it was likely just the shading in the computer software that generated those images that looked like a skull… Besides, with all the Skullduggery happening between the University and the various government agencies dealing with the find, we don't need another headache." Lucas snorted loudly at his intended pun.

"Skullduggery?" Stander smiled, then added, "More like Skulldiggery to get down to it…" He paused briefly before continuing. "Well, you're the archeologist. It's your job to figure all this shit out. That's what I'm paying you for, right?" Stander nodded at his new friend and newest employee.

"Sure, sure… You're the boss and owner of all this." Lucas gestured at the land extending out in front of them. The open fields that bordered the government and university work just beginning deep in the quarry. "So you still claim you didn't know you owned this place before you flew over?" Lucas cocked one eyebrow at Stander questionably.

"I swear it, man. Pinky swear even!" Stander solemnly pointed his smallest finger at the archeologist before bursting out in laughter as Lucas swatted it aside. "I told you before, I had no idea. Maybe my dad bought the land after my mom's accident. I don't know, man. But, if he did, I can't believe he wouldn't have told me. But hell, I'm about as sharp as a marble sometimes, so maybe he did tell me, and I just forgot. I guess I'll know more once all those fancy-ass expensive lawyers back in Chicago get through all the trust paperwork. Right now, I don't know shit. Maybe I own the fucking Eifel Tower too?" After laughing briefly, Stander grew more serious. "But it is kind of strange, isn't it?"

"I still can't believe when we went to research the ownership records for all this land and found the land was bundled up in a French trust named Noviodunum Suessiones, that some old guy from Michigan would turn out to be the owner. Much less that old guy would turn out to be…"

"Hey! Watch it now. That's two "old guy" references you used to describe me in back-to-back sentences. You know how fragile my ego is." Stander chided Lucas good-naturedly. "Especially at my advanced age."

"Oh? OK, how about venerable, rich guy? Maybe modern-day Methuselah Metal Head? Or tatted-up senior citizen? That better than just old guy?"

Stander casually turned slightly and began rubbing his cheek with one finger, his middle finger, toward the younger archeologist. Then let it rest on his jawline while pointedly looking directly at him. "So anyway, young blood, nothing else to report from the last couple of days? Any other news?"

Lucas nodded his head as he answered. "We did finally find the place where the villagers of Vieux hid during the bombing. It was up at the north side of the quarry. I can take you down there so you can see it for yourself. It's pretty interesting. The villagers must have left quickly, though, and never returned. There are lots of old artifacts of that era left behind. Pots, pans, toys, you name it." Lucas pulled out his phone and showed Stander a few pictures he had taken before continuing. "Some of these things would've been really valuable back then. See this old gramophone from the '30s? That would have cost a family back then a small fortune. Amazing, huh?"

"Yeah, you'd think someone would have taken that for sure. If not, then sometime later, come back for it at least." All the pictures showed belongings appearing to be untouched for decades.

"We also found a few places where there may have been some Germans hiding out. A couple rooms had parts of old crates and supplies, including some German munitions. We even found some remains that may have been a Nazi officer based on the scraps of uniform we put together. I took some pictures and sent them to a guy I know who specializes in Nazi memorabilia that can tell us for sure. We found some identification papers on him, but they weren't very helpful. About all you can make out is his rank and part of his name, Gunther something or other." He shrugged indifferently. "Some animals must have gotten to the body, though. The uniform and papers were all mostly torn up. The guy's bones were scattered and gnawed on. Hard to tell how he may have died."

"Interesting… Yeah, I would like to go down and see all that." Stander walked casually over to a cluster of yellow gentian flowers bobbing back and forth in the breeze. He ran his hands delicately over the tops of them. "Nothing else unusual? Makes you wonder why such a huge quarry so close to the village was completely abandoned. Unless they did know about the pit after all…"

"Or maybe they knew the actual owner was a dick." Stander didn't hide the middle finger he raised this time, and Lucas laughed.

"Anyway, if they do know, no one in town will admit it." Lucas gestured towards the village of Vieux on the other side of the hills. "We have tried talking to some of the older residents that would have either been alive or at least would have had parents that sheltered down there. But so far, they all claim ignorance." Lucas paused, "A couple workers say they have seen a big dog or wolf hanging around. We can't tell where it lives or where it is coming in and out from. But someone catches a brief glimpse of it every other day or so. I guess it lives down one of the old entrances or air shafts. Maybe has a den or some pups it's watching over. Probably thinks we are making too much noise and ruining the neighborhood. Or maybe it's upset we are getting ready to empty out what it regarded as its own personal stash of bones." Lucas guffawed loudly, laughing gregariously at his own joke.

Stander simply nodded, "Or maybe he is waiting for you to dig up what lies so close to the pit…"

FOR MORE INFORMATION

Gritzmonster.com

Book 1
Skulldiggery: The Relict

Book 2
Skulldiggery: The Quarry

Coming Soon
Book 3
Skulldiggery: The Lingering